BENEATH THE SHEETS

SHANDI BOYES

COPYRIGHT

DEDICATION

My one and only.
I love you, Chris.

ALSO BY SHANDI BOYES

Perception Series:

Saving Noah

Fighting Jacob

Taming Nick

Redeeming Slater

Saving Emily (*Novella*)

Wrapped up with Rise Up (*Novella - should be read after Bound*)

Enigma:

Enigma of Life

Unraveling an Enigma

Enigma: The Mystery Unmasked

Enigma: The Final Chapter

Beneath the Secrets

Beneath the Sheets

Spy Thy Neighbor

The Opposite Effect

I Married a Mob Boss

Second Shot

The Way We Are

The Way We Were

Sugar and Spice

Lady in Waiting

Man in Queue

Couple on Hold

Enigma: The Wedding

Silent Vigilante

Bound Series:

Chains

Links

Bound

Restrained

Psycho

Russian Mob Chronicles:

Nikolai: A Mafia Prince Romance

Nikolai: Taking Back What's Mine

Nikolai: What's Left of Me

Nikolai: Mine to Protect

Asher: My Russian Revenge

Nikolai: Through the Devil's Eyes

RomCom Standalones:

Just Playin'

The Drop Zone

Ain't Happenin'

Christmas Trio

Falling for a Stranger

Coming Soon:

Skitzo

Trey

ONE

HUGO

PRESENT DAY

My hand trembles as I yank my cell phone out of the pocket of my running shorts. My body is slicked with sweat, and my heart is pounding against my chest. There has only been one time in my life I haven't wanted to make a call. It was when I had to tell my best mate that my sister, his wife, had been critically injured in a tragic accident. If that wasn't bad enough, the same accident claimed the life of their unborn son.

My initial plan was to wait until Hawke's feet touched home soil before telling him about Jorgie's accident, but I didn't have the chance to wait that long. He knew something wasn't right the instant he heard me speak. I'll never forget the howl of a broken man that resonated down the line that day. It was a soul being shattered with no possibility of being repaired.

Against doctor's advice, we kept Jorgie on life support for three days so Hawke could return from duty in Iraq and say his final goodbye to the love of his life in person. Jorgie was buried the day after his return with their son, Malcolm, cradled in her arms. Part of me died the day my sister did. We were two peas in a pod, rebels cruising through life one adventure at a time. Her life was perfect. Until it was brutally ripped away.

Now, for the second time in my life, I have to tell a man the woman he loves is gone, snatched right under my nose by men who wish her harm. Protecting Isabelle is my job, the most vital task of my employment contract, but even if it weren't, I'd still protect her. Izzy has a lot of the same qualities as my sister Jorgie.

She's the same age as Jorgie was when she passed away. They have the same dark hair and fair skin, but instead of Izzy having Jorgie's cornflower blue eyes, hers are a rich chocolate brown color, but the biggest similarity of all is their personalities: little firecrackers who keep everyone surrounding them on their toes, making sure life never gets boring. I wouldn't necessarily say my life has been dull the past five years, but when Izzy crashed into Isaac's life, things certainly became more dynamic.

Before Izzy arrived in the picture, I'd spent the past five years as Manager of Operations in the background of Isaac's empire, hidden from prying eyes. I handled acquisitions and proposals presented to his company and assessed the capabilities of any nightclubs he was considering purchasing. Isaac knew the instant he met Izzy she was his game changer, so he took measures to ensure she would always be protected. The very first task he did was alter my job description.

Most would see my transition from Manager of Operations to a Protective Detail as a downgrade. I don't. Knowing Isaac trusts me enough to take care of Izzy when he can't is more rewarding than any fancy job title would ever be. Not only did I get the opportunity to thank Isaac for saving my life, I got to leave the stuffiness of my boring nine to five office job that was becoming as tedious as folding my overflowing laundry basket every Sunday morning.

The only bad thing that has come from Izzy's sudden inclusion in Isaac's life is realizing what I sacrificed by not taking the time to rationally consider the consequences of my actions. Instead of evaluating how greatly my life would change from the mammoth decision I made five years ago, I once again became a bull in a china shop, charging first and asking questions later. I live with the repercussions of my decision every day of my life, but seeing the way Izzy looks at Isaac makes the demise of my previous life even more apparent, but I can't change the past; I can only shape the future. And right now, my focus needs to remain on Izzy.

The muscles in my thighs burn as I sprint down 42nd Street, chasing the white Range Rover with an unconscious Izzy splayed in the backseat. I tried to get her out. I smashed the back window of the Range Rover with my fists trying to save her, but I failed. *Again.*

My feet stomping on the sidewalk drown out the thumping of my heart as I dial a number I know by heart. Lifting the cell phone to my ear, I push it in close, making sure I can hear Isaac over the shrill of my pulse in my ears.

"Hugo," Isaac greets me.

His tone is stern, like always, but with a slight hint of playfulness. I knew he would have seen it this morning, the spark in Izzy's eyes that told him she was coming back to him. I'd seen it emerging over the past few days: the way her ears would prick when my untraceable cell phone would ring, her long stares into space that would end with her arms prickling, and the way she finally stood up to the two-faced bitch, Clara. Seeing Izzy finally having the gall to stand up to Clara was all I needed to know she was ready to forgive and forget. To let love win. To stop fighting fate. Now, she may never get her opportunity.

"They have her. They've taken Izzy," I say, my words barely audible in my breathless state.

Isaac inhales a sharp, quick breath, no doubt his heart freezing in ice cold fear. It is the same feeling I had when he told me I had to walk away from Ava nearly five years ago when we stood out front of my sister's house.

"Walk away or risk her life. The choice is yours," he said that day.

To me, there was no choice. I was always going to protect Ava, until my very last breath. So I walked away. Not just for a moment, but for a lifetime. Although Ava and I were only together mere weeks as a couple, I gathered enough memories to last me a lifetime. I watched her sleep for hours, absorbing and categorizing every look that adorned her beautiful face.

Every smile and every frown was assessed in great detail. They're the memories that have kept me going the past five years. Even though our time together was short, I'm grateful I got to experience those moments with her. Not many people get the opportunity to meet their soulmate. I did and I'll be forever grateful for that. I know memories can't compete with the real life moments, but when they're all you have, you take what you can get.

"Who has her?"

Isaac's low tone drags me back to the present. "I don't know. They pulled her into a white Range Rover at the bottom of St.

Thomas Street," I answer, my words breathless. "Fuck, Boss, I'm sorry, I only left her for a minute."

As the remnants of a nightmare cling to my skin, Izzy's words about being a coward and hiding from my family hit me harder than normal. Although my nightmares have become a rarity the past five years, as the anniversary of the incident in Afghanistan creeps closer, my nightmares are resurfacing stronger than ever, but instead of absorbing the sting of Izzy's words like the man I am, I stormed off in anger, too over-whelmed with a barrage of emotions hitting into me at once to continue our argument. That was all it took for them to snatch her. Mere seconds.

My eyes lift to the Range Rover when it slams on its brakes and mounts the curb to avoid missing a blue sedan that suddenly pulled out in front of it. I barge my way through the dense foot crowd that always clogs Ravenshoe, pushing past a throng of people unaware of the danger surrounding them. In any other town, chasing a car by foot would be a fruitless effort, but thankfully for me, Ravenshoe has as many traffic issues as New York City.

Isaac's breathless grunt sounds down the line, reminding me I have my cell phone pressed against my ear.

"Where are you now?"

I cut across the T intersection of Tivot and Mark. My brisk pace halts when a truck comes out of nowhere, charging toward me. It slams on its brakes, infusing the air with the smell of burning rubber and smoke. The best parts of my life flash before my eyes as the grill of the truck inches toward me. Tires bouncing across the asphalt and a horn honking shrieks through my ears. Time freezes and everything goes deathly quiet.

I release a ragged gasp when the truck narrowly misses hitting me by half an inch. After gathering my heart off the floor, I recommence my chase. I jump over the tray of the truck and increase my speed. Motorists honk their horns and curse as I sprint by. My lungs are heaving, incapable of securing a full breath, but the strong mix of adrenaline and determination is keeping me going.

"I'm tailing them on foot," I inform Isaac, my words winded.

My body is beyond exhausted, screaming in pain, but I can't give up. I can't fail... *again.* The look in Izzy's eyes when she thrashed against her attacker as he held a white cloth over her mouth will haunt my dreams. Another item added to my already exhaustive list.

"They just pulled down Tivot," I advise when the white Range Rover mounts the curb, barely missing a pedestrian waiting to cross.

The veins in my neck thrum when the passenger of the Range Rover tilts his torso out of the window. He's a brute of a man, easily my height, and a good twenty pounds heavier. A snake tattoo slithers up his right arm toward a face only a mother could love. The corners of his mouth curve into an arrogant smirk at the same time he produces a black pistol. I inhale a sharp breath as my eyes scope the area.

"Fuck. Get down!" I scream at the mass gathering of people surrounding me.

The gunman aims his pistol at me, not the slightest bit concerned for the safety of the innocent bystanders milling around the space, enjoying their Sunday morning. I rush toward a middle-aged woman frozen in fear at the bus stop. A rustle of air escapes her lips when I push her out of the line of fire.

Burning hot lava scorches my veins as a jolt of pain shreds through my chest. I'm sent flying backwards, hitting the concrete sidewalk with an almighty thump. I try to get up, to fight through the pain, but my body won't co-operate. My breathing comes out in slow, uneven gasps, and a chill runs down my spine. The smell of copper mixed with sweat lingers in the air as my eyelids become heavy. A shadow hovers over me, blackened by the bright sun hanging in the sky. The sun bounces off the stranger's golden hair, haloing him, like an angel has fallen from heaven.

"My name is Brandon James. I'm an FBI Field Agent; my number is 443567. I need an ambulance sent to the corner of Tivot and Welsh."

"Blondie?" My words are garbled as the air from my lungs bubbles into my chest.

I cough, splattering my lips with the tangy taste of blood. A garble of incomprehensible words rumble from my mouth when someone pushes down on the scorching pain burning through my chest and shoulder. Hot, sticky blood puddles around me as my eyelids droop.

When the blackness overtakes me, my first thoughts go to her. *Ava.*

TWO

AVA

Washing my hands in the sink, I catch my reflection in the vanity mirror and grimace. Thanks to getting caught in an afternoon shower, my hair is a frizzy mess. The mascara I coated my lashes with this morning is gone, and my eyes are plagued with dark, heavy bags that haven't budged an inch in nearly five years. *I'm wretched.* After fluffing the wild mess of my hair, I grab my powder compact out of my purse and set to work on concealing years of restless sleep.

"I guess that will have to do," I say, staring at a slightly improved Ava reflecting back at me.

After a dab of lip gloss and spray of perfume, I rush out of the cramped bathroom of my office and scurry down the hall.

"I know, I know," I apologize when I catch the pursed lips of Belinda, dear friend and office receptionist.

She remains quiet while assisting me as I slip into my wool-lined trench coat.

"You know what he is like, Ava." She wraps a thick cashmere scarf around my neck as I slide my shaking hand into a pair of black leather gloves. "Being late is a way of saying you believe your own time is more valuable than the time—"

"Of the person who is waiting for you," I interrupt, quoting the saying I've heard *many* times the past four years.

Belinda smiles while handing me a cashmere beanie.

"But isn't it better to be late than arrive ugly?" I quip, my tone as unconvincing as the concern hampering my vocal cords.

Her dainty chuckle warms my heart.

"Please come with me," I beg, my words barely a whimper.

The corners of her mouth curve down, and the twinkle in her green eyes dampens. "I would if I could." She squeezes my forearm before guiding me to the office door. "Be careful, the grounds are slippery." She lean in to press a kiss on my cheek.

"I will."

After giving her a tight squeeze, I glide out of the reception area of my office. Cold winds pelt through me when I emerge from the foyer of my office building to the concrete sidewalk. The chill of winter has arrived early.

An invigorating buzz of excitement dashes through me as I pace through a gathering of people eager for the start of the weekend. I've always loved the anticipation of waking up on a Friday morning and knowing I only have to make it through another eight hours before I have two days of freedom to do whatever my heart contends. Slow, lazy weekends doing as much or as little as I please, those are some of my greatest joys.

When my cell phone buzzing in my clutch purse sounds through my ears, I increase my already brisk pace. I don't need to look at the screen to know who is calling; my five minute tardiness is all that's required.

"I'm so sorry, my last patient's crown took longer than expected," I say, pressing my cell phone to my ear. "I'm arriving now."

I hurry through the security turnstiles of the Belvedere Hotel, smiling a greeting to the elderly doorman welcoming me into the affluent foyer with a dip of his hat.

"We are in the west wing," my caller replies, his tone clipped.

The beating of my heart kicks up a gear when he abruptly disconnects the call, not allowing me the chance to reply. Generally, his mood can be quite curt, but his agitation at my tardiness would have increased his annoyance. Removing my coat, scarf, and gloves, I hand them to the grinning coat clerk and gather my ticket. My quick dash to the west wing wanes when the flash of a breaking news banner catches my eye. I slow my fast stride and amble toward a color TV sitting on the reception counter of the Belvedere Hotel.

"Col Petretti, notorious businessman and suspected Mob Boss has been killed in an FBI targeted sting," I read off the screen.

My throat painfully tightens as my eyes skim over the flickering screen, absorbing the snippets of information displayed. A female reporter is standing at the front of an old manufacturing warehouse, similar to the textile mill in Graham, North Carolina. The flashing of red and white lights bounce of the reporter's rich auburn hair as she hustles other reporters also vying for a prime position.

My pupils widen when a picture of Col Petretti flashes up onto the screen. Even though I'm looking at him through a television screen, his evocative gaze still makes my skin crawl. I've never forgotten the devastation I felt the night I first laid my eyes on him......

My heart leaps out of my chest when I'm suddenly grabbed at the side and dragged deeper into my corridor.

"You need to come with me," says a raspy voice I don't immediately recognize.

My rapid heartbeat slows when my head cranks to the side and I'm met with the worldly eyes of Patty. He holds me close to his side, bombarding me with his feverish body heat. Remaining quiet, his eyes drift around our location, similar to the way Hugo's did at the club months earlier.

Without speaking a peep, he guides me to an apartment at the end of the hall. He ushers me inside before securing a mass amount of deadlocks on his thick front door. The queasiness hampering my stomach earlier returns full pelt when Patty spins around to face me. His pupils are wide, and his face is gaunt.

"What's going on, Patty?" I query, my voice trembling.

He places a steel baseball bat against the entranceway table and paces closer to me. Seizing the crook of my elbow, he steers me into his kitchen, which is an exact replica of mine. He pulls out a wooden stool from underneath the counter and gestures for me to sit. I shake my head, too shaken to take a seat. I cross my arms in front of my chest and keep my eyes on Patty, never losing sight of him as he moves through the kitchen, gathering sandwich supplies like I'm an invited guest for dinner, not ushered here against my will.

"Patty--"

Any further words preparing to leave my mouth entomb in my throat from the wry glare Patty directs at me. My heart thrashes against my chest when I see the edge of calamity in his normally gentle eyes. Noticing my frightened expression, his face softens before he once again gestures for me to sit. Not trusting my shaking legs to keep me upright, I plop onto the barstool and swivel to face Patty. He places a loaf of crusted bread onto the countertop and runs his hand along the edge of his jaw.

"The man who followed you to Hugo's floor. Do you know who that man is?"

His voice is stern, but the concern in his eyes is causing my greatest worry.

I shake my head. "I've never seen him before."

"His name is Col Petretti," Patty advises, his tone deep and raspy.

My lips purse, certain I've heard his name before.

"He's a monster, Ava, a man who will decimate an entire family without a second thought."

My pupils enlarge as an overpowering sense of dread grips my heart.

"A brutal, heartless man who destroys everything in his wake, not stopping for anyone or anything."

"Hugo. He was at Hugo's apartment," I say through the tears clogging my words.

Patty steps closer to me. His face is set as hard as stone. "It is too late for Hugo. He made his bed; now he must sleep in it."

I violently shake my head, sending tears flinging off my cheeks. I slip off the barstool and rush to the door, my frantic steps only impeded by the fear wreaking havoc on my body. I can *barely breathe through my panic, but nothing can stop me. I need to get to Hugo, to protect him from the real life monster who has escaped his nightmares.*

Before I can reach the door, Patty beats me to it.

Pressing his back against the door, Patty's remorseful eyes dance between mine. "It is too late for Hugo, Ava. If he isn't already dead, he soon will be."

My eyes burn, unable to accommodate the rapid flow of moisture flooding them. My hand clutches my neck as I struggle to contain the emotions crippling me.

"He's gone, Ava. He can't come back from this."

Despair crashes into me when I see the candor in Patty's eyes.

"That is why he said goodbye." I hiccup through a stream of tears, incapable of catching a full breath. "He knew he was never coming back. He knew he was leaving forever."

Patty's glossed eyes stare into mine as he nods. My knees buckle as the fear paralyzing me becomes too much for me to inhibit. Patty catches me with his arms and cradles me close to his chest. Running his hand down my sweat-drenched hair, he whispers soothing words, encouraging me to breathe through the flood of tears flowing down my face......

"Ava," shouts a voice across the room, breaking me from my memories.

I run my index finger under my eyes, removing any evidence of my tears before spinning toward the voice. My attempts at making myself look presentable are fruitless when his narrowed eyes zoom in on the glistening of tears shimmering on my rosy cheeks.

"She doesn't need to sign in. She's with me," he informs,

peering over my shoulder at the receptionist standing behind me.

I smile warily at the receptionist, grateful she didn't refute his inaccurate statement. My high altitude stilettos click along the marble floor as I quickly span the distance between us. His eyes slit as he roams them over my Misha Collection Leyana dress. I run my hands down the knee-length skirt, smoothing out the invisible creases he *believes* are in my dress.

"Out of all the days to be late, Ava, you have to choose today," he grumbles, adjusting the neckline of my dress.

"I'm sorry," I mumble, my words weak.

After running the back of his hand roughly under my eyes, removing any traces of my smeared mascara, he clutches my hand in his and paces into the opulent ballroom. Once we are surrounded by elegantly dressed men and woman, his stiffened posture softens and the mask he regularly wears in public slips into place. I play the role of devoted spouse to a T. I smile at important dignitaries, ignoring their depraved assessments of my body, and praise the pompous-looking ladies in their hideous ball gowns.

By the time we make it into the middle of the elegant room, my cheeks are burning nearly as much as my hip from his firm clutch on my body.

"I said to smile at the important men, not give them an open invitation to your bedroom," he snarls, ensuring he's quiet enough only I can hear him.

"Believe me, no man in this room is getting an invitation to my bedroom tonight," I gabble under my breath before snagging a wine glass off a waiter ambling by, balancing a silver tray on his palm.

"Sorry, what did you say?"

From his tone alone, I know he heard what I said. My pupils dilate as a surge of anxiety courses through me. Thankfully, the clinking of a wine glass interrupts his furious glare. He strengthens his clutch hold on my body before gliding his gaze to Mr. Gardner standing near a podium in the middle of the ballroom.

Mr. Gardner, work associate and boss, looks dashing in a dark blue tailored suit and polished dress shoes. The vibrancy of his red tie matches the hue Mrs. Gardner's cheeks get when he bombards her with a flurry of compliments as he shares the story of how they met and married the day they attended a dental conference in Las Vegas twenty-five years ago today.

My heart warms when I see the love projecting out of Mr. Gardner's eyes as he speaks of his fondness for his beloved wife. He has the same gleam in his eyes Hawke would always get when he was in Jorgie's presence, the same gleam Hugo's eyes had when he woke me every morning before Jorgie's death. The sentimental tears Mr. Gardner's speech elicit allow me to conceal my heart break for the loss of Hugo and Jorgie.

A smile curls on my lips when the clinking of wine glasses jingles through my ears at the end of Mr. Gardner's speech. The color in Mrs. Gardner's cheeks amplifies as she prepares to comply with her wedding anniversary guests' request. A giggle bubbles up my chest when wolf whistles and cat calls bellow across the room as Mr. Gardner seals his lips over Mrs. Gardner's. Even though they're in their mid-fifties and have been married for twenty-five years, their love for each other is still in that giddy newlywed phase.

The uproar of cheers and hollering only simmer when a

deep voice rumbles over the excitement, requesting quiet. My heart hammers against my ribs when the procession of elegantly dressed party attendees swivel to face me. I can barely secure a full breath when my date releases his death clutch on my hip and kneels down in front of me.

My disbelieving eyes shoot around the room crammed with our work associates and important dignitaries as his hand delves into the breast pocket of his midnight black suit. My eyes rocket back to his when he produces a black velvet ring box from his pocket. The mad pulse raging through my body clusters in my ears as he cranks open the box to display the princess cut diamond engagement ring nestled inside.

"Marvin, what are you doing?"

My voice is low, ensuring the mass gathering of people surrounding us won't hear the fear in my voice.

Marvin's arduous eyes lift from the ring box to me. "Ava, will you do me the honor of becoming my wife?" His voice is as uneasy as the expression on his face.

Mrs. Gardner's hand shoots up to her mouth, muffling her excited squeal. I swallow, relieving the dryness impinging my throat. The room goes deadly quiet as I stare at Marvin, unable to comprehend what is happening, let alone articulate a response. The longer I stay quiet, the more Marvin's eyes glare into mine, reprimanding me for the delay. Tears pool in my eyes as I hesitantly nod, accepting his proposal.

The shake of my hand trembles my arm when he clasps my hand in his and slips the engagement ring onto my ring finger. The sternness in his eyes eases when he stands from his kneeled position and wraps his arms around my shoulders.

The crowd erupts into a loud cheer when he pulls me in and seals his lips over mine. The saltiness of the tears streaming down my face mixes with the whiskey lacing his tongue when he slips it inside my mouth, sealing our engagement with an emotion-packed kiss.

THREE

HUGO

My back arches off the mattress as a tormented scream tears from my throat. I thrash against the sheets wrapped around my withering body, fighting to loosen their deathly tight grip.

When another painful howl rumbles through my lips, my eyes snap open. They drift around the unfamiliar darkness swamping me as I rein in the panic scorching my veins. My body is covered in a thick layer of sweat, and my heart is pounding fitfully as the dark shadows of a nightmare cling to my body.

With the mellow-toned walls and stark white sheets, it takes me several moments to gather my bases. For the past nearly five years, I've become accustomed to waking up in the bedroom of my apartment, not a hospital room.

Five hours on an operating table, four pints of blood and more stitches than I can count were the aftermath of once again failing to rationally consider the consequences, but thankfully, this time, my failure didn't result in the harsh repercussions of my last debauched decision.

The relief I felt when I awoke to the remorse-filled eyes of Izzy staring down at me hit me like a ton of bricks. I should have known Isaac would have stopped at nothing to ensure she was safe. His protectiveness of Izzy is more vital to him than his next breath.

Ignoring my shoulder screaming in pain, I scoot across the hospital bed, desperately needing a shower to chase away the remnants of the nightmare still clinging to my sweat slicked-skin. The dull ache hampering my shoulder turns lethal when I raise my arm to clasp the silver lift dangling over my bed.

I need the pain, though. I want it as a somber reminder of what happens when I don't take the time to evaluate my decisions before making them. My lack in judgment yesterday could have ended a lot worse than it did, adding another item to the exhaustive list of mistakes I've made in my lifetime.

I grit my teeth and hoist myself into an upright position. A rush of dizziness clusters in my head, amplifying the swirls of my stomach. I throw my legs over the side of the bed and stand on a pair of wobbly knees. My shaky steps to the attached bathroom are hindered by the heart rate monitor strapped to my chest.

Leaning on the wheeled side table to steady my swaying movements, I use my free hand to rip off the heart monitor and defibrillation pads from my chest. As soon as the first pad is removed, an alarm sounds from the monitor, shrilling in my ears.

My fingers frantically punch at the buttons on the unit,

trying to shut up its irritating shrieks. The shake impeding my legs switches to my hands when a flood of memories pelt into me at once. You don't realize the significance of a ripple in a pulse line until you see one vanish before your eyes.

Allowing my anger to get the better of me, I rip the cords off my chest and stalk into the bathroom, dragging the IV stand with me. The pain shredding through my body is nothing compared to the ache crippling my heart. I step into the tiled hob of the shower, not bothering to remove my hospital gown.

Cranking the water on full pelt, I step under the spray. The freezing temperature of the frigid water sends a jolt through my body, restarting my frozen heart. I lean my good arm on the sparkling marbled wall and use my spare hand to rip off the thin gown before stepping deeper into the spray. The chilly water blasts the nape of my neck, relieving my overheated skin and chasing away the remnants of my nightmare.

The subzero temps have only just cooled my feverish skin when the bathroom door swings open and Raquel zips into the room.

"What are you doing out of bed?!" she reprimands me, her high-pitched squeal bouncing off the tiled walls and jingling into my ears.

Raquel is the nurse Isaac hired to look after me during my recovery. When Izzy spotted her sauntering into the room yesterday afternoon, her eyes popped and her elbow landed in Isaac's ribs, reacting the exact way any woman would when a girl with cock-twitching good looks like Raquel enters a room.

Raquel is the exact vision any man conjures when the term naughty nurse is mentioned. She has straight blonde hair, defined eyes, and curvy lips that accentuate her beautiful face.

Although Izzy is fooled by Isaac's reasoning in hiring Raquel as my nurse, I'm not. Isaac knows me well enough to know even though Raquel is gorgeous and has a body that would make most men fall to their knees, I'm not interested in purchasing what she's selling.

Although I'd never openly admit it, I have a *slight* fascination for a certain type of skin tone. It isn't an absolute necessity when I'm looking for a bed companion, just like every guy out there, but instead of the favorable characteristics of my *dates* being determined by their hair or eye coloring, my interests lie in the smooth richness of their beautiful skin coloring.

Don't construe my admission the wrong way, though. Although my preferences lean toward tanned skin, it isn't the only feature required to gain my attention. Raquel is a prime example of that. Just watching her nibble on the end of her pen last night sent a mass injection of blood to the lower region of my body, and her complexion is as white as a hospital sheet. I don't mean slightly pale. I mean, she doesn't have a hint of a tan, whiter-than-Casper-the-Ghost white, but Raquel's pasty skin coloring has nothing to do with why I'm not lining up to purchase the sweetness she's offering.

Although Raquel was hired as my nurse, I've known her for nearly two years, and I class her as a friend. Only once in my life have I crossed the fine line that separates friends from bed companions. I didn't just cross the line with Ava, I smudged it out with my foot on the way over, permanently erasing it from our lives. Just like Ava is the only girl I've ever lusted over, asked out and fallen in love with, she will remain the only girl I'll ever jump the friendship line for.

"You were told to buzz me if you needed anything," Raquel

scolds, rushing toward me without the slightest concern for my nakedness.

She encircles her arms around my waist and guides my shivering body to a shower chair sitting at the side of the stark white vanity.

"I was shot in the shoulder, not in my legs. I'm perfectly capable of walking," I remind her.

She snarls before pushing me into the chair, surprising me with her strength for her small stature. Her eyes reprimand me as she paces to my suitcase stored on a luggage table in the washroom. Her hand digs through the clothes laundered and packed by Catherine, Isaac's housekeeper. Suddenly, she stops rummaging through my belongings, cranks her neck and looks at me, blinking and confused.

"They didn't pack you any briefs," she informs me, her nose screwing up.

I lick my dry lips, concealing the grin attempting to spread across my face. "I don't wear briefs," I retort.

The scrunching of Raquel's nose amplifies.

"Boxers, butt huggers, nut huts, Calvin Kleins, whatever you want to call them. I don't wear them."

Raquel's brow cocks. "You go commando with *that*?" she queries, gesturing her head to my crotch.

I don't have a chance in hell of stopping the shit-eating grin stretching across my face. Come on, I'm a guy. You never turn down a compliment to your manhood, woeful mood or not.

A ragged gasp expels Raquel's lips when I nod. Swinging her bulging eyes back to my suitcase, she yanks out a pair of cotton blue-striped pajama pants, straightens her spine and saunters toward me.

"These will ensure there are no zipper incidents," she chides in a witty tone.

I gulp.

Noticing my panicked expression, a broad grin etches on Raquel's face. "Can you manage? Or do you need me to *shower* and *dress* you?" she quips, holding out the trousers.

I roll my eyes before snatching the pants out of her hands. "I've got this," I assure her, standing from my chair.

My abrupt movements send a rush of dizziness to my head, causing me to sway like a leaf in the hot summer breeze. Raquel grabs the tops of my arms, steadying my uncontrollable sways. Through gritted teeth, I use her and the IV stand as a brace as I slip my legs into my pants and yank them up my waist while internally grumbling at how pathetic I am since I can't even dress myself. *I got shot in the chest for fuck sake, not my legs.*

"You had a class four hemorrhage, Hugo. That's well over four pints of blood lost. Your muscles not only need time to recoup from that, you also chased a car for nearly five miles," Raquel explains, her tone sincere yet stern. "Even the best marathon runners in the world would need help getting dressed after that effort."

Once she secures the drawstrings on my pants, she wraps her arms around my waist and guides me back to my bed. Any agitation about my inability to care for myself dampens when I notice the strain hampering Raquel's face. The heavy crease in the middle of her eyes, and the way her lips are pursed, reminds me so much of a face Ava pulled years ago.

The groove crinkling Raquel's usually smooth forehead disappears when I flop onto the hospital bed. "There you go," she says, hauling my legs, which seem the weight of concrete, onto the bed.

"What happened to my personal belongings?" I ask. I try to keep my tone neutral, but my attempts are borderline.

Raquel's brows scrunch as her eyes shoot around the room. "Your clothing was given to a local detective, but your wallet should be here somewhere."

The heaviness weighing down my chest lightens. I have a very important item in my wallet I'd hate to lose.

Suddenly, Raquel's face lights up. "The triage nurse said she locked it in your drawer."

She ambles to the stack of drawers next to the double hospital bed. I release the breath I'm holding in when her hand plunges into the top drawer and she produces my black leather wallet.

"There you go." She hands it to me before walking to the bathroom.

Once she slips out of my view, I crack open the wallet. I inwardly sigh when the edge of a faded and cracked polaroid photo confronts me. I close my wallet and place it onto the side table. I don't need to see the photo to know what it looks like. I've studied it many times the past eleven years; I can recall it in photographic detail.

It is a picture my mom snapped of Jorgie, Ava, and me on our last family vacation at Lake George before Ava and Jorgie left for college. In the photo, Ava has a crazy mess of ringlet hair; she's wearing a teeny yellow bikini under a hideous Rochdale Village T-shirt she stole from my suitcase, and she has a knock-your-socks-off smile plastered on her face.

The smile she was wearing is the reason I carry the picture with me everywhere I go. That was the first time in the eight years I'd known Ava that I'd seen her smile like that. As if it wasn't rewarding enough being in the presence of such a beautiful smile, it was even more special because it was directed at me.

I'd spent a majority of the summer vacation hanging around Michael Scoller. Michael was a local boy who lived by the lake with his parents. He was four years older than Ava and Jorgie, but that didn't stop them slack-jawing in his presence. Jorgie nicknamed him Junior because she swore he was an exact replica of Freddie Prince, Jr. from Jorgie's favorite movie at the time, *I Know What You Did Last Summer*. Much to Jorgie's dismay, Michael only had eyes for Ava.

Unable to dampen the inane jealously that always swamped me when men paid attention to Ava, I spent the entire month of my summer vacation acting as if I was Michael's new best friend. Putting it bluntly: it was a fucking hard month. Being slapped with a cold fish would have been more entertaining than hanging out with Michael, but I did it. I gritted my teeth and spent the entire month talking about how dragonflies mate and the difference between the Harry Potter books and their motion pictures. It nearly killed me, but I would have done anything to stop him from getting close to Ava. My dedication paid off the final night at the cabin.

Every year, a bunch of local teens and a handful of college visitors held a final hoorah to summer down by the water's edge. It was generally held in a tiny pocket away from the prying eyes of gawking locals and the parents of the underage teens. After *pretending* to celebrate a little harder than I actually did, Ava aided me in returning to the cabin.

Cackling like the teenage boy I was over the excited gleam in her eyes when we made it up the two flights of stairs without incident, I stumbled on my monstrous feet right outside my bedroom door. In slow motion, I tumbled to the floor. Since Ava had her arms wrapped around my waist, she came crashing down with me. I was frantic, certain I'd crushed her to death. After rolling off her, I raked my eyes over her face and every inch of her body.

She remained silent, staring up at me wide-eyed and slack-jawed. When she spotted the mortified expression etched on my face, she laughed hysterically. Not the dainty, girly laugh I was used to hearing, a belly-crunching, full-hearted chuckle.

Like every time I heard her laugh, any hang-up I had about her being my little sister's best friend unraveled. Before I could blurt out that I'd been crushing on her for years, Ava leaped forward and planted her lips on mine. Fuck she tasted good. She was the perfect combination of sweetness and the watermelon punch she'd been drinking. Unlike our first kiss, I let Ava control the pace of our exchange. That kiss was just like Ava: sweet and tender.

We sat on the floor kissing for hours, like we were never going to get the opportunity to do it again. We didn't. Only a few short weeks later, Ava walked out of my life with a stream of tears flooding her cheeks and a one way ticket to San Diego. That was by far one of the hardest days of my life.

My attention reverts to the present when my hospital door unexpectedly swings open. I inhale a quick, sharp breath as my eyes roam over the man standing in the doorway. Even though nearly five years have passed since I last saw him, time has been kind to him. He's barely aged a day.

"Anyone would swear you just saw a ghost," Rhys mutters, pacing further into my hospital room. "I can understand your surprise. The only difference is, I have seen a ghost. A man who vanished without a trace five years ago. Missing, presumed dead."

Rhys walks to the end of my bed as he roams his vibrant hazel eyes over my body. "Imagine the shock of arriving in surgery to discover the patient you're there to save is already dead. Has been for years."

A smirk curls on his lips. "Well, dead on paper anyway."

"You're the surgeon who saved my life?" My voice comes out heavily drawled as fragments of my past crash into my present.

Although the full extent of my injuries hasn't been shared with Izzy, the bullet that entered my chest and exited through my left shoulder blade managed to not only nick my left lung on the way past, it also rocketed through a vital artery. From what Dr. Jae has informed me, it was the combination of the medical treatment received at the scene and the hands of a gifted surgeon that saved my life. I remember the events leading up to being shot, but everything after being knocked onto my ass is a complete blur.

Rhys nods. "I did everything in my power to save you... just like I did for Jorgie and her baby."

His words slam into me harder than his back hit the wall during our last exchange. When he told me he'd done everything in his power to save Jorgie and her baby, but he'd exhausted all avenues and had to let her go, I lost all rational thought. Even though Jorgie's death was over five years ago, I'm still grieving.

The smirk on Rhys' face fades as his eyes bounce between mine. "You have the same look on your face Ava did when she collected your death certificate two years ago."

My heart freezes at the mention of Ava's name, but fortunately, my outward appearance doesn't give any indication to the treason of my heart. I'm also flabbergasted by Rhys' admission. Normally, when a person disappears, they have to be missing for seven years before they will be declared dead in absentia. I've only been missing for five years. So why did Ava collect my death certificate?

My head shifts to the side when Raquel enters the room. "Next time you decide on a three AM shower, can you at least- -"

Her words stop when she detects an additional presence in the room. A vibrant grin stretches across her face when her eyes lift from the drenched hospital gown in her hands to Rhys. Although Rhys is discreet, I don't miss his eyes running over Raquel's body.

"Hi, Dr. Tagget," Raquel greets, her tone higher than normal.

Rhys nods in greeting at Raquel before shifting his eyes back to me. "My employment contract clearly stipulates the utmost diligence is to be given to any patients I serve in this hospital, giving me a clear conscience to pretend I've never seen you."

Raquel's brows scrunch as her eyes shift between Rhys and me. The tension in the air is so thick, it is palpable. After dipping his chin farewell to Raquel, Rhys spins on his heels and ambles to the door. Just before he exits, he cranks his head back to look at me.

"My conscience is clear; is yours?"

Not giving me the chance to reply, he walks out of the door and closes it behind him.

FOUR

AVA

"Thank you," I say through gritted teeth, sliding in the backseat of a taxi.

The coolness of the leather as I slide across the bench seat does nothing to simmer the fiery rage burning out of control inside of me. Keeping my gaze planted on the flow of dense traffic, I secure the seatbelt buckle and attempt to latch it into place. A silent squeal bubbles up my chest when my rough yanks on the seatbelt latch cause the safety mechanism to lock in, meaning I can't move it an inch from my shoulder. I stiffen when Marvin leans over my shoulder, gently pulls on the seatbelt strap and clicks it into place.

"Thank you," I say again, this time with less smear in my tone.

"157 McAllister Street," Marvin instructs the taxi driver. His flat tone doesn't have a chance in hell of hiding his anger.

The driver nods before cranking his neck to the side, seeking an opening in the thick flow of traffic. We've only merged mere inches from the curb before I lose the ability to rein in the aggravation scorching my veins with feverish heat.

"Why did you do that, Marvin?" I ask, shifting my eyes from the back passenger window of the cab to him. "You bombarded me in there, leaving me with no other option than to say yes."

I thought having my impurity announced to a room full of spectators would remain my number one most embarrassing moment, but Marvin's unexpected proposal is cutting it a close second. Not only was the room full of Marvin's family and friends, it was packed with our work colleagues and important associates. People who can aid or destroy any dental career of their choice. Mr. and Mrs. Gardner alone are allies I can't risk as I continue to strive for a prominent place in the notable dental conglomerate of Rochdale.

I dig my nails into my palms, fighting to bottle up my anger, storing it to be used at a more appropriate time.

"We are not ready for that." I keep my voice low, ensuring the taxi driver isn't subjected to the awkwardness of our argument. "I'm not ready for that." The last part of my sentence comes out with a quiver when Marvin swings his furious gaze to me.

"It's been five goddamn years, Ava!" he roars, the veins in his neck bulging.

Four years, nine months and three days, I gabble to myself.

"For fuck's sake, how much more time do you need?" Marvin yanks on the bowtie around his neck, unknotting it until it dangles around his heaving shoulders. "He's *never* coming back. He left you high and dry. Or did you forget that? He's *dead* and you still can't let him go."

My heart painfully squeezes, but I'm not surprised by

Marvin's outburst. He uses the same cruel words during every argument we have, not the slightest bit concerned about how the harshness of his words affects me. When my tearful eyes shift to the rearview mirror, my breath catches. The taxi driver's dark eyes are staring right at me. His gaze is full of worry and empathy. I return the cabbie's compassionate gaze as Marvin continues to unleash a torrent of vicious words.

"Without me, you would have ended up homeless, without a career, without a fucking thing. I fed you, clothed you, have taken care of you for years, but all you care about is a guy who left you. He *left* you, Ava."

The impact of his words is like a knife being stabbed into my chest, but, unfortunately, everything Marvin is saying is true. Hugo did leave me. He choose to go. Marvin didn't.

Inhaling a deep breath to clear my body of nerves, I tilt my torso to face Marvin. "I know that, Marvin, and I appreciate everything you've done for me, what you still do for me," I recount, saying anything to lessen his rambling tirade that always erupts when he drinks or Hugo's name is mentioned. "I'm thankful for everything you've done, but you know as well as I do, marriage isn't the solution for us. Neither of us are ready for that. I'm not ready, and neither are you."

He stares at me, his chest rising and falling with every breath he takes. It feels like hours pass, but it is mere seconds. Marvin's gaze is vehement and has my pulse quickening. When he braces his hands on his knees and drifts his eyes back to the heavy flow of traffic, I know it is the end of our discussion.

"THANK YOU," I say quietly, handing the taxi driver a bunch of crinkled notes from my purse. "Keep the change."

His pupils enlarge when he notices the generosity of my tip. A big tip is the least I can do for exposing him to the daily drama of my life.

I slide out of the taxi and walk up to my front door that's been left open, exposing my home to the chilly midnight temperatures. After ambling into the foyer, I close the door and kick off my shoes. I hang my coat on the coatrack next to Marvin's and pace further inside, seeking his retreating frame.

I discover his dark shadow standing in the middle of my compact kitchen, clasping a glass of hard liquor. Liquor is Marvin's go-to fix for any dilemma. Mine is a long, hot shower. Deciding I don't have enough strength for another argument, I leave Marvin to wallow in solitude and head to the main bathroom. Hopefully a good dose of scalding hot water can wash away some of the negativity choking my usually carefree attitude.

Upon entering my moderately sized bathroom, I remove my dress and place it in a dry cleaning bag draped over the bathroom door. Slipping into a satin knee-length kimono, I pace to the vanity, deciding to make quick work of the heavy makeup suffocating my pores before having a shower.

As I run a cotton cloth drenched in makeup remover on the dark shadow on my eyelids, I roam my eyes over the new ringlets sprouting through my hair. Since I had my hair chemically straightened over five years ago, my curls are returning stronger than ever. In the past six months, I've made three separate appointments to have my hair straightened again, but every time without fail, I neglect to attend my appointment.

Although it was well over ten years ago, the memories of Hugo twirling my hair around his finger when we watched re-runs of *Friends* was in the forefront of my mind every time I was working up the courage to walk in my local hairdressing salon. It might have been the smallest memory, but it still has the greatest impact to my suffering heart.

My reminiscing is interrupted when Marvin staggers into the bathroom. Whiskey and a cheap bottled cologne infiltrates my senses when he stands next to me and props his hip onto the vanity counter.

"I'm going to head to my place."

"It's past midnight, Marvin—"

"I know," he interrupts, his tone surly. "But I have some paperwork I have to take care of."

"It can't wait until the morning?" I shift on my feet to face him.

"No." His reply swift and short.

Keeping his eyes on the vanity, he leans in and presses a kiss to my temple. When he pulls away, his eyes drift down to the engagement ring nestled on my finger, shimmering in the bathroom light. I'll give credit where credit is due. The ring is beautiful, a princess cut three carat diamond of the highest quality, but just from looking at it, I know Marvin didn't choose it. He barely has time to look me in the eyes, let alone pick out my engagement ring.

Marvin lifts his bloodshot eyes to mine. "There could be far worse options for you than marrying me. You're lucky I came into your life when I did. You should remember that."

With that, he pivots on his heels and ambles out of the room.

I wait until I hear my front door slam shut before I call Marvin every curse name under the sun. I don't hold back. Words I swore I'd never speak come out of my mouth in a tirade of cursing a sailor on shore leave would be proud of. My loud rant is highly inappropriate but one hundred percent accurate. Every curse word I've heard in my life could describe Marvin in some form. *Asshole. Two-faced bastard. Motherfucker.* Those are a small handful of the words spilling from my mouth right now. And they're the tame ones.

After having a long, boiling hot shower, my annoyance at my exchange with Marvin is still firmly clutching my neck, asphyxiating me. I throw the frilly decorative pillows off my bed like they're missiles before diving under the thick down quilt.

Even surrounded by softness greater than a cloud, the tension tightly coiling my muscles is making me restless. My eyes drift to the bedside table on my left. I stare at it, willing it to answer my silent questions of whether it's able to calm the storm raging inside of me. *There's only one way I can relieve this type of tension.*

I scoot across the bed and fling open the cherry oak drawer. My heartbeat quickens when I delve my hand inside, hunting through the drawer full to the brim with odd knickknacks and ornaments. My breath hitches when my fingertips brush past a smooth, cool surface. I grasp the item tightly in my hand, knowing it is what I'm seeking without needing to physically see it.

I yank my hand out of the drawer, like I've been scorched by an ignited flame. My eyes dart around the room as I hold the article close to my chest. Once I'm sure the coast is clear of prying eyes, I slowly lower the shiny glass instrument from my heaving chest.

I snap my eyes shut, urging my tears to stay at bay as I twist the lid on the bottle and inhale deeply. Hot, salty tears roll down my cheeks when the invigorating smell of Woods of Windsor aftershave fills the air surrounding me. Even though it doesn't have the scent of his skin mixed with it, it is an energizing smell that sends a flurry of emotions coursing through my mind.

After placing the smallest dab of the aftershave Hugo left sitting open on my bathroom sink nearly five years ago onto my pillow, I put the bottle back safely into the drawer and snuggle into the pillow. No matter how hard I try, no matter how many days, months or years pass, I can't forget. My heart will never forget him.

When my eyelids become as heavy as my heart, I allow my mind to drift. My very first thoughts go to him. *Hugo.*

FIVE

HUGO

FIVE DAYS LATER....

"Hugo!" Izzy squeals at the top of her lungs when I wrap my good arm around her and hoist her off the ground.

I've just arrived at the annual Christmas Eve party billionaire Cormack McGregor holds every year. Cormack is one of Isaac's oldest and dearest friends. Even though he's filthy rich, he's one of the most stellar guys I've ever met.

Just like Isaac, his heart is bigger than his bank account. Although Cormack's Christmas Eve party isn't as extravagant as his other numerous functions I've attended the past five years, it is my favorite. The atmosphere is always relaxed, focused more on guests having a good time than attempting to drain their pockets for the various charities Cormack and Isaac chair.

When I place Izzy down onto the ground, she spins around to face me. Her jaw is hanging low and her eyes are opened wide. After running her eyes over my face, they drop to vigorously access every inch of my body. She has done the same thing every day for the past week. No matter how many times I assure her my injuries were a result of my lack of due diligence, Izzy still harbors guilt over what happened.

"Is the sling a necessity, or are you trying to get sympathy points from the ladies?" she quips, her tone playful as she peers at the sling holding my injured shoulder up.

I throw my head back and laugh. "A little bit of column A, a little bit of column B," I retort, loving that the guilt plaguing her eyes the past week is diminishing as time passes.

I drift my gaze from Izzy's glistening chocolate eyes to Harlow, Izzy's best friend. "Are you going to share one of those?" I ask, gesturing to the bottle of tequila she's clasping. "Since I'm officially not on duty and can't get fired by Izzy misbehaving, I may as well have a little bit of fun."

My deep chuckle booms around the room when Izzy screws up her nose and sticks out her tongue. If I squint, I could pretend she was Jorgie. Harlow waggles her brows before pouring four shots of tequila into gold-flecked shot glasses.

After handing me a shot glass, Harlow playfully winks. "Bottoms up."

Just as the scent of tequila hits my senses, the shot glass is snatched from my hand.

"Or not." Regan downs my nip of tequila.

I balk, surprised when she doesn't attempt to grab a wedge of lime sitting on the round bar table after she swallows the entire nip of tequila in one quick gulp.

"Come on, Regan, one shot won't kill me."

Regan is Raquel's older sister. If that doesn't already make her a ball crusher, she's also Isaac's friend and lawyer.

Regan quirks her lips. "No, but Raquel might if she finds out you were drinking alcohol after taking pain medication."

I scoff. "If she stopped ramming them down my throat, I wouldn't have to worry."

Regan smiles a bright grin. As much as she would deny it, she loves that Raquel is following in her footsteps. Raquel's hard ass, take-shit-from-no-one stance has been wearing my patience thin the past week, but in all honesty, even with her busting my chops at every opportunity, Raquel is good at her job. Without her pushing me, I'd most likely still be laid up in a hospital bed, stewing over my confrontation with Rhys.

Only now, years after the incident do I realize I was in the wrong from the way I reacted when Rhys informed me Jorgie wasn't going to pull through her injuries, but in my defense, part of me died the day Jorgie did. And no matter how hard I fight to piece back the shattered pieces of my heart, it never happens. *It will never happen.*

My eyes float from the floor when Isaac asks, "How did you get out of Raquel's clutches for the night?"

"I didn't," I grumble, my mood balancing dangerously between somber and playful. "She sent her evil twin in her place."

My mood sways to playful when Regan throws her clutch into my chest, winding me from the power of her hit. I chuckle while ribbing her with my elbow. Although Regan acts like she hates me, the tears frequenting her eyes every time she visited me in the hospital tells me she likes me a little more than she's letting on, but just like Raquel, as much as taming the beast raging inside Regan would be a compelling feat, she's too much of a friend to tread over that line.

I cringe when a high-pitched voice shrieks through my ears. "Holy crap! What is that?"

My eyes missile to Cormack's little sister, Cate. Her bugging eyes are planted on a glistening of color sparkling on Izzy's hand.

Izzy's teeth munch on her bottom lip. "We're engaged."

I can't hold in the grin that morphs across my face. Although Izzy and Isaac have only been a couple a few short months, time is no barrier when you find your other half. It shouldn't matter if it is a week or a year, if they're who your heart desires, that's all that matters. *Oh god, would you listen to me? Maybe I did get shot in the cock instead of my shoulder.*

My brows furrow from the stern glare Isaac directs at me when I issue my congratulations to Izzy with a friendly hug. He knows me. I never cut another man's turf. Shrugging off Isaac's newly acquired second green head of envy, I slip away from the group and amble to the bar. I raise my chin in greeting to the bartender preparing a spritzer for a slightly overweight lady wearing a dress five sizes too big for the luscious curves of her body.

"Can I grab a beer?" I request, sitting on the barstool.

The bartender places a coaster in front of me before setting an open bottle of beer on it.

"Where have I seen you?" I ask, raising the beer to my parched mouth.

He seems familiar to me, but his name has been misplaced, which is unusual for me. I have a stellar knack for matching names with faces.

"Dante," he introduces himself.

After wiping his condensation-covered hand down a white tea towel hanging off his waist, he offers it in greeting.

I accept his hand. "Hugo."

He tries to mask his surprise, but I didn't miss his quick intake of breath that relays he knows who I am. Not the Hugo Jones everyone in Ravenshoe knows. The real Hugo. The Hugo Marshall who vanished from Rochdale nearly five years ago.

The pulse thrumming in Dante's neck increases when I squeeze his hand with more force than I was originally instilling. He tries to pry his hand out of my grasp, but his small frame is no match for a man of my size.

"Please don't break my hand. I'm starting my internship to be a surgeon next month," he begs, his eyes pleading into mine.

"How do you know me?" I query, my tone low as anger envelopes me.

I've reached my quota of run-ins with people from my past. First, I had to deal with Col Petretti sniffing around Ravenshoe, then Rhys, now Dante.

"My brother," he stammers as the bones in his hand creak from my brutal pressure. "My brother is Rhys."

My eyes dance over his face. Same mocha skin coloring, hazel eyes, and prominent nose. I don't know how I missed it. He's the spitting image of his older brother. The strain hampering Dante's face eases when I release him from my grip. His hand shoots across the counter, ensuring it isn't within my reach. I swig on my beer. Dante follows my every movement.

"Why are you in Ravenshoe?" I ask, my voice low.

I shift my eyes around the room, ensuring no one witnessed my small confrontation with Dante. Isaac is talking to Clara at the side, and Izzy is pacing toward the makeshift dance floor with Cormack's younger brother, Colby, closely in pursuit. Happy no one is watching, I shift my eyes back to Dante.

"Rhys is my guardian," he mutters. "Until I finish my studies, I go where he goes."

My brows stitch together. "What happened to your parents?"

Mr. and Mrs. Tagget have been members of the Rochdale community as long as my parents. Mrs. Tagget was my fifth grade teacher and Mr. Tagget was the local obstetrician.

"They were killed in a traffic accident nearly five years ago," Dante informs me.

My eyes snap to Dante. The devastation of his loss still weighs heavily in his readable eyes. They're full of remorse and anguish.

"I'm sorry for your loss."

Although my eyes issue my sympathies for the loss of his parents, they also deliver my repentance for my earlier overreaction. Dante nods, accepting my apology before moving down the bar to serve another patron.

My attention lapses from perusing the dance floor when a flurry of red catches my eyes.

"Hi," Peta breathes out heavily, slipping into the space beside me.

"Hey." I swig on my beer to conceal my assessment of her face and body.

Peta is Cormack's secretary, and the second sexiest woman alive. She has flawless, rich, tan skin; unique light brownish-yellowish eyes; and a face hand-carved by sculptors. She's no doubt gorgeous, and even better than that, she's not a friend of mine.

"Did you want to dance?"

My lips purse, shocked by her request. Although we've

openly flirted the past year, it's never gone any further than a few corny one-liners. That may have something to do with the fact I refuse to ask anyone out. Not to a date, to the movies, or even to dance. No one has been asked out before Ava, and no one will be asked out after her.

When Peta runs her shaking hand over the curve of her top lip, I realize I failed to answer her question.

"Sure, I'd love to dance," I say with a grin.

I guzzle down the last of my beer before guiding Peta to the dance floor by placing my hand on the small of her back. My eyes scan the area as we approach, ensuring it is clear of any encumbrances. Screening the premises is as natural as breathing to me. It is a habit that was engrained in me years ago, way before Ava and I reunited. Although I'd always done it, it became more important after Ava was nearly attacked in a dance club right under my nose. Some may see my constant surveillance as an annoying practice. To me, it isn't. Keeping an eye out for safety means I won't get blinded by other people's bad habits.

After nearly an hour of dancing, my dress shirt is limp, weighed down by a mountain load of sweat, my throat is parched, and my shoulder is wailing in pain, though I'd never admit the latter to Raquel. I lean in to Peta's side, ensuring she can hear me over the loud rumble of music booming out the speakers.

"I'm going to grab a quick drink," I shout in her ear. "Did you want anything?"

She spins on her heels, revealing inches of skin on her luxurious thigh when the split in her dress gapes open. Spotting her mouth-watering legs has me wanting to reconsider what hankering I want to tackle first. My thirst, or another irrepressible hunger only a woman can quench.

"A bottle of water?" Peta replies. Her unease makes her request come out as more of a question than a demand. "Then maybe we can get out of here?" she adds on, her voice trembling.

My heads slants to the side and I peer into her famished eyes. The unsure grin curling her lips morphs into a full smile when I nod. Winking at the excitement crossing her face, I pivot on my heels and make my way to the bar. Dante's throat works hard to swallow when he notices me approaching. If I weren't in the midst of thinking with my lower head, I'd take the time to properly apologize for my previous reaction, but for now, that will have to wait. After gathering my beer and a glass of iced water, I amble back to the dance floor. My pace is fast, eager to wash off the funk I've been sporting the past week.

My brisk strides only falter when a deep voice says, "If I squint, I can see the similarities."

I crank my head to the side faster than a rocket launching into space. Rhys is standing behind a round bar table. Unlike last week, he has forgone his surgical scrubs and stethoscope, choosing the classier look of a sleek black suit with pale green dress shirt.

With the air saturated with mugginess from a large gathering of people in a small space, he's removed his suit jacket and rolled up the sleeves of his shirt, exposing his vast collection of tattoos. Just like my arms, every inch of skin on Rhys' forearms is covered in artwork. Just seeing Rhys floods my mind with memories I try to keep buried. *Imagine what it would be like if I ever saw her again?*

After lifting my chin in greeting, I continue with my initial objective.

"Poor girl. Does she even know you're looking at her as a doppelgänger?"

I grit my teeth and continue walking, choosing to ignore Rhys' taunt. I'm not the same man I was five years ago; I've learned to hide my spikes well.

"She may look like Ava, but you sure as hell know even someone as beautiful as her can't compete with a woman of Ava's qualities. No one can compete with Ava's sweetness."

I freeze halfway between the bar and the dance floor. I inhale quick, rapid-fired breaths to calm the anger bubbling in my veins, but no matter what I do, no matter how much I try to suffocate the jealousy building like an out-of-control wildfire, I can't squash it. I've never been able to rein in my anger when it comes to Ava.

Before I can contemplate what I'm doing, I spin on my heels and charge toward Rhys. He doesn't balk. He doesn't even blink an eye when he notices me storming his way. He just stands his ground, like a man who is on a mission to unravel me one thread at a time.

"Even after all this time, she's still under your skin." His eyes bounce between mine. "She's right where you left her, Hugo. If you want her that much, why don't you go get her?"

"I left for a reason." My angry snarl booms over the blaring music.

"Yeah and that reason is now dead."

I balk and take a step backward.

"Come on, Hugo. Give me some credit. I'm a lot smarter than I look." He takes a step closer to me. "The man who was charged with running down Jorgie goes missing the exact day the victim's brother falls off the face of the earth, never to be seen again."

In the corner of my eye, I catch Hunter watching the exchange between Rhys and me. He runs his hand along the edge of his scruffy beard, signaling he's positioned to step in at any time. I crack my neck, advising that I've got this. Although Hunter moves deeper into the crowd, I can feel his eyes on me.

"You may want to get your facts straight before you go running your mouth. This town isn't Rochdale," I warn.

Rhys smirks, not the faintest bit intimidated by my threat. "Col Petretti wanted your blood. When he couldn't get it, he went after the next closest thing."

"That is why I left!" I snap, incapable of inhibiting my anger any longer. "That is why I stayed away. To protect my family!" *To protect Ava.*

Rhys' strong stance weakens. "I know that, but you can't use that excuse anymore. Col Petretti is dead. I saw his body myself. So if you want to keep hiding, pretending you're dead too, you'll need to find another excuse, because your last one expired."

My nostrils flare as my lungs fight hard to cool my overheated body. Even though everything Rhys is saying is true, it doesn't stop the anger pumping my veins with ferocious heat.

Rhys rolls down the sleeves of his shirt and puts on his jacket. Once his suit coat is buttoned up, he lifts his penitent eyes to me. "It took courage to walk away like you did. To sacrifice everything to keep your family safe. To keep Ava safe, but a man who can admit he made a mistake would be even more courageous than that."

With a flash of an uneasy smirk, he ambles out of Destiny Records' head office without a backward glance.

By the time Peta finds me standing where Rhys left me, her glass of water is sitting at room temperature, and my mood is woeful.

Peta's unique light brown eyes dance between mine. "I'll catch you at the next function?" she says, reading my pitiful mood without me even needing to speak.

I nod, place a kiss on her cheek and make my way to my truck. Everything Rhys said plays on repeat for the entire drive to my apartment building, but it isn't as simple as he makes it out to be. Just because Col is dead doesn't mean I can waltz back into my old life like nothing happened. I'm also dead. The Hugo Marshall who was born in Rochdale is dead. I can't come back from that. And even if I wanted to pretend the facts didn't matter, there would be no possibility a woman like Ava would still be single and waiting for me to return. *Would there?*

Hawke's head lifts from his laptop monitor when he hears me entering the front door of my apartment. Although Isaac offered him his own apartment, he was happy to camp in the spare bedroom of my place while I was recovering at Regan's. He watches me cautiously but remains quiet. I rip the stupid shoulder brace off my body and dump it into the bin in the kitchen. Grabbing a cold beer out of the fridge, I crack it open on the marble countertop.

"Good night?"

I grunt before flopping onto the white leather sofa in my sunken living room. After grabbing a few extra beers, Hawke ambles into the room and sits in the seat next to me. If I ignore the cracks in my heart, I could pretend we are sitting back in his den, laughing and drinking beers like we did every Sunday afternoon when he wasn't deployed.

As the hours tick by on the clock, the beers settling into my belly lessen the anger coursing through my veins.

"Come back with me," I blurt out, my mouth choosing to speak before my brain can object. "Come back with me to Rochdale."

Hawke stiffens but remains as quiet as a church mouse. "I can't," he eventually replies, staring straight ahead. "I can't go back there without her."

"Do you think she'd want this, Hawke? Do you think Jorgie would want you to be living like this? Either of us living like this? If you can even call it living. You're fucking miserable," I shout, my voice rising as a surge of emotions pummel into me. "Jorgie would be rolling in her grave--"

Before any more of my drunken tirade can escape my lips, Hawke's stealthy moves have me pinned against the wall of my living room. The veins in his neck bulge as he tightens his grip around my throat. His nostrils flare as his broken, desolate eyes burn into mine.

"She's never coming back, Hawke," I sputter, my words cracking.

He yanks me forward before slamming me back with brutal force. My body doesn't register the pain of my head slamming into the hard wall; it's too focused on the hurt projecting out of Hawke's lifeless eyes to register anything. I don't put up a fight because I know he needs this even more than I do.

My watering eyes drift between his. "She's gone, Hawke."

"You don't think I know that?!" he roars, the veins in his neck bulging. "I wake up every fucking day praying it was all a nightmare, praying that Jorgie and Malcolm are still here, but it never happens. I never wake up! I don't need you to tell me she's gone. I'm stuck in this fucking nightmare. I live it every fucking day. I know she's gone!"

His jaw quivers as a flood of moisture forms in his eyes. His chest heaves up and down as he struggles through the same emotions that cripple me every time I think of the loss of Jorgie and my nephew... *and Ava.* Hawke's grip on my neck loosens as his eyes dart between mine.

"But you don't have to live in this nightmare if you don't want to. Ava can pull you out of it." Hawke's eyes flick between mine. "But only you can choose if you want her to save you."

My feet return to the ground when he releases his grip on my neck. "I'd give anything for another day with Jorgie. To have her in my arms. To hold my son, but I don't have that opportunity. You do."

After picking up the reclining chair he knocked over as if it is weightless, he staggers out of the room without a backward glance.

SIX

HUGO

My hand darts down to the window crank of my car – *Jorgie's baby*. Shifting my eyes between the road and the window mechanism, I wind the window up, easing the thick blast of cold air blowing in from outside.

It's colder here than I remember.

The crisp wind, chilled with sleet has the tip of my nose turning a shade of red.

I didn't even pack a jacket.

Every mile I get closer has my heart rate quickening. Even though it's been years since I've been here, I know the way. It is engrained in me. I took the same route I used when I left. All back roads hidden from prying eyes. The candy apple coloring of my car is now a murky brown thanks to the thick dust lifting off the dirt roads I've driven down.

The tremble pounding my heart extends to my hands when the "Welcome to Rochdale" sign peers over the horizon. I've been driving for hours, nearly nine straight. I only pulled over for gas before I continued on my mission, not giving my brain the chance to formulate an objection to my rushed decision I made while hungover and licking my wounds from my tussle with Hawke.

Noticing my gas gauge sitting close to empty, I pull into a gas station on the outskirts of the main town district. The quietness that surrounds me when I switch off the ignition and curl out of the driver's seat is disturbing. When there is too much silence, my mind tends to wander. Ducking back into the cab to grab my wallet, I snatch a baseball cap and pull it down low over my head.

While filling up the gas tank, my eyes roam around my surroundings. Five years has passed, and its looks like nothing has changed. The graffiti on the brick wall attached to St. Mary's church is still where it was, only faded and accentuated with new tags. The half shackle sign dangling out of the front of Gus's Grease Box is still rusted and askew, and the inquisitive gawks are still present. *Nothing's changed.*

I place the gas nozzle back into the pump and amble into the service station, eager to pay for my gas and continue with my trip. It's late and I'm beyond tired. The beat of my heart kicks up when the glass automatic doors swing open and numerous pairs of eyes turn to me. I lower the sleeves of my shirt, concealing my tattoos that normally conjure nosey gazers.

Several pairs of eyes track me as I walk across the space. My long steps have me reaching the counter in four strides. Even with a cap hanging low on my face and my appearance altered from the effects of age, I know their curious stares aren't associated with a stranger arriving in the middle of the night. No, they come from recognition.

I was born and raised in Rochdale, the beloved quarterback of the high school football team crowned State Champions two years in a row under my leadership, but even if they're too young to remember my glory days, or too old to care, my family are well known members of the community and I'm the spitting image of my father. My eyes, my nose, hell, my entire face is an exact replica of his.

"Pump four," I say, tossing three rolled up twenties onto the counter before spinning on my heels. I always pay with cash. No cards means no chance of being tracked.

My brisk strides slow when the cashier shouts, "You forgot your change."

I raise my arm into the air. "Keep it."

I stop frozen in my tracks when the cashier replies, "I can't do that, Hugo. It's against the rules."

The automatic doors open and close, unable to sense if I'm coming or going. They aren't the only ones confused.

After exhaling a big breath, I spin on my heels. The walk back to the counter is painstakingly long. I raise my chin high enough to peer at the cashier, but low enough my face isn't fully exposed.

A grin carves on my mouth when the petite frame of Mary Walker pops into my peripheral vision. Her glistening corn-flower blue eyes stare into mine, her excitement building with every step I take.

"Hey." Grinning broadly, she fiddles with the hem of her floral skirt. "I knew it was you."

Mary was in Ava and Jorgie's grade at school. Since she was born ten weeks premature, she has always been a tiny little thing, looking much younger than her real age. Her older brother Mitchell was a good friend of mine in high school. We lost contact when his life took a ride down a very steep hill at the same time mine hit a brick wall.

"How are you going, Mary?" I ask, accepting the crumpled up notes she's holding out and shoving them into the pocket of my jeans.

The smile on her face broadens, both shocked and happy that I remember her.

"Good," she replies quietly. "If you're in town long, come on over to the house one day, Mitchy would love to see you."

I nod. "I will. I'll try and get there later this week."

She smiles even bigger. With a dip of my chin, I bid farewell to Mary before walking out of the service station, not missing the extra sets of eyes I gained from my brief exchange with her.

I slide into my car and crank the ignition. As I pull onto the road, I roll the window back down, needing the crispness in the air to calm the mad beat of my heart. One more mile is all I have left to travel. The town is quiet, not surprising since it is late on Christmas day.

My eyes scan my surroundings as I pull down a familiar street. The same wrought iron lights line the edge of the cracked concrete sidewalks, clapboard houses in a range of pastel colors and rolling lush green front yards.

Nothing's changed.

I release my heavy compression on the accelerator, slowly creeping my car closer to my childhood home. When I come to a stop in front of the two story house, I'm not surprised when I spot a light flicking in the back right-hand corner of the property. No doubt, my mom still packing away the dishes from the Marshall Christmas party she hosts every year.

I wonder what her reaction will be when I stroll back into her life? Will she greet me like she did the morning I turned up for family brunch? Or will she be angry for the way I left?

"There's only one way to find out," I mumble to no one.

I pull into the driveway and park behind my mom's station wagon. *I can't believe she still drives that old thing.* My hand trembles as I open the car door and step out onto the concrete driveway. The smell of pumpkin pie and mashed potatoes filter in the air as I briskly stride down the side of the house.

My steps are fast and uninhibited, ensuring I don't give myself the opportunity to back down on my quest. I've daydreamed about this day for years, but I never thought it would come to fruition. I grip the handle of the screen door, willing for the memories of the last time I exited these doors to slip my mind. Sucking in a lung-filling gulp of air, I pull open the door. The old wood gives out a slight creak, but I barely hear it over the Christmas music playing on a radio in the middle of the kitchen counter.

As I pace into the kitchen, my eyes drift around the room. *Nothing's changed.* It is exactly the same. My mom's hair, although a little grayer than I remember around the temples, is pulled back in a bun. She has a pair of pink gloves on her hands as she works her way through a pile of dirty dishes stacked at her side.

Her hips swing, bobbing side to side as she sways to "Jingle Bell Rock" by Bobby Helms drifting from the speaker on the island counter. Half-eaten pies and containers of food are stacked on the countertops. No doubt the fridge is too crammed to fit in all the goodies she bakes every Christmas.

Pacing in closer to my mom, I open my mouth, preparing to

speak. My words entomb in my throat when the swinging door between the kitchen and the dining room swings open and Ava glides inside. My heart freezes along with my feet. *My god, she's even more beautiful than I remembered.*

Her hair is a crazy mess of ringlet curls sitting a few inches past her shoulders, her face is fresh and unmarked, like she hasn't aged a day in five years, and her body is captivating. Her lush tits are only just hidden by a dusty pink cashmere sweater, the hem sitting on her curvy rounded hips. Her stomach is smooth and flat, and although I can't see her legs that are covered by a pair of black jeans, I'm sure they're just as stellar as the rest of her. She's captivatingly beautiful and has me wanting to drop to my knees.

My heart leaps out of my chest when a screeching scream rips through my eardrums. My mom's focus is no longer on the dirty dishes. She's staring at me wide-eyed, her face pale and full of disbelief. Her squeal demands Ava's attention. Following my mom's fretful stare, Ava pivots around to face me. She intakes a quick, sharp breath as a flood of tears wells in her eyes. The wine glass she's holding plummets to the ground as she lifts her hand to clamp it over her gaped mouth, muffling her shocked scream.

The wine glass shatters as the first tear slides down Ava's cheek.

SEVEN

AVA

When an ear-piercing scream rattles my core, I pivot on my heels, panicked beyond comprehension at what has caused Mrs. Marshall to react in such a way. Her entire body is uncontrollably shaking, her face pale and clearly in shock. She looks like she has seen a ghost. I swing my eyes to the side, both eager and fearful to discover what has caused her unusual reaction.

The air is vehemently removed from my lungs when my eyes lock in on a face I only see in my dreams. My hands slick with sweat, causing my wineglass to slip from my grasp and plummet to the floor, shattering into a million pieces at my feet. My stomach swirls, threatening to spill its contents at any moment as my brain tries to comprehend what I'm seeing. It can't be true. It can't be him. He's dead. Gone. Never coming back.

I lift my hand to cover my gaped mouth while ensuring the contents of my churning stomach have no way of escaping. I snap my eyes shut and shake my head, compelling myself to wake up. I must have fallen asleep, or perhaps I'm in a food-induced coma from eating too many carbohydrates during Christmas dinner.

My breath hitches halfway between my lungs and my throat when my eyes slowly flutter open and the visual of both my nightmares and dreams still stands before me. Even with half of his face shadowed by the brim of a baseball cap, I'd never forget that face: his plump, delicious lips, perfectly straight nose, and eyes that captured my soul and never gave it back.

The shock on Mrs. Marshall's face hasn't lessened any as her head flings between Hugo and me. Even though she has tears streaming down her face, her excitement at seeing her youngest son again is evident all over her beautiful face. She graces me with a shaky smile before she dashes to Hugo. Her steps are slow and unstable, overwhelmed with the same emotions that are keeping my feet planted on the ground.

Mrs. Marshall crashes into Hugo with so much force, a rustle of air parts his lips. She slings her arms around his neck as a tormented sob tears from her mouth. I lower my shaky hand to my thigh and pinch hard, urging myself to wake up. I pinch so hard, I'm going to be sporting a nasty bruise in the morning, but I don't wake up. *Surely, I'm dreaming. I have to be.*

Mrs. Marshall's loud sobs secures the attention of the remaining Marshall residents still clearing away the mess of a chaotic Christmas day. Although we are all exhausted, none of us wanted to leave the burden solely on Mrs. Marshall's shoulders. Mr. Marshall's brisk strides to his wife falter when Hugo lifts his head from his mom's neck. She's accidentally knocked the cap off his head, fully exposing his Marshall family heirloom: his glistening baby blues.

I bite the inside of my cheek hard, battling to keep my tears at bay when Mr. Marshall's knees buckle and he lands on the ground. Tears seep from his eyes as joy overwhelms him. I fling my tears off my cheek when Chase and Helen rush into the kitchen, their faces morphing from panicked to astounded in record-breaking time. They rush to aid their father off the ground before greeting Hugo with the same amount of enthusiasm their mother showed. I stand still, numb and in shock. My brain can't comprehend the complexity of the situation, let alone command my legs to move.

The final person to enter the kitchen is Marvin. He appears more annoyed about the interruption to the football game he's watching than concerned for what caused Mrs. Marshall's screams. Marvin props his shoulder on the doorjamb and swings his eyes around the room. My attention reverts to the gathering of Marshall members reuniting when Hugo loudly pats his brother on the back before stepping past him.

My heart thrashes wildly against my ribs when his gaze locks with mine as he slowly paces to me. His eyes blaze into mine, rendering me even more motionless than my shock. A smirk curls on his lips as his heavy-lidded gaze runs over my face before lowering to absorb my body.

Suddenly, his pace slows as he swallows harshly. His eyes are arrested by the diamond ring on my finger. I battle hard not to squirm when his fervent gaze burns the skin surrounding my engagement ring.

When his eyes float back to my face, he musters up a fake smirk before continuing with his strides. The glint of happiness sparking his vibrant eyes dampens when I'm suddenly clutched around the waist and pulled into a heated body.

"We should go, Ava," Marvin jerks me in tighter. "Our taxi has arrived." He gestures his head to a yellow and black taxi parked behind an unfamiliar car in the driveway.

I'm too dazed, stuck in an illusory state to form a response. Hugo's eyes dart between me and Marvin as Marvin guides me past him and into the foyer. In a blur, Marvin shoves my coat into my hands and places my beanie on my head. Freezing cold winds blast my face when we step onto the back patio. My body is shaking intensely. I don't know if it is from the crispness of the cold winter night or because I'm in shock.

"Ava," says a voice from behind. A voice I immediately recognize. *A voice I'll never forget.*

"Keep walking, Ava," Marvin demands, seizing my elbow and dragging me toward the waiting taxi.

"Ava, wait." Hugo leaps off the patio to follow us down the concrete path. "Just give me a minute. That's all I'm asking."

My eyes shoot up to Marvin, stupidly requesting permission. Marvin's lips thin, and he briskly shakes his head. Yanking open the taxi door, Marvin snatches my coat from my hand, throws it into the taxi, and gestures his head to the cab, demanding for me to enter.

The disbelief hazing my normally astute mind clears when Hugo says, "Nothing's changed. You're still letting a man tell you what to do. First your dad, now Marvin."

Something inside me snaps, and for the first time in years, it isn't my heart. I pivot on my heel, preparing to storm toward Hugo. Marvin snatches my wrist, halting my angry steps. Gritting my teeth, I yank out of Marvin's tight grasp, my anger too great for him to stop me. A jolting pain spasms my arm, but I'm too irate to register it.

"Give me one goddamn minute!" I request to Marvin, snarling through clenched teeth.

Marvin's furious eyes burn into mine, but they hold no threat. Even if they did, nothing could stop me. My entire body shakes as I charge toward Hugo, stopping only when I'm within an inch of his face. I'm so close, our chests connect with every breath of air we inhale.

"Don't you dare judge me!" I scream, ignoring the tears threatening to spill down my cheeks. "You don't know what I've been through. The hell I went through."

My anger is so strong, I can barely breathe.

I pound my enclosed fists on his chest. "You can't come waltzing back into the picture, acting like nothing happened. It's been five years, Hugo! Five goddamn fucking years!"

I step back, angrily brushing away a string of curls that have fallen in front of my face. "You can't come back from that amount of time. You can't pretend it never happened."

"We have before," he argues, stepping closer to me with his remorseful eyes bouncing between mine.

My back molars snap together. "We were kids. Stupid pathetic kids too young to know any better." My voice lowers as the pain in my heart cripples me.

Hugo shakes his head and steps closer to me. "The past cannot be changed, forgotten, edited, or erased. It can only be accepted."

I hold out my hand, keeping him at a safe distance. "You can't change the past, but you can learn from it. I let you back in my life once. I learned from my mistake. I'm *not* going to make it again."

With that, I pivot on my heels and race back to the taxi.

Ignoring the furious wrath of Marvin, I slide into the back seat of the taxi and slam the door shut, forcing Marvin to enter the taxi from the other side.

When I raise my eyes from my balled fists, I'm met with the tormented face of Hugo, struggling to get out of his brother's clutch. The silence in the cab amplifies the devastating sound of my heart being torn in two from the melancholy look on Hugo's face as he furiously fights against Chase.

Hugo yelling my name and begging for a chance to explain bellows into the cabin when Marvin enters the cab from the opposite side. Marvin's tone is curt when he recites my address to the driver, but thankfully, he spends the entire trip back to my house giving me the silent treatment. I spend the drive gathering my skewed composure, bottling it away for another day, not to be used until I'm alone and without the fear of repercussions.

EIGHT

HUGO

Everything's changed.

"Ava!" I shout, shrugging out of Chase's hold.

My steps to the retreating taxi are sluggish, weighed down by the heaviness of my maimed heart. Seeing Ava's tears hurts more than I could have ever imagined. Knowing I'm the one who caused them makes the deathly tight grip on my heart even firmer. It killed me seeing the tears streaming down her pale cheeks. I just want the chance to wipe them away. To beg for forgiveness. To explain what happened. Why I did what I did, but I didn't even get to say hello... *or goodbye.*

I crouch down on the ground still misting from the taxi's engine to run a shaky hand over my head. I don't know what I was expecting. I knew Ava's reaction wasn't going to exactly replicate my mom's, but I was hoping it would follow a similar path. That she was going to have happy tears flowing down her face, not ones filled with heartbreak and despair.

In all honestly, on the drive here, I was hoping Ava had

moved on, was married and had kids. Because if she did that, I would've known I didn't shatter her heart and break her spirit. I was hoping my absence would have only caused a little ripple in her pond of water, not a tidal wave, but from the devastated look in her eyes when she banged her fists on my chest, screaming about the hell she's been living in, I realized my prayers were left unanswered, just like Ava's.

I'll admit it, it felt like a grizzly bear was clawing my chest when I noticed the sparkling diamond ring flickering on her ring finger, but that was nothing compared to the pain I felt when Marvin clutched Ava's waist. That grizzly didn't just maim my heart, he ripped it out of my chest and shredded it to pieces.

Chase squeezes my shoulder before squatting down in front of me. "Give her some time, Hugo. It's been a really long, and now emotionally draining day."

It's been the longest fucking day of my life.

Chase stands before me offering me his hand. Snubbing the guilt creeping into my veins, I accept his hand. A sharp jolt of pain rockets through my shoulder when Chase clasps my hand in his and yanks me from the ground. *Pain is good. A reminder of how far I've come.*

"Getting a bit soft in your old age," Chase jests, noticing the wince I failed to stifle.

"Something like that."

He curls his thick arm around my shoulder and guides me back into the house. My mom's eyes are plagued with red rims and tears. My dad is still shocked, his hand rattling as he sips on the glass of water Helen gave him. I can't believe after all this time I thought nothing would have changed. Everything has changed. Even me.

"YOU'RE FUCKING KIDDING ME!" I say, my words barely audible from the breathy chuckle escaping my lips. "It's exactly the same!"

Chase nods and laughs. "Mom didn't want to change anything." He places my overnight bag onto my childhood bed with its camo bedspread. "Even Jorgie's room is the same."

It doesn't hurt hearing Jorgie's name as much as it normally does, since it is coming out of Chase's mouth. I have to remember I'm not the only one who loved and lost Jorgie. Everyone in this house did too. *Ava as well.*

"How long has Ava been engaged for?" I ask. I try to get my tone neutral, but it slightly smears with agitation. Out of all the men in the world, I can't believe Ava paired up with Marvin.

Chase's face scrunches. Apparently he isn't a fan of Marvin either. "From what Helen told me, it only happened last week. Ava hasn't officially announced it yet."

My lips quirk. Sensing my piqued interest, Chase glides his blue eyes to me. Although his eyes are creased with wrinkles I've never seen and his jaw covered with a thick beard, he's still the same Chase who stood by my side when Hawke married Jorgie five years ago. The same Chase who dared me to eat a bee to see if it tasted like honey. He's my brother. My blood.

"Fuck. I still can't believe you're here."

A whizz of air escapes my nose. "You're not the only one."

"You missed so much, Hugo. *So much...* Jesus, what Ava went through. Fuck. You have no clue."

I do understand what Ava went through. Leaving her broke

my heart too. Losing Jorgie gutted me. Losing Ava devastated me.

"Don't expect her to just forgive you, Hugo. It isn't that simple. You didn't just walk away leaving her with a broken heart. You shattered her soul."

The constrictive hold strangling my heart strengthens. "I know, Chase. I live with the guilt of what I did to her every day."

He runs his hand over his tired eyes. "It's been a long ass day. I'm tired. You look dog-ass tired."

I throw my head back and laugh. Chase has always been direct.

"I'm heading out. If you're not busy tomorrow, come and meet your nieces," he suggests.

My eyes missile to his. "You have kids?"

Chase smirks while nodding. "Yeah. Two little girls."

I take a step backward when my eyes shoot down to his hand and I notice a thick platinum band wrapped around his ring finger.

"Holy shit, you're married? Chase No-Girl-Is-Ever-Going-To-Catch-Me Marshall is married? Fuck, I've missed so much."

Chase chuckles at my use of his old nickname in high school. "You have no clue how much you missed these past five years." He slings his arm around my injured shoulder and pats me on the back. "No fucking clue."

He inches back to glance into my eyes. His gaze is packed with unease. "See you tomorrow?"

I smirk, trying to ease his uncertainty. "I'll be here."

After throwing a punch into my chest, Chase ambles out of the room. I stare at the door, utterly dumbfounded. Chase was adamant no girl was ever going to tie him down. He always joked that is why our parents called him Chase. Because women would be chasing him across the country. Now he's married with two kids. *Fucking crazy.*

I rub a painful knot in my shoulder while pacing around my room. It looks exactly like it did the last time I was here. *When I snatched Ava's virginity.* Same bedspread, faded border, even the pictures hanging on the wall are the same. There are so many memories here. Good ones, and ones that still haunt me.

Being surrounded by silence makes my memories even stronger.

As memories I try to keep hidden flood into me, the walls of my childhood room close in. I shake my head, begging for the images that plague my dreams with nightmares to vanish. When they become too great, I leap from my bed, snag my duffle bag from the floor and bolt down the stairs. I can't stay here. It reminds me too much of her, and the time I stole Ava's virginity.

The house is eerily quiet, not a peep can be heard. I'm halfway out the back door when recollections of me running five years ago smack into me. *I can't do that to them again. I can't run.*

Snatching my mom's shopping list off the fridge, I scribble down a quick note saying I'll be back first thing in the morning. For extra reassurance, I add my untraceable cell phone number at the bottom of the note.

FORTY-FIVE MINUTES HAVE TICKED by before I pull my car into the driveway of Jorgie's house. I've tried every motel in town, but due to the late hour and being Christmas, every motel within a twenty-mile radius is either booked up or closed. Although the memories of Jorgie are strong in her house, for the majority, they're good memories.

I turn off the ignition and crank open the door of my *baby* before walking up the cracked concrete path. After barely a wink of sleep last night and the events of today, I'm exhausted and barely standing straight. After rubbing my tired eyes, I run my hand along the top lip of the door, knowing it is the spot every Marshall family member hides their spare key.

"Third pot on the left," whispers a voice to my side a short time later, scaring the living daylights out of me.

After gathering my heart off the floor, I focus my attention to the voice.

"Mrs. Mable?" I ask, my surprise evident.

Nothing against Mrs. Mable, but she would have be getting close to ninety, and that's on a good day.

"If you're looking for the spare key, it's under the third pot on the left," she instructs.

I nod before moving to the scattering of pots lining the edge of the patio. A puff of air whizzes from my nostrils when I find a shiny gold key hidden under a small pot of Japanese Yew.

"Thanks," I praise, holding the key into the air.

Pushing the key into the lock, I swing my eyes to Mrs. Mable. "Why aren't they hiding the key on the door lip anymore?" I query.

"Jeez, do I look like a giraffe?" she gibes, waving her hand in the air like she's swatting a fly.

A chuckle escapes my lips. Mrs. Mable reminds me of Estelle Getty, the actress who played Sophia Petrillo in *The*

Golden Girls. She's small and compact, but more explosive than dynamite.

"I keep my eyes on the place, make sure no one is up to any mischief," Mrs. Mable explains, her tone bitchy. "You're not up to any mischief, are you, Hugo?"

She eyes me with suspicion. A brick lodges in my throat before I shake my head. *Not today I'm not.*

"Alright, then don't let me hold you; it's nearly three AM."

She turns around and enters her house, only to stop and spin around two seconds later. "And take your boots off. Their noisy stomping woke me up," she snarls.

"Sorry," I apologize, my lips twitching to crack a smile from the derisive stare she's awarding me with.

I kick my boots off and throw them to the side of the patio before unlocking Jorgie's front door and ambling inside. I don't bother switching on any of the lights. I've walked the floors of this house so many times that I can recall every inch in photographic detail.

My plan is to catch up on a few hours of sleep before wrangling a way to force Ava to talk to me. Until I've hashed out all my guilt for what happened, I'm going to relentlessly nag her. Even if she never wants to talk to me again, I still want the opportunity to explain why I vanished. Maybe once she realizes I did it to protect her, she can release some of the pent-up anger she's harboring toward me.

I massage a kink out of my neck before pulling my long-sleeve shirt over my head. My eyelids are heavy, exhausted from being awake nearly thirty-six hours. I take a left at the end of the hall before entering the second door on the right.

Although never officially given the title, this room was my

room anytime I stayed at Jorgie's house. I unbutton the fly on my jeans and slide down the zipper. By the time I hit the end of the double bed, my jeans are discarded on the floor and I'm wearing nothing but a pair of socks. The bed gives out a creak when I sit down to yank off my socks. After tugging back the thick duvet cover, I slip into the bed.

The brisk coolness of the night becomes a forgotten memory when I sink into the heavenliness of a warm bed. There's a beautiful smell infusing the air. A homely smell. It smells fresh. Sweet even. Sweet with a dash of aftershave. It's kind of like a smell of a man and woman mingled together. It's intoxicating.

My eyes balk when a body curls around my torso. My heart leaves my chest when a loud, high-pitched squeal booms through my ears, sustaining me permanent hearing loss.

When the warmth heating my body darts out of the bed, I scamper, freaked that I've just entered a stranger's bed. I send a quick prayer to God, hoping their husband or father doesn't own a gun.

My eyes wince when a bedroom light flicks on, illuminating the room with unnatural light. Adjusting my eyes to the sudden brightness, I notice a blurry figure frantically pacing around the room.

"Where the hell is it?"

Just as my vision clears, a wildly swung steel baseball bat misses hitting the side of my face by a mickey whisker. If I were an inch closer, my head would have been knocked into the next century.

"Jesus," I say, taking a step backward when it flings past my head again, grazing the tip of my nose.

Through the distorted vision of a wildly swinging bat, I

catch the quickest glimpse of a profile I'd never forget. A vision that's burned into my retina.

Ava steps closer to me, swinging the bat like Babe Ruth is standing out on the pitch. "If you come near me, I'll shove this bat.... where... where.... the sun don't shine," she warns.

My head flings back and the loudest laugh I've ever cackled in my life tears from my throat. My lungs burn when they lose the ability to fill with air. Tears stream down my face, and my whole body shudders as I laugh like a man who has lost his marbles. I can't help it. Ava's never been good at issuing a threat. Clearly, nothing has changed.

Recognizing my laughter, Ava stops swinging the bat. She rests it at the side of her barely covered legs and stares at me with a gaped mouth. Her chest is thrusting up and down, and her eyes are wide. My laughter halts when I realize she's standing before me in nothing but a tiny pair of satin sleeping shorts and matching cami that doesn't have a chance in hell of hiding her perfect, cock-twitching body.

With a body crafted by the Almighty Himself to bring men to their knees, Ava is like a bottle of fine wine. She keeps getting better and better with age. Her lush, pert tits are straining against her meager satin cami top, and inches upon inches of her glorious, toned legs are peaking out the bottom of a pair of satin sleeping shorts. She has a rocking body that makes my cock as hard as stone. *She's perfect!*

She stands across from me as quiet as a monk on a vow of silence as her massively dilated eyes run over my body. The more she absorbs the tattoos covering every inch of my torso and arms, the more her brows pull together. Other than the squadron tattoo on my forearm, every tattoo in my collection was added after I vanished. Every one of them reminds me of her in some form.

Ava's eyes widen and she inhales a quick, sharp breath when her gaze becomes arrested on something lower than my stomach. Following her shocked gaze, I mumble a curse word under my breath and run my hand along my jaw. Once again, I'm standing before her as naked as the day as I was born. And hard enough to drill through the Arctic circle.

"Shit, sorry," I mumble, raking my eyes around the room, seeking anything that could cover my primed and ready-to-plunge-into-Ava's-tight-pussy cock.

I cringe while grabbing a ball-shrinking pink lace scatter cushion off the floor to place in front of my stiff cock. I'm not joking when I say this is the most hideous pillow I've ever seen. If Ava wasn't standing across from me, practically naked, it would have made quick work of the hard-on turning my brain to mush from the mass loss of blood being directed to my cock, but even looking like I'm about to go dance on a float at Mardi Gras, my dick isn't softening any. If anything, it's getting harder. That probably has something to do with the smile tugging on Ava's mouth. *She's even more beautiful when she smiles.*

"What is it with our reunions always ending up with me being naked?" I ask, my tone cheeky.

The happiness on Ava's face vanishes in an instant, replaced with a look of a woman who is ready to castrate me. I swallow harshly as she storms around the bed, reaching me in two heart-thrashing seconds. She places her open palms on the middle of my back and pushes with all her might.

"Get out!" she grunts, her words coming out in a strain.

"It's three AM," I plead.

"I don't care," she retaliates, increasing the strength in her pushes. "You're not staying here!"

My feet skim across the carpet from her determination. "Come on, Ava. It's late. I already checked every motel in town. They're either full or closed."

I could dig my feet in the carpet and refuse to budge, but I'm not going to. At the end of the day, I'm an intruder in her home, and I don't want her to feel like she can't protect herself in her own house.

I crank my neck to the side and peer at her. A grin forms on my lips when I'm met with her crazy ringlet curls wildly bouncing from her heavy stomps and her raspy grunts.

"Just one night. I'll be gone first thing in the morning," I beg, returning my eyes front and center.

Ava's brisk pace across the living room eases, as do her windless pants. Sensing her resolve slipping, I continue with my plea.

"Before you've even woken. Please, Ava," I shamefully beg. "I'll get down on my hands and knees if I have to." I use the same voice I regularly used when begging for her to make me blueberry pancakes for dinner when we were younger.

A cool breeze zaps down my spine when Ava drops her hands from my back. When tiny feet padding along the wooden floor of the living room resonate through my ears, I spin around. Not wanting to give her any more incentive to kick me out, I cover my half-masted cock with my hands.

Ava moves swiftly through the house, gathering a sheet and blanket from the hallway cupboard and a spare pillow from her bed. Keeping her narrowed eyes firmly rooted on me, she walks into the living room, only stopping when she reaches the side of a two-seater sofa. With a sly smirk etched on her face, she gestures her head to the couch. I cringe. A man of my size won't fit half of my body on that tiny couch.

Ava cocks her brow. "The sofa or the patio. The choice is yours."

"I'll take the sofa," I mumble, ambling toward her.

Ava slants her head to the side and peers into my eyes, pretending she isn't affected by my nakedness. I'm not buying it. I can see her internal battle in her readable eyes. She's not the only one struggling. My eyes are fighting the same tortuous battle, but not wanting to risk the chance of sleeping in below freezing temperatures on her front patio, I keep my eyes planted on her face instead of her cock-twitching body.

It is fucking hard feat.

"Why are you staying here anyway? What happened to your apartment?" I ask with curiosity in my tone.

A winded grunt parts my lips when Ava shoves the bedding into my chest with force. Snarling, she storms into her room, slamming the door behind her.

NINE

HUGO

An inaudible groan rumbles up my chest as I reluctantly flutter my eyes open. The furious migraine pounding behind them worsens from the blindingly bright rays of the early morning sunshine beaming through the fully-opened living room drapes. I run the back of my hand over my tired eyes before sitting up. My back is kinked and screaming in protest about sleeping on a couch harder than a rock.

My eyes drift around the room, seeking the grandfather clock I heard ticking all night long. *What the hell. It's not even 7 AM.*

I know I told Ava I'd be out of her hair before she woke up, but she failed to mention she gets up before the birds. She's been bashing and crashing in the kitchen for the past forty-five minutes. I did my best to ignore the noise, yearning for a few more hours of sleep, but the longer I've stayed sprawled on the couch, the louder the noises emerging from the kitchen become.

Rubbing the sleep out of my eyes, I stagger toward the

kitchen. My stomach grumbles when a delicious aroma fills my senses. I've only smelled one thing sweeter in my life: *Ava.* My eyes bug out of my head when an even more ravishing visual greets me. The heaviness weighing down my eyelids is a forgotten memory as my eyes absorb every scandalous inch of Ava's body.

She's wearing an old faded Columbus State University shirt, and her hair has been pulled up, sitting in a messy bun on top of her head, exposing her long, delicate neck. I angle my head to the side and dip it down low. My brow cocks. *She's wearing pants – barely!* But you wouldn't know it. Her teeny tiny pair of denim shorts would be best described as panties.

I prop my shoulder on the doorjamb and let my eyes drink her in. It's been years since they've been enticed by such a stimulating visual. "How Does It Feel" by D'Angelo is playing out of a little speaker sitting on the two-seater table at the side of the room. Ava has her back to me, facing the upright oven. She has a spatula in one hand and a tea towel in the other.

When the song hits the chorus, her hips swing, naturally seducing me without even trying. My cock jumps when she grips the edge of the counter before slowly bobbing down and doing a seductive twerk. *Only Ava could make twerking look sexy.* Even spotting a massive pile of pancakes resting on the counter, I can't tear my eyes away from the sexy curves of Ava's ass peeking out of her tiny pair of short as she dances with such ease and grace. Ava's always been innately sexy. *Nothing's changed.*

Scraping my hand along my unshaven jaw, a shameful groan tears from my throat when the visual becomes too enticing not to spark a reaction from me. Hearing my shameful response to her seductive dance moves, Ava straightens her spine and spins on her heels. A massive grin stretches across her face as her eyes run my covered body. Not wanting another naked incident, I slept in my jeans and long-sleeve shirt, further hindering my ability to sleep.

When Ava's eyes return to my face, I chew on my lip. Her nipples are budded against her shirt; her eyes are wide and exposed, and there's no denying the spark blazing in her beautiful eyes. Ava is famished and it isn't a hunger for food.

"How did you sleep?"

"Good." *I spent the entire night dreaming of you.* "You?"

She shrugs. "Could've been better."

When she prances toward the fridge, swings open the door and dips her lower half inside, my heart rate kicks up a notch. *Ava and I have many fond memories in fridges.* I lick my dry lips when she emerges from the fridge holding a can of whipped cream. Keeping her eyes locked on me, she walks to the massive stack of freshly prepared blueberry pancakes on her right.

"Cream or syrup?" Her voice drips with sexiness, like hot lava erupting from a volcano.

"Syrup."

Ava places the whipped cream onto the counter and opens the cupboard above her head. My cock, now hard, strains against the zipper of my jeans when she stands on her tippy toes, struggling to reach the maple syrup sitting on the top shelf. I push off the counter, walk toward her and arch over her back. I easily reach the syrup, but take my time, pretending I can't quite reach it so I can relish in her closeness for a few seconds longer. My nostrils flare when her sweet smell engulfs the air surrounding me.

"Thank you," she says when I hand her the syrup, her voice as sweet as her scent.

She slips under my arm and walks to the other side of the kitchen, taking the stack of pancakes with her. Even with her standing at the other side of the room, the kitchen is so small in size, we are still close enough to feel the sexual energy zapping between us. It is electrifying and has my cock hardening more.

Ava slathers the pancakes with syrup, ensuring every inch is covered in the sugary goodness I love. A provocative moan tumbles out of her lips when she pops her thumb into her mouth and licks a smidgen of syrup off the tip. The hardness of my cock turns lethal.

I've never been so hard. Nothing's changed. *Not a single fucking thing.*

It wouldn't matter if a year had passed or a hundred, Ava will always be the only girl who can knock me onto my ass. Although, I'll admit, I'm surprised by the quick change in Ava's behavior overnight, but I'm loving her new-found playfulness.

"Hungry?" Her tone is laced with sexual undertone.

"Fuck, yes." *For you.*

My eyes drift between the stack of pancakes balancing precariously in her hand and her soft pouty lips. *I know which one I want to taste first.*

My eyes rocket to hers when she asks, "What do you want to taste first?" like she can read my internal dialogue.

"I have a choice?"

She bites her lower lip before she nods.

"You."

Her eyes spark with fervor as a smile furls her lips . "Who said I was on the menu?"

I run the back of my fingers down her flushed cheeks. "These."

She always blushes when she's turned on.

The ravenous fire in her eyes dampens, and her throat works hard to swallow. "Well, I'm not... *yet*, but these are." Her eyes dart down to the massive stack of mouthwatering goodness in her hands.

Her lips tug high as she outstretches her arm, offering the pancakes to me. My mouth salivates as my eagerness to taste their scrumptious goodness thickens my blood. It's been years since I've tasted anything as good as Ava's pancakes.

My pupils widen and a dramatic gasp escapes my lips when Ava releases her grip on her end of the plate before I've secured my end. Time slows to a snail pace as the pancakes plummet toward the ground. I scramble, trying in vain to save them before they land in the bin I'm standing next to.

I'm too late. The pancakes are history.

"Oh no," Ava gasps, her hand darting up to cover her gaped mouth.

"It's okay, we can save a few of them," I assure.

Although they've landed in the bin, the top ten pancakes are sitting straight, not touching anything that resembles rubbish, giving me the all clear to salvage them. "The top few haven't touched anything gross."

"Oh."

With a smile on her face, she grabs a bowl of empty egg shells from the kitchen sink and dumps them onto the pancakes.

Her lips purse. "Can they still be saved?" Her voice no longer has the sugary sweetness it had earlier.

My brows meet my hairline. I've never witnessed Ava

unleash such cruelty. What did the poor defenseless pancakes ever do to her? My eyes lift from the ruined pancakes covered in eggshell pieces to Ava. Gone is the little sex kitten who was prowling around the kitchen, replaced by a lady whose heart looks like it was carved by an ice sculptor.

Ava's eyes blaze into mine. "I'm going to take a shower. You better be gone by the time I get out. If not, I'll call the police."

TEN

AVA

Oh my god! I can't believe I did that! I've never been so... *rude!* Jorgie would be so proud I've finally grown a backbone. It might have taken me twenty-nine years, but it is better late than never.

I barely slept a wink all night, unable to comprehend that the man who snatched my ability to enjoy a restful night was in my living room, sleeping on my rock-hard couch. I'd dreamed of nights like last night, praying that one day Hugo would suddenly reappear. What I wasn't expecting was the flood of emotions that would return with him.

At first I was shocked, not believing what my eyes were relaying, thinking it was a cruel, twisted joke. It was only when the fog cleared did the reality of the situation dawn on me. Hugo isn't dead. He's far from it. So where has he been the past five years? And why did he wait so long before emerging again? He would have had to have known what his mother was going through. He saw firsthand the pain she endured when she lost

Jorgie and her grandson. How could he put her through that again? How could he do that to me?

That is when my anger surfaced. It festered and boiled my blood all night, overheating my body with more fury than I've ever felt. I'm furious Hugo was so selfish, that he could do that to his own mother. I at least got a goodbye. Mrs. Marshall didn't even get that. Hugo took the coward's way out when he left. He left his family. Left me. *Left us.* It was his choice, so he doesn't get to waltz back into my life acting like nothing's changed.

Everything's changed.

A grin tugs on my lips as I slip out of a pair of the denim shorts I rustled from the back of my walk-in closet this morning. Hugo's always been a legs man, and even though his physical characteristics have changed from the man I used to know, his insides are the exact same. The shell of an egg can be painted any color you like, but the inside is still a heartless yolk.

Knowing Hugo loves legs nearly as much as he loves blueberry pancakes, I decided on my little ploy. Was it childish? Yes. What is over the top? Yes. Would I do it again? Yes! In a heartbeat. The look on his face when his beloved pancakes toppled in the bin was priceless. Totally worth the hour I slaved over the open-flamed cooktop to make them.

I raise the hem of my shirt, throw it over my head and step into the steam-filled shower. In an effort to regain some of my usual down-to-earth composure, I take my time in the shower, lathering and pampering my exhausted body.

As I run a washcloth over my body, images of my run-in with Hugo last night pop into the forefront of my mind. Although his torso is covered with more tattoos than my eyes could ever absorb, his body was... *panty-drenching good.* Ripples of hard muscles, smooth planes of colorful skin and his cock, *my god,* I thought I was letting my imagination get the better of me the past five years. I wasn't. *Jesus.* If I was in a cartoon, my eyes would have comically bugged out of my head.

My body. Well... a lot has changed there the past five years. My boobs are no longer sitting where they should be, their perkiness dwindling away with my youth. My thighs are a little larger, and my stomach is anything but smooth. We couldn't be more opposite if we tried. Hugo is hard, colorful, and accentuated. I'm squidgy, plain, and boring.

Hold on! Why am I even comparing us? Hugo is a nobody. He's the equivalent of a barfly, buzzing in and out of my life as he saw fit. Not anymore. I'm putting my foot down. *This isn't just about me anymore.*

After a long, hot shower, I make my way out of the bathroom. The house is eerily quiet, only the grandfather clock pendulum swinging can be heard. Hugo must have heeded my warning. *Good, because my warning wasn't an idle threat.*

I walk into the laundry room and slip out the back door. The rusty-hinged gate separating the land between my house and Mrs. Mable's gives out a small squeak when I open it. The gate was Mrs. Mable's idea. She figured it would save me scaling her fence again if I ever felt the need to add some additional fertilizer to her award-winning rose garden. My cheeks flamed as I stumbled out the worst apology of my life. I'd never been more embarrassed.

Even though I was joking about adopting Mrs. Mable as a grandmother at Jorgie's wedding, she has become exactly that. She's a little bundle of mischief who keeps my life interesting. I would have loved to have introduced her to Patty, but unfortunately Patty's gigantic heart gave out a few weeks after Hugo disappeared. *It really has been a shit couple of years.*

Mrs. Mable walks out of the kitchen, drying a china teacup in her hand when she hears me opening the glass sliding door on her back patio. Her lips purse as her rheumy eyes roam over my face. Her gaze is full of suspicion, and it has my curiosity piqued. I arch my brow and return her ardent stare. When I notice the scoundrel look on her face, my jaw drops.

"I'm revoking your key holder privileges," I say, staring into her rascally eyes. "You told *Hugo* where the spare key was, didn't you?" I squeak when I say *his* name.

Mrs. Mable doesn't deny my claim. Not a single word seeps from her lips. It wouldn't matter even if she did refute my allegation; the truth is projected by her wholesome eyes.

Mrs. Mable places the china cup into the display cabinet before shifting her feet to face me. "I thought you could do with a night of fun. Get your knickers out of the twist they've been in the past five years," she informs me with her pencilled brows raised high into her tight silver ringlet hair.

"Knickers?" I query, glaring into her beaming-with-mischief eyes.

Mrs. Mable rolls her eyes. "I'm British. Can't you hear my accent?"

My eyes bulge. Mrs. Mable's tone couldn't be anymore Southern if she tried. She sounds like Reese Witherspoon... after smoking three packs a day.

Ignoring my wide-mouthed expression, Mrs. Mable continues, "But I'm gathering, from the way you strolled in here looking like you still have that stick stuck up your bottom, my ploy didn't work? What was it? The tattoos? Or are you not a fan of his shorter hair?"

A snarl forms on my lips as my eyes narrow.

Mrs. Mable pats her translucent, wrinkled-covered hand on my forearm. "Don't pretend you weren't interested in what he was hiding under his clothing. That body...oh, he could crank my engine anytime he likes."

My cheeks get a rush of blood behind them. Although this type of jeering is nothing new for Mrs. Mable, I've never been one to air my dirty laundry in public.

"So what was it?" She eyes me with curiosity. "The tattoos or the hair?"

Thankfully, I'm saved from answering her highly inappropriate question when a little pair of arms wraps around my legs. "Hi, Mommy."

I crouch down to scoop him into my arms. "Hi, baby. I missed you so much." I plant a sloppy kiss on his cheek. "Were you a good boy for Grandma?"

His expressive eyes enlarge before he nods. "Uh huh. We stayed awake until it was *really* late watching cartoons." He turns his eyes to Mrs. Mable. "Well, I stayed up. Grandma fell asleep, *again*." Air hits my cheeks when he huffs dramatically.

I snort when Mrs. Mable waves her hand in the air, shooing off Joel's tease. I'm not worried about their late night adventures. Anything past eight PM is late to Joel. Running my fingers through his thick afro curls, I fix them into place before setting him back onto his feet to put on his jacket. He cranks his head to the side as his eyes roam over my face. He stares at me like he's seeing me for the first time.

"You look pretty, Mommy," he mumbles.

He places his cool hand on my inflamed cheeks. "Did you have fun at the party?" He stutters when he says the word "party."

My eyes shoot up to Mrs. Mable when she fails to conceal her deviant snicker by pretending to cough.

"It was very interesting." I clasp Joel's hand in mine before standing from my crouched position. "Thank you for watching him."

"It was my pleasure, sweetie. Anytime."

She has said on many occasions that Joel keeps her young. She loves babysitting him. Although I do make sure her hearing aid batteries have been replenished before she watches him, I never hesitate to leave him with her. They have a unique bond that grows stronger with every moment they spend together, so I refuse to let Mrs. Mable's age create a barrier between them.

After thanking Mrs. Mable with a kiss on the cheek, Joel and I exit the back sliding door.

"What did you want to do today?" I ask, opening the gate so Joel can enter before me. "I was thinking DVDs and a pizza?"

Joel screws up his nose and gags.

"No?" I say with a shake of my head and pursed lips.

"We had pizza last night. Grandma likes olives and anchovies." His face pales like he's going to be sick at any moment.

I laugh. "Okay, so no pizza. What about--"

"Pancakes!" he pipes up, his voice high as excitement takes hold of his vocal cords.

I grimace. "I'm sorry, honey, Mommy used all the eggs this morning." *Teaching a bad man a valuable lesson.*

Joel's lower lip drops into a pout.

"But I can duck down to the store later this afternoon, and we can have pancakes for dinner," I suggest.

Joel's eyes bulge. "Really?"

I smile and nod. "Really."

Joel shares the story of how Mrs. Mable fell asleep with her mouth open as we walk into the back entrance of our home.

"She was drooling too. It was gross--"

He stops talking, and his head lifts in slow motion. The more his neck tilts back, the larger his mouth gapes. "Who are you?" he asks with his head fully cranked back.

My head swings to the side so fast, my neck screams in protest. There standing before us in all his six-foot-five glory is Hugo.

Shit.

ELEVEN

HUGO

My eyes dart between Ava and the little boy standing at her side, clutching her hand. I stare at him. Not a general stare—I stare, stare at him, absorbing every little feature of his adorable face. Big plump lips, smooth caramel skin, a crazy mess of ringlet hair on the top of his head, and the biggest pair of blue eyes I've ever seen. I take a step back, flabbergasted.

Holy shit. It can't be.

The little boy's eyes run the length of my body, from the tips of my toes to the top of my head. When his eyes reach their final destination, his jaw slackens. I'm not surprised to see little white pegs of perfectly straight teeth in his mouth. His mom is a dentist after all.

"Who are you?"

Even his voice is adorable.

Ava flinches before her head rockets to the side. Her eyes travel the same path the little boy's just did, but when she reaches her final destination, her mouth doesn't gape open in surprise, but her eyes do.

Ava musters a fake smile across her ashen face before she bobs down in front of the little boy. "Sweetie, go into your room. I'll be there in a minute."

"But, Mom—"

"No arguing. Go!" Her voice is stern and authoritative, a tone I've never heard her use.

The boy clenches his hands into balls as he screws up his nose. With a loud huff, he storms down the hall. "You're not being fair!" he yells before slamming his bedroom door shut.

His abrupt closure of the door is so powerful, the picture frames lining the hallway rattle from his force, making Ava balk. She runs her hands down the front of her white-washed jeans before standing from her crouched position. When I step toward her, she holds her hand out in front of her body, demanding for me to stop.

Her moisture-glistening eyes lock with mine. "He isn't—"

"Don't you dare," I interrupt, my words coming out sterner than I was anticipating. "I *know* he's my son."

He's the perfect mixture of both Ava and me. My hair coloring, her curls. My eyes, her lips. His nose is a combination of us both. He's my son, and nothing Ava could say would change my mind on that. Even if I wasn't looking at an exact replica of my eyes, I can feel it in my bones. He has my blood pumping through his veins. *He's my son.*

My eyes bounce between Ava's. "Why didn't you tell me?"

Ava's head flings back as she laughs. It isn't the beautiful, soulful laugh I'm used to hearing. It is a laugh that expresses how much she's hurting. It is crammed with pain and sorrow, and it breaks my heart just hearing it.

Once her laughter settles down, her eyes glare into mine. "And exactly how was I supposed to tell you? Put an ad in every newspaper in the state... or perhaps the entire country since I didn't know where you'd gone?"

She glides her hands through the air, dramatically expressing herself like a fight promoter holding a press conference. "Naïve virgin fucks high school crush in his childhood bedroom, stupidly forgot to check if he's wearing protection, falls pregnant the very first time she has sex. If this sounds like someone you know, please call 555-I'm-a-naïve-idiot!"

Ice-cold fear grips my heart when tears prick her eyes. I take a step closer to her, wanting to offer her comfort. She angrily shakes her head and takes a step backward. My heart hammers from the dejected look in her eyes. She looks broken. Utterly heartbroken.

Stuffing her hands into the pockets of her jeans, Ava's gaze strays to her feet.

"Babe."

Her eyes snap to mine. "Don't call me that," she sneers, her words dangerously low. "You lost the right to call me a nickname, *any name*, when you left me pregnant and heartbroken."

My stomach twists. "If I'd known, Ava..."

"If you didn't run, you would have known! You would have!" she yells. "But you ran. You were a coward who ran!"

The pounding of my heart increases, but I remain quiet, unable to negate her truthful statement. I was a coward who left, but if I'd known she was pregnant, I would have... Fuck, I don't know what I would have done.

When Ava's angry voice bellows down the hall, she intertwines her hands and gathers her composure, not wanting to startle her son... *our son.* I stare into her heartbroken eyes as she takes a step closer to me. Her legs shake with every stride she takes. Her eyes are packed with hot, salty tears threatening to spill at any moment.

"Hugo." She stops talking and scrunches her brows. "Is that even your name anymore?"

Even though she's asking a question, she continues talking.

"Maybe you changed it. What is it now? Slade, Jesse... Oh, I know! You're the *asshole* who has five seconds to get the *hell* out of my house before I call the police and tell them a *stranger* is standing in the middle of my home."

"I get it, you're pissed."

"I'm not pissed, Hugo, or whatever the *fuck* your name is now. I'm *way* beyond pissed. You have no clue what I've been through the past five years. I walked through the gates of hell to keep our son fed, to keep him looked after. Because of you, I nearly lost everything! And now, just as everything is *finally* panning out after an *exhausting* five years, you come waltzing back into the picture, throwing a wrench into the works. I'm not the stupid and naïve Ava you remember. I'm not going to let you ruin everything I've worked so hard for—again."

Her words cracks as the first lot of tears splashes down her cheeks. I take a step closer to her, aspiring to stop her tears. Every one that falls down her face adds more cracks to my already decimated heart.

"*Please* leave," she begs, her pleading eyes on mine.

The constrictive hold on my heart tightens. "He's my son, Ava. I can't leave him. I can't leave *you.*"

Tears flood her cheeks. "*Please,* I'm begging you. I'll fall down onto my knees if I have to."

The squeeze on my heart turns deadly when she locks her dispirited eyes with mine. "If you cared for me at all, if you ever loved me, you'll walk away. *Please* don't drag our son through the hell we've both walked through."

My heart is a massive mess of confusion, torn between wanting to ease Ava's pain and wanting to meet my son.

Her lips quiver as a fresh batch of tears streams down her face. "If you can't do it for me, then do it for him. He doesn't deserve to be thrown into this mess. *Please,* Hugo, I'm begging you."

As hard as it is for me to do, I walk away.

TWELVE

AVA

When Hugo slips out my front door, my knees buckle and I crumble to the ground. I gather my legs in close to my chest and cry. I cry for all the years we missed. I cry for my son who has never had a chance to know his dad, and I cry from the sheer pain that washed over Hugo's face when I begged him to leave. My words cut him deep, but I'm angry, and rightfully so.

I went through hell the past five years. I lost my best friend, my soul mate, and a man who was like a grandfather to me within a matter of months. It was one horrific blow after another.

With everything going on, it took me a while to realize the churning upsetting my stomach every morning and late afternoon wasn't caused by grief. It was a baby, a baby I'd created with Hugo. Even after six pregnancy tests, I still didn't believe it. I was pregnant. After attending an appointment with Dr. Tagget, it was clear I'd gotten pregnant the very first time Hugo and I were together.

That night, I was so caught up in the moment, I didn't even consider checking to see if Hugo had used protection. I'd never filled in the birth control prescription my local gynecologist gave me. I didn't see the necessity since I was not sexually active and my periods were as regular as clockwork.

At first, I saw our baby as a blessing, a final gift from both Jorgie and Hugo. It was only when I discovered I was due two months before I officially took my position at Gardner and Sons did my opinion on the matter change. Although Mrs. Gardner is a lovely lady, she's also a business woman. Like any rational business woman, she handled my situation respectfully while assuring her business wasn't negatively impacted by it, which meant my offer of partnership was given to another intern, leaving me unemployed and heavily pregnant.

In my seven month of pregnancy, I sold my apartment on Hamilton Street. The impressive nest egg I'd been ecstatic about growing was put toward my hefty tuition debt. Although my payment chewed a sizable portion off my debt, I was still left with an outstanding balance. For the following two weeks, I stayed at Mrs. Marshall's house.

Although it has always felt like home to me, the house had too many memories of Jorgie and Hugo, and my restless sleep worsened during my weeks there. After a heartfelt discussion, Mrs. Marshall suggested I move into Jorgie's place. It took days of deliberations before I agreed to move in, and even then, only on one condition: I wasn't going to use the master bedroom. That room belonged to Jorgie and Hawke. I didn't feel comfortable sleeping in there.

A few weeks after I moved in, Marvin started sniffing around. He would turn up with bags of fancy restaurant food any pregnant lady would salivate over, and sneakily paid my heating bill when I got a little behind on a payment. He asked what I was planning on doing once the baby was born, and reminded me that just because I was becoming a mom, it didn't mean I had to give up my dental career. I could have both if I wanted. I'll admit it, I was shocked. Marvin had never been a positive man, but he was the only one encouraging me not to give up on my dreams.

Over the next few weeks, the reasoning behind his interest was exposed. Marvin and Hugo are as opposite as they come. Hugo is a tall brute of a man; Marvin is waif-thin and average height. Hugo favors females with rich, caramel-colored skin and dark features; Marvin prefers blondes with fair skin and blue eyes. *Hugo has a large cock; Marvin doesn't.*

Although Marvin loves beautiful blonde bombshells, his father is a proud African American man, and he wanted his son to follow in his footsteps. During my vulnerable state, Marvin convinced me that aligning could be beneficial for us both. He said if I agreed to pretend to be his girlfriend, he would assure my position at his family practice was waiting for me after giving birth. He benefited from our situation by getting his dad off his back about settling down and getting married. He was convinced it was a win-win situation for us both.

It was... until twelve months ago. Marvin didn't want to pretend anymore. He wanted us to become a real life couple. I was hesitant. Joel knew of Marvin, but their contact was severely lacking. Neither was interested in getting to know the other. When I hesitated, Marvin was quick to remind me how he guided me through the storm and that without him, I would have had nothing. After swearing his indiscretions would end and promising to put more of an effort into our relationship and Joel, Marvin and I became an official couple nine months ago.

Nothing changed.

Our relationship followed the exact same path as the previous four years. Marvin's indiscretions never ended. Not that I mind as it keeps his focus off me. He continued to live in his apartment on Pinter; I remained in my house, and he has never spent any time at all establishing a relationship with Joel. That is why I was so shocked when he proposed. Neither of us are ready for marriage. We are barely a couple, let alone ready to walk down the aisle.

Although Marvin is an asshole and he irks the living hell out of me, I would have been lost without him. He did save me. So like all things in life, I accept the good with the bad. People believe Marvin is using me, but I've used him just as much. We are as bad as each other.

My head lifts from my knees when Joel rushes out of his bedroom and charges down the hall. His little face is lit up, and his eyes are wide and clearly excited.

"I knew it!" he squeals loudly, his eyes bouncing in all directions.

"It's him, isn't it? The daddy in the pictures, my daddy," he says, his words coming out in an excited flurry.

When he fails to locate Hugo, he runs into the kitchen, clutching a photo frame in his hand. My heart squeezes painfully when he emerges from the kitchen not even two seconds later. The excitement on his face has dampened, and his shoulders are slumped and hanging low. He looks utterly devastated.

"Where did he go?"

I gesture for him to come sit with me by outstretching my arms. Tears pool in his eyes as his slowly trudges to me. All the excitement on his face has vanished, and his lips have turned downwards. When he sits into my lap, I run my fingers through his thick hair before pressing a kiss on his sweat-beaded forehead. After peering down at the photo frame in his hand, Joel locks his tear-drenched eyes with mine. My heart breaks when I glance into his beautiful eyes. His eyes are identical to his dad's in every single way.

"Was it him?" Joel hands me the picture frame.

Fresh tears spring in my eyes when I look at the photo he's offering me. It is a picture Mrs. Marshall snapped of Hugo and me dancing at Jorgie's wedding. It was taken mere seconds before Marvin interrupted us, requesting to dance with his date. I'm not ashamed to admit that nothing but love is projecting out of me in this picture. I loved Hugo for years, and Mrs. Marshall's photo captured that.

"Yes, sweetheart, it was him," I answer, my voice shuddering from the pounding of my heart. Although I could lie to him and say Hugo isn't his dad, I've never been one for deceit. *If you tell a lie once, all of your truths become questionable.*

Joel inhales a quick, sharp breath. "Is he coming back?"

His eyes stare into mine, begging for me to say yes. I run my hand across his forehead. His heart is beating so fast, I can feel his pulse raging through his temples.

"I don't know, sweetheart." I run my index finger under his eyes, removing a few stray tears seeping free. "Maybe he'll be back?"

His tears dry as his eyes drift between mine. His eyes are like his father's in another way: they can see straight through to my soul. He also knows I'd do anything in my power to ease his pain. Even breaking my own heart.

———

I DON'T NEED to see Hugo to know he's here. I can intuit his presence without needing to physically see him. We round the corner of the Marshall family residence, moving toward the back patio where the monthly Marshall brunch is held. To celebrate Hugo's return, Mrs. Marshall organized an special invited attendees-only brunch. I've never missed a Marshall brunch the past six years, and today won't be an exception. I have many treasured memories from the Marshall family brunch. I even went into labor at one.

Joel spots Hugo before me. His grip on my hand firms and a dimpled grin stretches across his face. I've never hidden Joel's dad's identity from him. I shared photos and stories of Hugo with him many times the past four years. Joel even has the Marshall last name. No matter how often Marvin begged for me to pretend Joel was his biological child, it was never going to happen. The Marshall family suffered enough loss to last a lifetime. I wasn't going to add another name to their already extensive list. Hugo is Joel's father, and no amount of hurt or anger will ever change that fact.

Exhaling a deep breath, I drift my eyes to Marvin. "I'll be back in a minute," I advise, my words low.

Marvin slits his eyes as his jaw gains a tick.

"Please don't create a scene," I say, stopping his callous words before they can escape his lips. "He needs this." I gesture my head to Joel, who hasn't taken his eyes of Hugo.

Marvin aggressively crosses his arms in front of his chest, but thankfully he continues giving me the silent treatment. The thrum of Joel's pulse jolts up my arm as we pace to Hugo, hand in hand. His excited smile enlarges with every step we take. Hugo is flanked by two gorgeous blondes, and for the first time in my life, my claws are sheathed. His nieces, Katie and Angie, Chase's two-year-old twin daughters, are climbing over him like he's their personal play fort. They appear as smitten as every female does when they're awarded with Hugo's attention.

When Hugo notices me approaching with Joel, he wrangles them off his jean-covered thighs and hands them to Chase. His eyes are still crammed with the despair he wore two days ago when I begged him to leave, but with every step we take toward him, it lessens, and a new glimmer of hope brightens in them.

I stop in front of Hugo and muster a small smile, pretending my heart isn't hammering against my ribs.

"Hugo, this is your son, Joel Marshall," I introduce him. The mad beat of my heart causes my words to come out with a judder.

Hugo intakes a sharp breath, clearly shocked by my introduction.

I swing Joel's arm into the air, trying to settle the nerves trembling through his little body. "Joel, this is your dad."

Hugo crouches down in front of Joel and offers him his hand to shake. My heart swells when Joel swats Hugo's hand away and wraps his arms around Hugo's neck. *He's always believed actions speak louder than words.* Joel's quick movements make Hugo stumble onto his knees in front of me, staining his jeans with dirty sludge and leftover snow.

Tears prick my eyes when Hugo chuckles. "You're a strong little thing," he says, pulling Joel in nearer to his chest.

My tears threaten to fall when Joel pulls away from Hugo and clasps my hand in his while still holding Hugo's, undoubtedly proving he's our little connection that will tether us together for eternity. I bite the inside of my cheek, refusing to relinquish my tears when I see nothing but sheer joy beaming from Joel's expressive eyes. My simplest decision has given him the utmost pleasure.

Lifting my eyes to Hugo, I say, "Maybe after brunch, you could take Joel somewhere? Get to know him a little better?"

Even though my tears have kept at bay, my rickety voice is giving away the surge of emotions flooding into me. I prayed for years for this exact moment to happen, and I can't believe it is finally coming true.

Joel's eyes rocket to Hugo. His mouth is ajar, and his pupils are as large as saucers. "Will you?"

A vast smile etches on Hugo's face before he nods. Joel throws his fists into the air and squeals an ear-piercing scream, forcing an immature giggle to seep from my lips. Joel's reaction alone verifies that my decision to include Hugo in his life was the right choice to make. He wants his dad in his life more than anything.

After running his hand over Joel's crazy, ringlet curls, Hugo's baby blues lock with mine. "*Thank you,*" he mouths. The gratefulness in his eyes adds strength to his simple statement.

I gently smile and nod. I'd do anything in the world to ensure Joel is happy. Even if means I have to side with the man who broke my heart and shattered my soul.

"I'll be just over there if you need me," I inform Joel, pointing to Marvin standing at the side, watching the exchange between the three of us. His arms are crossed in front of his chest, and he's giving us a poignant stare.

"Okay," Joel says, wrapping his arms around my thigh. "I love you, Mommy."

"I love you, too." I run my fingers through his ruffled hair, fixing it into place.

I'm not going to lie, walking away is one of the hardest things I've done. My heart is thrashing against my chest, and my eyes are crammed to the brims with tears, but the decisions I make aren't just based on what I want anymore. Every decision affects Joel as well. He wants this, and he deserves this. Every child has the right to have their father in their lives. I just hope Hugo doesn't break his heart. If he does, it won't matter how much I still love him, I'll never forgive him. That is unforgivable.

"This wasn't part of our agreement," Marvin sneers the instant I stand beside him.

I intertwine my hands together and pivot around. A smile tugs on my lips when I spot Joel showing Hugo his hidden finger trick Mrs. Mable has been teaching him since he was old enough to sit. It is nothing more than cupping your hands together and sticking your middle finger out and wriggling around, but Joel thinks it is magic.

"Joel was never part of our deal, Marvin. Not once," I retort, keeping my eyes on Joel and Hugo as they move to the back deck. "He's *my* son and any decision I make regarding him falls solely on *my* shoulders."

The hairs on the nape of my neck prickle when Marvin

leans into my side and snarls. "When Hugo vanishes for another five years and shatters *your* son's heart, don't come crying to me."

After throwing a garden chair out of his way, Marvin storms down the driveway. I'd like to say this is the first time he has thrown a tantrum like a child, but, unfortunately, it isn't. Perhaps that is why Marvin and Joel don't see eye to eye. Marvin sees Joel as a competitor instead of an ally. If he was smart, he would realize my son is the key to obtaining my heart. Gaining his approval is the biggest hurdle any man will need to jump to secure my devotion. His failure to realize that proves he doesn't know me at all.

Marvin slides into his red BMW convertible, throws the gearstick into reverse, and pulls out of the driveway like a bat out of hell. Tires squealing and the smell of burning rubber filters through the air. After rolling my eyes at his childish nature, my eyes return front and center. Marvin's little spectacle has gained me a handful of spectators, including Hugo. His eyes have narrowed, and even from this distance, I can see his jaw muscle ticking. Thankfully, Joel is too enamored with Hugo to be paying any attention to Marvin.

I jump when an arm unexpectedly wraps around my shoulders. I don't need to look up to know who is embracing me, her baked cookies and honeysuckle smell is all the indication I need.

"Sorry about that," I apologize, raising my eyes to Mrs. Marshall's face.

"It's fine, Ava. I have five grand-babies. Believe me, I've handled much worse tantrums," she replies, patting me on the shoulder with her translucent-skinned hand.

A giggle bubbles up my chest and erupts from my mouth.

Joel could give any kid a run for his money when it comes to chucking a tantrum – until three weeks ago. I never laughed so hard when he threw a wobbly in the middle of a department store because he wanted a new Spiderman toy. When I suggested he should wait until after Christmas, he dropped to the ground, kicked his legs and wailed. That isn't the funny part of my story. It was when Mrs. Marshall replicated his tantrum, howling sobs and all, did I lose it. I'd never laughed so hard in my life. A nearly sixty-year-old lady on the ground thrashing her fists against the tiled floor in the middle of a bustling department store was more than I could bear.

Her weird tactics worked, though. In an instant, Joel's tantrum stopped. His tear-soaked face popped off the floor, and he glared at his grandma, open-mouthed and wide-eyed. He looked utterly mortified. He's never chucked a tantrum since that day.

"Maybe we should test your logic on curbing tantrums on Marvin?" I suggest, my lips pursing into a grin, vainly trying to portray I'm not embarrassed by Marvin's childish antics, where in reality, I'm humiliated.

Mrs. Marshall smiles a deviant grin. "The only thing that boy needs is a good walloping."

I laugh. Marvin is the reason I'm making sure Joel is raised with morals. I do not want him to grow up to be spoiled little brat like Marvin. Although Joel will always be my baby, there's a big difference between coddling a child and just letting them be a brat. The biggest difference between Joel and Marvin is Joel knows the difference between right and wrong. Marvin doesn't.

Mrs. Marshall firms her grip on my shoulder. "I'm so proud of you, Ava," she whispers, her words full of admiration.

I peer into her glistening eyes, confused by the sudden shift in our conversation and her praise. Mrs. Marshall has never been one to hold back praise, but it's been a few solid months since she has been so frank. Actually, the last time she was forthright was when she urged me to reconsider my partnership with Marvin. Although she said she would support me in any decision I made, I saw her disappointment relayed in her wholesome eyes when I informed her of my decision.

"I'm proud you're not holding Joel against Hugo," she explains to my bemused expression. "You have every right to be angry at Hugo. Hell, I'm still peeved at him, but you're handling this situation with grace and dignity. Like a true lady. That makes me *very* proud of you. Not just today, but every day."

My nose tingles as fresh tears well in my eyes. Unable to articulate how much her words mean to me, I return her embrace with an extra squeeze.

THIRTEEN

AVA

THREE DAYS LATER...

"Where the hell are you?" I mutter, lifting a plastic sheet off a half-assembled desk.

My eyes frantically dart around the space, trying in vain to locate my handbag. The faint sound of my cell phone ringing has been shrilling into the room the past two minutes, but I can't locate my phone under all the mess.

"Check the boxes near the door," suggests Belinda, pointing to a three-stack of moving boxes near the front entrance door.

The volume of my cell phone ringing increases as I urgently pace to the boxes.

"There you are!" I scold, yanking my handbag out of the top box.

My heart rate kicks up a gear when I peer down at the screen and notice it is Hugo calling.

"Hello," I greet him, pressing the phone into my ear.

"Hey, where are you?" Hugo replies.

No matter how many times I've heard his deep voice the

past three days, it still causes a peppering of goosebumps to form on the surface of my skin every time I hear it.

"We've been knocking on your front door the past five minutes," Hugo adds on.

My eyes dart around the space, seeking any type of time-telling contraption. When my gaze comes up empty, I peer out a small tear in the newspaper taped around a window. *Shit, it's dark outside.*

"I'm so sorry, I lost track of the time. The plumber was a moron, and between his stupidity and--"

I stop talking when Hugo's deep chuckle sounds down the line. "It's fine, Ava. I'm more than happy to keep Joel for a few more hours if you're busy," he offers.

My heart clenches. I've missed Joel so much the past three days, but I've taken a step back from my parenting role to give him and Hugo time to become acquainted with each other. For the past three days, every morning, bright and early, Hugo arrives and collects Joel. They've visited the Central Park Zoo, been to see a Knicks game, and even took a day trip to Liberty Island. Although I feel like I'm missing my right arm, Joel needs this just as much as Hugo does.

Any concerns I have of Hugo breaking Joel's heart are diminishing as the days go on. Joel has never been so happy. He even wakes up smiling. I'm confident to say in a short period of time, Joel has fallen in love with Hugo. I can't blame him. Hugo is a lovable guy. I fell in love with him in days too. Although I'm still harboring anger at Hugo for the way he left, I can't help but feel joy when I see the way Joel's face lights up around him. When I collected Hugo's death certificate two years ago, I never thought I would have the opportunity to see them standing side by side. That makes it a precious memory I'll treasure for a lifetime and proves what I've always known: Joel is the key to my heart.

"Could you bring Joel here?" My question is low as I struggle to keep my sentimental tears at bay.

"Sure. Where are you at?"

Just from the change in his tone, I know he's detected the unease in my voice. Hugo's always been able to read me. More often than not, he's known my response before I even formed one.

After reciting the address to Hugo, I throw my cell phone into the box and rush into the crammed bathroom. Belinda, the receptionist from Gardner and Sons, and my friend, laughs at my frantic dash. I grimace when I catch sight of my disheveled reflection in the mirror. I have smudge marks all over my face, my hair is a wild, frizzy mess from the scattering of snow I scurried through earlier today, and my eyes display my lack of sleep. I look wretched.

Wetting a napkin in the grime-covered sink, I run it over my face. It isn't that I'm trying to impress Hugo, I just don't want him to think I'm a slob. *Oh, who am I kidding?* I've been waking up before the sun rises the past three days just to ensure I'm presentable before Hugo arrives. It is stupid and I don't have the faintest idea why I keep torturing myself, but no matter how many times I reprimand myself, I continue to do it. Hugo has seen me at my worst; no amount of makeup will change that fact.

Huffing, I throw the napkin into the bin and pivot of my heels.

"You look fine. You have that artsy look going on," Belinda chuckles when she spots my scowl.

I stick my tongue out at her snickering face before setting to work.

By the time Hugo and Joel arrive thirty minutes later, I'm covered with a dense layer of sweat, splatters of paint, and I'm way behind schedule.

"Mommy!" Joel charges across the room, sidestepping numerous boxes on his way.

"Hi, baby." I crouch down to return his embrace. "Did you have fun today?"

He nods excitedly. His elation increases when he notices Belinda standing in the corner of the room. His eyes expand as he licks his lips. He loves Belinda as she sneakily hands him jelly beans when she thinks I'm not looking.

"Go on," I say, nudging my head to Belinda. "But don't eat too many jellybeans as we haven't had dinner yet. And you'll have to brush your teeth once you've finished."

Flashing his adorable grin, Joel hotfoots it to Belinda.

His fast steps slow when Belinda says, "Sorry, Joel, I'm all out of candy."

His lip drops into a pout as tears form in his eyes.

"But there's an ice cream store half a block down," Belinda says with her lips quirked.

Joel's downcast head rockets up as his eyes bulge. He loves ice cream nearly as much as he loves pancakes. When Belinda shift her focus to me, seeking permission, I nod. Joel jumps into the air, throwing his fists up high before he drags Belinda out of the office and onto the sidewalk, not bothering to bid farewell to Hugo or me.

I rub a kink out of my neck as I pace to the other side of the room. After placing a rolling brush into a bucket of water, I shift on my feet to face Hugo. His brows are furrowed together tightly, and his vibrant eyes are absorbing the room.

"What is this place?"

I bite the inside of my cheek, battling to keep in my smile as I move to the middle of the room. An immature giggle bubbles in my chest when I pull a plastic protective sheet off the dental chair and catch sight of Hugo's fretful face. Anyone would swear I just told him I'm going to extract his teeth without any form of pain relief.

As quick as a flash of lightning sparks a darkened sky, the fret marring Hugo's face vanishes. His eyes get a renewed spark as a smirk etches on his face.

"Ava, is this your practice?"

My chest swells, honored by the pride in his tone.

I smile and nod. "I've been tucking away money the past few years. It's nothing flashy, but it's mine."

While Joel has been busy with Hugo, I've occupied my time setting up my new practice. When I first walked into this office space six months ago, it took a lot of imagination to visualize the space as anything, let alone a dental practice. It was filthy dirty and roach-infested, but with a little bit of vision, and a hefty loan from the local bank manager, I'm slowly transforming the place from a rundown dump to a small, but clean practice. I'll be living off my credit cards for the next twelve months as I build my patient list, but it will be worth the sacrifice to have my own practice. *And to be out of Marvin's clutches.*

My pulse quickens when I lock my eyes with Hugo's twinkling baby blues. He has a venerable smile stretched across his face, and his eyes are sparked with admiration.

"You did it," he praises proudly.

I cringe. "Not yet, but I'm trying."

My eyes drift around the half-painted walls and boxes of furniture waiting to be assembled. "I've got a long way to go. My doors are supposed to be opening in the New Year, but with how far behind I am, I might have to delay it."

Hugo removes his thick coat and throws it over an half-assembled office chair.

"Where do you want me to start?" he queries, rolling up his shirt sleeves.

I wave my hand in front of my body. "It's fine. I'm sure you have other more important things to do."

Hugo arches his brow. "Let me do this. Please, Ava. Not just for you, but Joel as well."

My breathing quickens when I peer into Hugo's eyes. It isn't just Joel who has fallen in love. Hugo is smitten with him as well.

"Please, Ava," he pleads, staring into my eyes. "Give me a chance to make up from some of the wrongs I've done."

My eyes return his beseeching gaze for several heart-clutching seconds.

"Are you sure you're not busy?" I ask, my tone hesitant. With everything going on with Marvin, I'm apprehensive to accept assistance.

Hugo grins a heart-fluttering smile before nodding. My eyes dart around the space, not just endeavoring to find a chore to assign Hugo, but struggling to ignore the ludicrous surge of excitement dashing to my core from his panty-wetting smile.

Even angrier than the Hulk stuck in a beehive, my body reacts to Hugo as if he owns me. That, in itself, is a truly terrifying notion.

"There's so much to be done," I mumble, pretending I'm not at all affected by his heart-stopping smile. The jittering of my voice gives away my deceit.

"The quicker you assign me a task, the quicker we can get out of here," Hugo replies to my quiet ramblings, his smile enlarging.

The sexual innuendo laced in his reply proves he isn't buying my act of decorum.

Sneering at his heckling face, I ask, "Can you paint?" wiping his smirk straight off his face.

"I'M BENT," I groan, flopping onto an office chair Hugo has just finished assembling.

For the past six hours, Hugo and I have been painting and assembling furniture. We had a quick break when Belinda and Joel came back from the ice cream parlor carrying a bundle of greasy cheeseburgers and fries. An hour later, when Joel became bored spinning in an office chair Belinda assembled, she graciously offered to take him home for a bath and to put him in bed.

Even though Hugo and I have been working tirelessly the entire time, we've talked a lot the past six hours. Like all parents concerned about the welfare of their child, most of our conversation revolved around Joel. It hasn't been tight or restrictive. It's been free flowing and easy. *Like it has always been between us.*

Thankfully, our chosen topic of discussion has meant we've avoided a majority of the sexual sparks that always ignite when we are in each other's presence. Although I'll always be attracted to Hugo, I'm trying to look at him as the father of my child and not an old flame. Let me tell you, it's been an uphill battle. Age has been kind to Hugo. *Very kind.*

Hugo plops his backside onto the ground and chuckles. "Bent?"

"Yeah, bent. Tired. Exhausted. *Bent.*"

He chuckles even louder. "*Bent* is when you're under the influence of alcohol or drugs. I was so *bent* after that party."

My brows scrunch. "No, it isn't! It means you're tired." *Doesn't it?*

A majority of my adult time is spent hanging out with a four-year-old, so I'm a little out of the loop.

Hugo's brows become lost in his hair as he ogles me with a mocking grin carved on his face.

"Whatever," I mumble, snagging a paint brush out of a bucket of water and flinging it across the room.

My mouth gapes open when my throw has perfect aim, hitting Hugo smack bang on his left cheek, smearing half of his face with the vibrant sun yellow paint now lining the exam room walls of my office.

"I'm so sorry!" My words come out in a shudder since my entire body is shaking, battling hard to hold in my laughter at the shocked expression on his face.

"Oh, yeah, you're going to be sorry," Hugo replies, launching for me.

I squeal and dart to the other side of the room. A ragged grunt expels from my lips when Hugo wraps his broad arm around my waist and tackles me to the ground. I roll onto my side and scamper across the floor on my hands and knees. *I'm too old to be subjected to a tickling attack.* Hugo snags my ankle, sending me tumbling onto my stomach. I'm laughing too hard to register the pain of crashing onto the rigid ground.

The plastic sheets we laid to protect the newly laid wooden floorboards crinkle under my body when Hugo drags me backward. I kick out of his hold, roll onto all fours and scramble onto my knees, mimicking his position. Even with my insides dancing like a stripper on crack, I force a stern mask to slip over my face, trying to pretend I'm not loving his playfulness. *I haven't mucked around like this in years.*

"Don't you dare tickle me," I warn, waving my index finger in the air like I did when I disciplined Joel for eating an entire box of frosty flakes in one serving last week.

A grin stretches across Hugo's face as he waggles his brows. We kneel across from each other, staring but not speaking. Only our chests thrusting up and down as we endeavor to fill our lungs with air is heard as we undertake a sweat mustache-provoking stare down. *I really shouldn't look into his eyes. His eyes are his biggest ally in repairing the damage he inflicted on my heart.*

"What happens if I do?" Hugo asks a short time later, tilting his torso closer to me. "What happens if I tickle you?"

I swallow, relieving my parched throat from the seductive purr of his voice.

"I'll... I'll—" *Come on brain!*

A crass grin morphs onto my lips. "I'll use this against you." I yank the drill off the dentist chair we're kneeling next to.

All the color drains from Hugo's face when a dentist drill

breaks the silence between us. His widened eyes dart between the functioning drill vibrating in my hand and my leering face. *I've got him exactly where I want him.*

Right before my eyes, the fretful mask Hugo is wearing slips off his face. "It will be worth it," he says with a wink before diving at me.

Before I can react, I'm pinned to the ground by Hugo's large frame and subjected to his tortuous, tinkling hands. I squeal a window-shattering scream as his hands unleash a torrent of tickles on my ribs and stomach. Tears stream down my flushed cheeks as I buck and wail against him, but no matter how hard I fight, a woman of my size is no match for a beast of a man like Hugo.

"Mercy!" I try to scream, but I can barely breathe, let alone speak.

"Mercy! Mercy!" I scream again. If he doesn't stop soon, I'm going to pee my pants.

I suck in a deep breath when Hugo finally hears my roaring pleas and rolls off me. My heart is beating wildly against my chest; my cheeks are sore from the giant grin I've been wearing all night, and my throat is hoarse from the childish laughter that tore from my lips. It feels like we've stepped back in time thirteen years and are once again two teens lying on the floor in the middle of Jorgie's bedroom. *Oh what I'd give to really step back in time.*

My exam room falls into eerie silence. It is so quiet, I'd hear a pin drop. Suddenly, one of the most wonderful noises I've ever heard in my life thunders through my ears, startling the living daylights out of me. Hugo's head is thrown back, and he's laughing. Not a small, brief chuckle—a full-hearted laugh that shreds straight through my soul and heals some of the cracks in my damaged heart.

Just hearing his boisterous chuckle spurs on my own laughter. Before I can stop myself, laughter bubbles up my chest and erupts from my mouth. Hearing my hearty giggles spurs Hugo to laugh even louder. And thus begins the vicious cycle of belly-crunching laughter. We lay next to each other loudly cackling until we don't even know why we are laughing. Then we laugh some more.

By the time Hugo wipes the tears from his cheeks and scrambles off the floor, my stomach is riddled with cramps as I've laughed more the past twenty minutes than I have the past twelve months.

A smile stretches across my face when Hugo thrusts out his hand, offering to assist me off the floor. After settling my erratically beating heart, I accept his offer. A girly squeal emits from my lips from his strengthened tug on my arm. My nipples bud and a shameful, husky moan topples from my mouth when my chest crashes into the hard ridges of his pec muscles. The shift of air between us is so great, they would feel it all the way in the city.

As Hugo stares down at me, flicking his gaze between my lips and my eyes, I drink him in. Other than the small wrinkles in the corners of his eyes when he smiles, he hasn't aged a day in five years. His eyes are youthful and full of life. They're identical to Joel's in every way, the boy who had to grow up without a father the first four years of his life.

With a twisted mess of a confused heart, I maneuver out of Hugo's embrace. I can feel Hugo's eyes tracking me, but he stays quiet as I gather my bag and cell phone from the newly assembled reception desk in the foyer of my office.

"Can I give you a ride home?" Hugo offers.

I shake my head. "No, I'm fine. I have my car."

I continue gathering my stuff, not trusting myself to spin around. When I look into Hugo's eyes, I want to pretend the last five years never happened. I want to act like he isn't the man who shattered my heart and left me broken. I want to stare up at him in awe like Joel does and pretend there's nothing else in the world that matters more than gaining his attention, but that isn't real life. I'm not a sixteen-year-old girl gushing over her high school crush. I'm also not a twenty-four-year-old naïve virgin seducing a man into her bed. I'm a mom who will do everything in my power to ensure her son's heart is protected. *That my heart is protected.*

"You don't have your car here, Ava. Remember?"

I pivot on my heels to face him. My brash movements cause a rush of dizziness to cluster in my sleep-deprived brain.

"You asked Belinda to take your car so Joel had a car seat," Hugo explains to my confused face.

Shit, I completely forgot.

"Come on," Hugo says, gesturing to the door. "It's only a lift, Ava, nothing more than a friend offering another friend a ride home."

He can say that. He isn't the one who has snuggled into a pillow drenched in his aftershave the past five years just to get a few measly hours of sleep. I've been struggling the past six hours to ignore his intoxicating woodsy smell, and that was in the space of an office. Imagine how impossible it will be in the small confines of a car?

Before I can answer Hugo's suggestion, the shrill of a cell phone vibrates through the quiet. The mask of fretfulness that slipped off Hugo's face thirty minutes ago settles back into place when he realizes the noise is resonating from the pocket of his jeans. His brows furrow as he digs his hand into his pocket to retrieve an outdated silver cell. He flips open the phone and presses it against his ear.

"Boss," he greets, his tone packed with apprehension. "Alright. When?"

His eyes snap to mine. They're full to the brim with guilt. I turn my focus to my newly decorated office, pretending my heart is hammering against my ribs from the devastated look crossing Hugo's face.

When he finishes his phone call, he moves to stand in front of me. My eyes travel his body, from his paint-splattered boots to the week-old stubble on his chin. After exhaling a nerve-cleansing breath of air, my eyes finalize their journey, landing on his Marshall family heirlooms: his glistening baby blues.

"I have to go... My job... My boss needs me." His words sounds as tormented as he looks.

Snubbing the tears pricking in my eyes, I fake a smile and nod.

"When do you have to go?" I ask, my voice quivering.

He rubs a kink in the back of his neck. "*Now.*"

My heart plummets into my stomach as quickly as the first tears escape my eyes.

"I'll be back, Ava. I promise you, I'll be back," he vows.

He steps closer to me, engulfing me with his delicious scent, making my tears flow even more quickly. He wraps his arms around my shoulders and pulls me into his thrusting chest. His heart is beating so fast, it is pulverizing my eardrum.

"I'll be back. Nothing could keep me away from Joel. *From you*," he assures me, locking his eyes with mine.

The truth in his eyes weakens the stranglehold crippling my heart. He runs the back of his fingers across my cheeks, removing my tears in one quick sweep. Once my face is free of any moisture, he lifts his sorrow-filled eyes to mine.

"I know its late, but can I please say goodbye to Joel?" he requests, his eyes pleading into mine.

I bite the inside of my cheek, refusing to let any more tears spill before nodding.

The drive back to my house is somber, the mood void of our earlier playfulness. Even the shock of Hugo driving Jorgie's *baby* hasn't fully registered. I assumed it was still rusting in the back garage at the Marshall's residence. When Hugo pulls into the driveway, the shake of my hands has converted to my entire body. I walk up to the front door with mute Hugo in tow. If I didn't hear his feet stomping, I would have assumed he was still in his car from how quiet he is.

When I press the key into the front door and swing open the door, Hugo asks, "Where does Marvin live?" His face is fettered with confusion.

My eyes stray to my shoes. "Marvin still lives in his apartment on Pinter," I strangle out, ashamed.

"You're engaged but you don't live together?"

The unease in his tone demands my attention.

"It's complicated," I mumble, ambling into the foyer.

"First door on the left," I advise, happy to end our awkward conversation while also forgetting Hugo knows the layout of my house just as well as I do.

Hugo smirks a tight smile before walking down the hall. His strides are long but heavy.

After seeing Belinda off, I hesitantly pace down the corridor. A small sheen of light is drifting into the hall from Joel's room, no doubt the nightlight he sleeps with. Ever since his uncle Chase read him *Der Struwwelpeter,* he has requested to sleep with the light on.

When I reach Joel's room, I lean my shoulder on the wall just outside the doorjamb and prick my ears.

"Are you gonna come back?" Joel's voice is groggy from being woken so late.

The mattress springs creak before I hear, "Yeah, buddy, I'll be back soon."

I smile when Joel says, "Will you bring me back a present? When Uncle Chase went to Disney World, he brought me back a present."

"I'm sure I can wrangle up something. What do you like?"

"Do they sell candy where you're going?"

Hugo chuckles. "I wouldn't live there if they didn't."

When the room falls into silence, I sneak a peek. My heart squeezes when I realize what has caused the quietness. Joel has his little arms flung around Hugo's neck, squeezing him tight. Hugo is embracing him just as robustly. When Joel releases Hugo from his embrace, Hugo's face strains. My heart beats double time. Hugo doesn't want to leave Joel any more than I want him to go.

"I'll see you soon, buddy," Hugo assures him, standing from the bed.

Joel nods and dives back into his bed. After tucking Joel in and placing a kiss on his forehead, Hugo pivots around and ambles out of the room. Tears spring in my eyes when I see the confounded look crossing his face.

"He isn't going anywhere," I comfort him, saying anything to ease the uncertainty clouding his eyes. "He will be waiting for you when you come back."

Although words cost nothing, sometimes they're the most valuable thing you can give a person.

When Hugo places a kiss on the side of my mouth, his lips quiver against mine.

"I'll see you soon," he mutters into my ear before he spins on his heel and races to the door, exiting without a backward glance.

FOURTEEN

HUGO

"You take Hugo, or you don't go, Isabelle."

My eyes drift between Isaac and Izzy. It feels like I've been transported to a different universe. When I left Ravenshoe, five days ago, they were announcing their engagement to the world and blissfully in love. Now, they're standing across from each other as if they're strangers. Trust me, after the five days I've just endured, I know a lot can happen in a short span of time, but I'm still surprised to return to this. Izzy and Isaac are solid. They remind me a lot of Hawke and Jorgie, so I know they will get through the latest debacle, but it makes me wonder what happened the past few days to tilt the axis of their relationship so viciously.

My past few days have been surreal. I have a son. A precious little boy who captured my soul in under a second. Just glancing into his eyes heals wounds I never thought would have the chance to mend. I'm not biased when I say Joel is perfect. He's perfect in every way. It's not surprising, though, considering who his mom is. Joel has so much of Ava in him. The way he screws up his little nose when he's thinking, his crazy curly hair, and how his eyes can see straight through to my soul.

But I also see some of my qualities in him as well. His love of sweets for one. That's the only thing the poor guy lucked out in having Ava as his mother. I laughed hysterically when Joel told me Ava sings him the "Brush the Teeth" nursery rhyme every morning and night to ensure he brushes his teeth for the recommended timeframe. He also disclosed that she limits the amount of sugar he's allowed to consume. When he argues, declaring she isn't being fair, Ava says she doesn't need his praise, because his teeth will thank her when he's older.

My attention reverts from reminiscing when Izzy paces out of Isaac's office. Her face is gaunt, her eyes full of tears. I pace quietly behind her, still reeling too much from my own emotions to handle any more. Izzy moves around the master suite of the home she shares with Isaac, hastily gathering a small bag of bare necessities.

"Is that it?" I ask when she hands me the overnight bag.

When she nods, relief engulfs me. From how light she has packed, the hope our trip to Tiburon will be a short one increases. Isaac was vague on the phone last night, simply requesting for me to accompany Izzy to her hometown. He didn't give any stipulations on how long we will be away or why we were going, he merely said he "needed me." After everything Isaac has done for me the past five years, I couldn't deny his request.

My heart was maimed leaving Joel and Ava. It was one of the hardest things I've ever endured, but I know it is only a matter of time before I see them again. I'll never be parted from them for an extended period of time ever again. I just have to steer Isaac and Izzy through their latest crisis, then I'll sit down and work out how to balance both my loyalty to Isaac and my family.

"Alright. I'll meet you in the foyer. Roger will take us to the airport," I advise Izzy, pivoting on my heels and rushing down the stairs.

My steps are eager, because the quicker we get to Tiburon, the faster I'll return to my family.

BY THE TIME the private jet Isaac hires touches down in Tiburon, I'm a wreck. I haven't slept in over thirty-six hours. I assumed the sleep I missed during my nine-hour car trip from Rochdale to Ravenshoe would be caught up on the flight over. It wasn't. Anytime I closed my eyes, the image of Ava's tear-filled face would haunt me. It was only halfway across the country did it hit me why the image haunted me so much. If she reacted so fearfully with me promising to return, how many times have I been the cause of her tears the past five years? The thought of her crying over me riddles me with guilt. I hate that I've caused her so much heartache.

That message I left on Ava's voicemail the day I vanished is as solid now as it was back then. I still love her. I always have, and I always will. I just hope one day she can find it in her heart to forgive me. Not just for vanishing without a trace, but for breaking her heart.

My eyes lift from the eat-in kitchen floor when Izzy says,

"You can put your bag in the spare room. It's the third door on the right."

I nod before ambling down the hall. Photo frames ranging in size are scattered on the walls of the corridor. They're all pictures of Izzy at various stages of her life, from a freckle-faced little girl to a stunning teen all dolled up for a school dance. In a majority of the photos, she has her arm wrapped around a large brute of a man. He would be nearly as tall as me, but double my weight. The flash of the camera bounces off his shiny bald head. Even looking like a trained killer, nothing but admiration beams out of Izzy's eyes as she stares up at him.

Placing my black bag onto the double bed in the middle of the room, my eyes drop to my watch. It is a little after five PM local time, so it's close to eight PM at Rochdale. Nearly Joel's bedtime. Swallowing a lump in my throat, I pull out my cell phone and dial Jorgie's old home number I have memorized, hoping Ava's number is the same. I push the phone in close to my ear, ensuring I can hear her over the mad beat of my heart.

"Hey, you've reached Ava and Joel. We're not home right now so leave a message after the beep," Ava and Joel say in sync.

A grin tugs on my lips from the corniness of their message.

"Hey, it's me... umm... Hugo. Joel's dad." *Jesus, I sound like a moron.*

"Just wanted to say goodnight to Joel. Goodnight, buddy, I hope you had a good day. And to let you know I'm thinking of you... both of you. Bye."

I'm pulling the phone away from my ear when it suddenly dawns on me what I said. I raise the phone back to my ear in a sense of urgency. "Not goodbye. I'll see you so--"

I stop talking when a loud clink sounds over the line. "Hey, you're home," I greet with a smile.

"Yes, they are," advises a male voice I don't recognize. "Home with me, where they belong."

My teeth grit when I recognize the condescending tone shrieking down the line. *Marvin.*

"Leave my family alone, Hugo," Marvin sneers.

"They're not your family," I snap back. "Joel is my son. He has my blood." *And Ava owns my heart.*

"Joel may have your blood running through his veins, but I'm the man who raised him, fed him, and clothed him. Without me, he wouldn't even have a roof over his head."

Fury blackens my veins, but even fuming in anger, I can't negate Marvin's claims. I haven't been there for Joel, but that is only because I didn't know he existed. If I did, I would have done everything in my power to ensure he was looked after. To ensure he didn't have to endure the pain Ava and I went through the past five years.

"Put Ava on the phone," I demand, my words coming out rough as a surge of emotions flood into me. "I want to talk to Ava."

"Do everyone a favor, Hugo. Stay away. That will be the kindest thing you could ever do for you son," Marvin snarls before disconnecting the call.

I throw my phone onto a bed then run my hand over my head. I can't give them up. It isn't possible. It was hard enough staying away from Ava the past five years. Many times I've jumped into my car and headed to Rochdale, dying to see her again, needing to know she was safe and protected. I never made it any further than the Welcome to Rochdale sign four miles out. I couldn't risk her life, but I also didn't want to see the pain in her eyes knowing I was the one who put it there. So with a heavy heart, I turned around and steered my car back to Ravenshoe, back to the town that sheltered me during my roughest storm. I've always quoted that your home isn't where you were born and raised; it is where your family is. For the past five years, Ravenshoe has been my family, but not anymore, the woman who owns my heart lives in Rochdale, as does the boy who has captured my soul.

I peer out the window when I catch the shadow of a figure in a room at the back of the property. *Shit! I'm supposed to be here protecting Izzy.* I house my firearm in the back of my jeans and rush in the direction I saw the figure.

"Izzy," I call out when I enter the backyard.

The furious beat of my heart lessens when Izzy's faint voice emerges from an office attached to the side of the house. When I sprint into the space, my eyes scope the room, ensuring it is free of any threats. Other than stacks of moldy boxes, Izzy is the only living thing inside the room.

"What is this room?" I ask, pacing deeper into the space.

Izzy huffs. "Years of hard work wasted. My Uncle Tobias never relied on computers. He said they were too risky. I guess he never met a cracked tile before."

When she rolls her eyes while dragging a stack of sagging boxes across the room, I chuckle lightheartedly. I've never been a fan of computers either, preferring to communicate in person rather than over the internet. Perhaps if I hadn't been so stubborn, I would have discovered Joel's existence years ago.

Hours pass in an instant as I aid Izzy in saving years of her uncle's FBI paperwork. I've never had a fondness for law enforcement officers, but the way Izzy speaks about her uncle tilts the pendulum in his favor. My lack of respect for law enforcement wasn't engrained in me until my sister's death. I know I made a mistake five years ago when I allowed my grief to overrule my moral compass, but in my defense, I did try to handle the situation legally. It was only when it failed did I let my anger get the better of me.

A giggle spills from Izzy's lips when my stomach loudly grumbles. I'm not surprised by its reaction. I haven't eaten anything since the cheeseburgers Joel and Ava's friend brought back last night.

"I'll climb up onto the roof tomorrow morning and patch the hole the best I can, but you might need to get a professional out to look at it," I offer.

Izzy smiles. "Thanks. I guess I should feed you then, to make sure you don't fade away before tomorrow morning," she jests.

I laugh. Given the chance to meet, Izzy and Ava would get on like a house on fire. Both can make me laugh even when my mood is woeful. My stomach is still cramping from the amount of laughing I did in Ava's office. I can't believe how immature I acted last night. I'm nearly thirty years old, but that didn't stop me from tackling Ava to the ground and tickling her until she begged me to stop. It's been years since I fooled around like that. I'm not surprised, though. Only Ava has the ability to make it seem like I've stepped back in time. Anytime I'm around her, I once again become a teenage boy chasing his high school crush.

"I don't think there's much chance of me fading away," I quip, my tone playful as the memories of last night drastically improve my mood.

"Just give me a chance to get the box I originally came in here for and then I'll order us some pizza from Maria's," Izzy advises, pacing toward a large stack of shelves housing document boxes.

I slant my head to the side and stare into Izzy's eyes when she paces back toward me with a box marked O01P10. It isn't the box gaining my attention, it is the fretful mask slipped over Izzy's face causing my greatest concern. I follow Izzy into the main house, noticing her positive stance has also faded away.

"I'll order in some pizza, then I'm going to take a quick shower."

Not waiting for me to reply, she steps into the hallway. My eyes incessantly peer at the box she left sitting on the dining room table as I prepare myself a cup of coffee, hoping a good dose of caffeine will give me a boost. No matter how much I try to keep my focus off the box, my eyes consistently stray to it.

Unable to assuage my curiosity any longer, I set down my half-empty mug of coffee and amble toward the box. My eyes dart to the hallway, ensuring the coast is clear before I lift up the box flap. The air is vehemently removed from my body when my eyes zoom in on the first photo in the box. *Him.*

I throw off the lid with brutal force, sending it flying halfway across the kitchen floor. My hand shakes when I snatch the photo from the top of the pile. *Why is Izzy investigating the man who killed my sister?*

As I continue to delve through the box of photos and handwritten records, my concern grows. Numerous photos of Isaac are stored in this box, taken around the age he was when I first met him. Izzy isn't investigating Robert Petretti. She's investigating Isaac. Why would she do this? Why can't she just leave it alone? What's done is done. It can't be taken back.

"What are you doing? You can't go through that. Those files are highly confidential," roars across the room.

"Confidential?" I sneer, glaring at Izzy storming across the room. "You're invading his privacy, and you're worried about confidentiality. Is this why you came here? Searching for answers to questions he can't answer yet?" *Questions he shouldn't have to answer.*

Izzy gathers up the articles and photos spread across the table. Her face is pale, and her eyes are welling with tears.

"If you want answers, you should've kept asking, not go behind his back and investigate him." *He doesn't deserve your interrogation. I do.*

"I'm not investigating him," she retaliates.

"Then what do you call it, Izzy? You're looking into his past, digging through his *personal* life."

"I'm not prying into his personal life!"

I slam a surveillance photo of Isaac onto the wooden table-top. "You're not prying into his personal life, hey, then what the fuck is this?" I yell, no longer able to harbor my anger. Isaac has sheltered and defended me for years, all to have the woman he loves investigate him like he's a criminal.

"He isn't a criminal, but you're treating him as if he is one, and not the man you've agreed to marry."

A tear rolls down Izzy's cheek, calming my anger. I inhale a deep breath and count backwards from ten, a trick Avery taught me to do when I feel my anger is spiraling out of control.

"Ten seconds can be the difference between a lifetime of mistakes or a lifetime of memories," she has often quoted.

Izzy snaps her eyes shut, battling against her tears. Her hand slips into the back pocket of her jeans to remove a folded up piece of glossy paper. My eyes roam over her face as she unfolds the piece of paper before handing it to me. Even though the blood surging through my body has turned potent, the spark of fear ignited in Izzy's eyes sets me on edge. When she hands me the piece of paper, a freight train crashes into me. My eyes bounce between the photos of Isaac and his girlfriend before her untimely demise sprawled on the table and the photo in my hand of a girl who looks eerily similar to Isaac's deceased girlfriend. *No way, it can't be.*

"This can't be true," I mutter, my tone quickly shifting from angry to sympathetic.

"It is," Izzy mumbles. "This file proves it is. Ophelia is alive, and she's been living in Tiburon the entire time."

She paces toward me and matches up the photos, proving without a doubt the lady in the new photo is the same girl photographed with Isaac. Everything about her is similar: her face, her eyes, and a small mole in the corner of her neck.

"I gathered she was here because that's Old St. Hilary's church on Esperanza Street in the background. It is a well-loved landmark in Tiburon."

My eyes lift to Izzy. She isn't devastated to discover the secret Isaac's been hiding the past five years. She's devastated because she thinks she's losing him.

"Jesus Christ," I mumble under my breath. "Does Isaac know about any of this?"

Izzy bites on her lip and shakes her head. "No, I wanted to come and see for myself. I couldn't risk hurting him if it wasn't true. If it wasn't really her."

"If it is her, are you planning on telling him?"

Izzy lifts the newest photo of Ophelia off the dining table before gently nodding. A heavy weight slams into my chest from the defeated look on her face.

"What can I do to make this easier on you?"

New tears form in Izzy's eyes. "Just remind me that he loves me. And that I'm doing this to ease his pain."

FIFTEEN

HUGO

I climb the stairs of a private jet with Izzy cradled in my arms. She hasn't stopped crying since we left a pharmacy nearly thirty minutes ago. I've always been a communicator, but I'm too shocked at the events that transpired today to configure a response.

The hunch Izzy was running with was solid. She found Ophelia. Isaac's girlfriend who was killed in an "accident" well over five years ago is alive and well. As if that isn't shocking enough, Ophelia has a child, a small boy who would only be a year or two older than Joel. Isaac could be a father and he doesn't even know it.

I'm honestly at a loss on how he will react. Isaac protects every member of his empire as if they're his family, as if they're his blood. Imagine how great his response will be to discovering he has a child?

A few hours into the flight, Izzy's tears finally dry and her head lifts to me. "How old do you think Ophelia's son is?"

I want to lie. I want to tell her there isn't a possibility Ophelia's son is Isaac's, but I can't. I can't deceive her like that. I'm not a deceitful person.

"Five or six."

Her hand rattles as she takes a sip from a bottle of water. "So the dates could add up? He could be Isaac's son?"

She tries to put on a brave front, but she isn't fooling anyone. Izzy's eyes are very expressive. I can read her like a book. I move to sit in the spare seat next to her. A whimper escapes her lips when I wrap my arm around her shoulders and pull her into my chest. Flashes of the time I comforted Jorgie in my parent's kitchen weeks before her death come rushing to the forefront of my mind.

"You can't fight fate, Izzy, but that doesn't mean you should give up. Isaac gave you that engagement ring as a promise." I peer down at the dark gray and purple gemstone on her finger. "He's never spoken those words to another woman before, so that alone shows your importance to him. You need to have faith that things will work out the way they're meant to."

As do I. I fought my attraction to Ava for years, using any pathetic excuse I could find. She was my sister's best friend. My parents treated her like a daughter. I didn't want to settle down. Only now do I realize why it has only ever been Ava occupying my thoughts.

She was the first girl I ever lusted over, the first girl I ever asked out, and the first girl I've ever loved. My very existence begins and ends with her, and I'm going to make sure she's fully aware of that. Even though she's wearing another man's ring and has agreed to be his wife, I'll fight to my very last breath. I'll never give up.

AFTER WATCHING Isaac participate in a charity UFC match, I understand why he is feared by his rivals. The smile he wore in the cage didn't reflect the viciousness of his attack. I'm considering changing his nickname from Boss to the Smiling Assassin.

"Are you alright?" I ask Izzy, punching in the security code for Isaac's private residence.

Keeping her gaze fixated on the arched window of Isaac's house, she faintly murmurs, "Yes."

When I pull to the side of the driveway, I turn off the engine and grasp the door handle latch. My quick exit is foiled when Izzy places her hand on my knee.

"I want to talk to Isaac alone," she advises, her words weak. "He's a private man and wouldn't appreciate an audience."

Izzy's uncle should be proud. She has grown up to be an admirable woman. Even with her heart breaking, her priorities remain on protecting Isaac. She harbors so many of Ava's qualities. Even though I left her heartbroken, she has been nothing but encouraging of my relationship with Joel. For that, I'll be forever indebted to her.

"Alright. I'll wait here until Isaac arrives, then I'll head out, but if you need anything, Izzy, you have my number."

Izzy nods before leaning over and pressing a kiss against my cheek. "Thanks, Hugo, for everything."

Not long after Izzy has peeled out of my car, the headlights of Isaac's Bugatti illuminate the driveway. When he notices Izzy standing at the entrance of his house, he tries to keep his face passive. He fails miserably. Just like the night I officially introduced Hawke to Jorgie, anytime Isaac and Izzy are together, the dynamic between them is explosive. Like fireworks in a blackened sky.

Once Isaac joins Izzy on the porch of his home, I jump into my Chevelle and tear out of the driveway. My mind is jumbled, trying to pick between driving back to Rochdale now, or grabbing a few hours of sleep.

"You're not going to do anyone any good if you end up wrapped around a telephone pole," I mutter to myself.

My excessive speed down the winding roads of Isaac's estate slows when I notice a blue BMW parked on the edge of Isaac's property line. A snarl forms on my lips when the headlights of my car light up the number plate on the BMW. *Blondie.* What the fuck is he doing here?

When I pull in behind Blondie's BMW, he climbs out of the driver's seat. I don't know what it is, but there's something about Blondie that sets me on edge. I can't tell if it stems from the way he looks at Izzy when he thinks no one is looking, or if it is the cloud of secrets his wholesome eyes are concealing, but no matter how well he portrays the image of a humble Boy Scout, I ain't buying the shit he's selling. I can't comprehend why Izzy can't see the darkness impinging his eyes. To me, it is as obvious as the sun hanging in the sky, but Izzy seems oblivious to it. I know Blondie is hiding something, and I'm planning on exposing his deepest, darkest secrets.

"What are you doing here, Blondie?" I ask, pacing toward him.

I've nicknamed Brandon Blondie. It isn't his blond hair that has given him the title. It is the fact I don't believe Brandon is his real name. Hunter, Isaac's head of security, is one of the world's best hackers—not Adrian Lamo on a good day. He's Adrian Lamo on his best day. After completing a search on Brandon that Phillip Marlowe would have been proud of, Hunter couldn't find a trace of information on him. Not a single smidge. Brandon is even more of an illusion than I am. From experience, I know only men with something to hide keep their information locked up tighter than Fort Knox. That is why I know Brandon is hiding something, and it isn't his fascination with Izzy. That's even more obvious than the sun shining in the sky.

"You sniffing around hoping Isaac left out a bone?"

Brandon smirks, misconstruing my statement as a joke. I wasn't joking. He fidgets on the spot, kicking dust up from the loose gravel when he notices my furious wrath.

"I just want to make sure Izzy is alright," he replies, peering sheepishly into my eyes.

"Then why not go knock on the door like a real man?" I ask, my brow arched.

He laughs and shakes his head. "Been there. Done that."

I stare into his eyes, confused by his statement.

"I've tried numerous times to see Izzy since she left the hospital. My attempts were always denied... by Isaac."

I'm not surprised by his confession. I thought the jealousy issues that plague me with Ava are fierce. It is nothing compared to the jealously Isaac has when it comes to men getting close to Izzy. I can't say I blame him, though. From the gleam Brandon's eyes get when Izzy is in his vicinity, I have no doubt he would trample anyone in his way if Izzy was ever placed back on the market.

"Izzy is fine. She's with Isaac, where she belongs," I inform him before pivoting on my heels and ambling back to my car.

My brisk strides halt when Brandon mutters, "Even with Ophelia being alive?"

The beat of my heart kicks up as I turn around to face him. His face is washed with confusion, and his brows are furrowed tightly.

"How do you know about that?" I ask.

Brandon's pupils enlarge as his throat works hard to swallow.

"You gave Izzy the photo, didn't you? You thought it was your way in. The key to breaking up Isaac and Izzy."

Brandon's lips form a snarl and he shakes his head.

"Bullshit," I retaliate, pacing to stand in front of him, wanting to look him in the eyes as I call him out as the weasel he is. "You weaseled your way into Izzy's life by pretending you're her friend, all so you could undermine her relationship with Isaac. I've got news for you: you can't fight fate, so I suggest you give up while you're ahead."

"I'm her friend," Brandon responds, his tone surprisingly strong. "Everything I've done is because I'm trying to protect her."

"She doesn't need your protection," I roar when I spot the gleam in his eyes. "She has Isaac. She has me. She doesn't need you. So go jump on your white horse and find another damsel in distress to save, because Izzy doesn't need saving."

I count down to ten as I walk back to my car. If I don't control my anger, I'm going to burst.

"Are you going to protect her like you did Gemma?" Brandon shouts, his voice crammed with anger.

I freeze when Gemma's name seeps from his lips. Surely I didn't hear him right. My pulse is blaring in my ears, so I must be mistaken. *I have to be.* When I spin around to face him, I have no doubt he said what I thought he said. The look of fear in his eyes in the only indication I need to know he's aware of the night that still haunts my dreams......

"If only you liked white chocolate," Gemma gabbles, plopping onto the barstool next to me.

My hearty chuckle rumbles over the music blasting out of the jukebox in the corner of the room. I've spent a majority of my night with members of my squadron at a dime a dozen watering hole in the middle of a town we are stationed at. Although rundown, Cantina Vault is a buzzing hive of activity. Line dancers and regular nightclub patrons share the floor space; Air Force officers from Second Lieutenants to Brigadier Generals are spread as far as the eye can see, and the beer is the coldest I've ever guzzled. What more could a man ask for?

I toss down half a bottle of beer before turning my eyes to Gemma. Gemma is the first female Lieutenant in my squadron. With her wittiness and willingness to give anything a shot meant we became close friends in a short period of time, but in all honesty, when I was first introduced to Gemma, I was concerned about how she was going to cope with the rough conditions we'd immersed ourselves into. It wasn't that I was a chauvinistic asshole; I was just raised by my father to protect my mother and sisters, so I assumed it would take me a bit of time to adjust to Gemma being a fellow officer, not my little sister who needed protecting.

The adjustment didn't take as long as I was predicting. It lasted all of one week—the time it took for me to walk in on

Gemma showering in the male latrine. The boiler in the female dorm broke so Gemma ducked in our latrine, expecting my squadron to be longer at our TI drill than we were. After raking my eyes over Gemma's naked body, any worries about treating her like my sister flew right out the window.

Although she's a little on the short side and couldn't weigh more than a pile of feathers, Gemma is gorgeous. No doubt about it. Cascading blonde hair falling to her shoulders in a satin waterfall; rich, prominent green eyes that dazzle even in the poor overhead lighting; and perfect unblemished skin, except for the smallest mass of freckles sprinkling her tiny nose. She's beautiful – a prime example of both looks and personality, but even being hot enough to cause my dick to stir, nothing has ever happened between us. Gemma likes to say it is because she has the wrong skin coloring, but it isn't that. There has only ever been one girl I want to jump the friendship line for: Ava. So as much as Gemma's offer is tempting, I've never taken her up on it.

I angle my body to the side, tilting in closer to Gemma. "Who said I'm not a fan of white chocolate?"

Gemma drifts her glistening eyes from the diverse gathering of people cavorting on the crammed dance floor to me. She cocks her brow before pulling her "I'm not buying the shit you're selling" look she regularly uses when dealing with her male counterparts in the Air Force.

"How long have we been stationed together? Nearly ten months?" Gemma queries with her lips pursed.

I nod, agreeing with her assessment.

"In that whole time, I've not once seen you share the love with your fairer companions."

I laugh. It is the only plausible reaction to her absurd

misconception. For one, the week before we deployed, I had a very compelling meeting with one of Gemma's sorority sisters from Alaska. Two, any time we go out, Gemma spends her night dancing like the floor is on fire, too busy to be paying attention to my female companions. And third, but not at all least, just from the impish glimmer in her eyes, I can tell she's full of shit. She has eyes like Jorgie, I can see straight through to her soul.

"Jealously has never looked so good," I quip, my tone doused with smugness.

Gemma's head snaps to mine. "Jealous? Please! You had your opportunity—you lost it. No second chances around here," she remarks, wiggling her index finger in front of my face.

I chuckle at her sassiness before taking a swig out of my beer.

Malted liquid sprays out of my mouth, dousing the wooden countertop and Gemma's face when she says, "I also snuck a peek at the photo you hide in your foot locker. Ava is very beautiful. I can understand your fascination."

My heart freezes at the mention of Ava's name, but thankfully my outward appearance gives no indication to the treachery of my heart.

"I'd like to say this is the first time I've had beer sprayed in my face, but, unfortunately, it isn't," Gemma mutters, dabbing her face with a midnight black napkin.

Once all fragments of my spit beer have been removed from her face, she lifts her expressive eyes to me. "Ava is in San Diego, not on the moon. You know that magic tin can we're flying home in on Monday? They have similar ones that can fly you to any destination of your choice. San Diego included."

I smirk against the rim of my beer before taking a mouthfilling gulp. "You sound like my sister, Jorgie."

Gemma smiles broadly. "I need to meet this Jorgie. She sounds a little too good to be true," she jests before placing an order with a bartender for a virgin margarita.

"Loose lips sink ships," I mutter to myself.

I learned the meaning of that saying the weekend following Warrior Week. That week of training should be called Hell Week. We slept in tents, ate funky combinations of beans and rice and practiced war-like conditions, but it wasn't the unappetizing setting or the less-than-stellar accommodations that gave it the coveted title of Hell Week. It was TI Drill Sergeant Cody Spencer. He was the hardest, bare-knuckled and bloody drill sergeant I'd ever encountered. After a week in his presence, I could barely crawl, let alone walk. Deciding we needed to celebrate surviving our trip to hell and back, our regiment went out to a local salsa bar. After celebrating as if it was Cinco de Mayo, my lips become as loose as the salsa dancers' hips. One slip up during a game of twenty questions saw me mentioning my high school crush's name. Ever since that night, Ava's name is mentioned at every celebration.

I slam down the remainder of my beer and signal to the bartender for another. My squadron only has two days remaining in Afghanistan until we return home from our second stint. We're guzzling down our drinks like we aren't paying fifteen dollars for a can of bootleg beer, but when you're celebrating a successful end of our tour without any casualities to your unit, you'll happily pay the premium price, because you can't put a value on that – it is priceless.

"Why aren't you out there dancing?" I ask Gemma, noticing the direction of her gaze. Her glistening eyes are absorbing the hot sweaty bodies mingling on the dance floor.

Her nose screws up. "Grabby McGee is being extra grabby," she replies.

My eyes rocket to the dance floor. Madden McGee is a fucking sleaze, and that's putting it nicely. He was born and bred with Air Force blood pumping through his veins. His uncles, grandfather, and brothers all served in the same squadron of the Air Force. Although his predecessors honored his family name, Madden has done nothing but tarnish it. He ignores any instructions given by his superiors, he treats the female members of his squadron as if they're inferior, and he has his nose so far up his own ass, he thinks his shit doesn't stink. He's the type of guy who gives Air Force Officers a bad name. I also have a knack for reading people, and I didn't like him from the moment I met him.

I drift my eyes back to Gemma. "Do you want me to talk to him?" I offer.

"No," she says, dramatically drawing out the short word. "I can handle Grabby McGee."

A smirk tugs on my lips. After seeing the way Gemma handled Warrior Week, I have no doubt she can handle a worm of a man like Madden. After accepting her virgin margarita from the bartender, Gemma hip bumps me before making her way to a handful of female squadron members mingling at the side of the dance space.

"Come find me when you're ready to go," she yells.

———

AFTER A HANDFUL OF BEERS, I decide to call it a night and head back to base. I straighten my spine, extending to my full height so I can seek Gemma in the crowd of people cavorting on the dance floor. Although we aren't a couple, we always arrive and leave together when we go out drinking. When my search fails to locate her shiny blonde locks, I move to the bar. A bartender with inky black hair and a neck tattoo stops wiping the counter and paces toward me.

"Have you seen Gemma? Blonde hair, green eyes, around this tall," I ask, holding my hand across my chest. "She's been ordering virgin margaritas all night."

He smiles. "White floral dress?"

"That's the one."

Gemma is the only girl who can pull off a floral dress in a war-torn country.

He stops drying a glass and gestures his head to the entrance door. "She left a few minutes ago."

My brows furrow. "She left?" Skepticism radiates from my voice. I normally have to drag Gemma out of any bars we visit.

"Thanks," I say, tapping my knuckles onto the wooden bar top before spinning on my heels.

As I walk to the double swinging doors, the churning hampering my stomach revs up a gear as the feeling of something not being quite right overwhelms me. My steps to the door become urgent, only hindered by the beer sloshing in my twisted stomach. When I emerge out the double wooden doors, a blast of humid air hits me in the face, making my stomach churn even more. My neck cranks to the right before drifting to the left. There's a handful of late-night, drunk partygoers scattered on the sidewalk, but Gemma is nowhere in sight.

My head shifts to the side when a young blond-haired man stumbles out of a side alley. His face is ashen and his pupils wide. I lift my chin in greeting as I eye him with curiosity. I've never seen a kid look so rattled before, even after serving in Afghanistan for two years. The blond kid's eyes stare into mine. His chest thrusts upwards as he battles to secure a full breath.

His eyes snap to the side at the same time a faint scream overtakes the hum of music pumping out of the bar. My head rockets to the side at lightning speed. I freeze and take a step backwards, winded like I've been sucker-punched in the guts. The shock of what I witness quickly converts to fury as the scene unfolds in front of me. I charge down the alleyway, my steps no longer impeded by the alcohol I drank. The blood rushing through my veins turns potent, blackened by the fury scorching it.

"Get off!" I scream, my deep angry snarl bouncing off the stained brick walls.

"Stop it! Stop it! Get off!" I scream again.

Blinded by rage, I grab the first man I see and throw him against the trash can he is standing next to. His head connects hard with the steel edge, sending a stream of blood running down the side of his face. He stands, dazed and confused. Holding his wounded head in his hand, he staggers down the alleyway. I storm toward a group of men, dragging them away from a pair of fear-filled green eyes staring up at me, pleading for me to save her. A man I've seen before but misplaced his name stops in front of me. He cracks his knuckles and sneers at me.

A bone being fractured bellows through the eerie quietness when my clenched fist connects hard with his jaw. When he falls to the ground, I grab another man, and then another, unleashing hit after hit in a haze of rage. Even outnumbered, the scent of fear never approaches me. I'm running on pure adrenaline, too enraged to stop the anger burning me from the inside out.

My sweat-drenched shirt clings to my chest when I fist the shirt of another man.

"Stop, Hugo. It's me. It's Brody," says a voice quieter than a mouse.

My wildly swinging fist freezes mid-air, inches from a terrified face. The same face of the man who stumbled out of the alley mere minutes ago stares up at me, terrified and confused. My clouded eyes dart up and down the alley. I unclench my fist when I find the alley empty of the men who were here ten minutes ago. My chest rises and falls as my body fights to rein in my usually carefree composure.

Any sense of normality vanishes when a painful sob shreds through my ears. My eyes dart down to Gemma, huddled against a brick wall. The roughness of the brickwork scratches her skin as she scrambles across the cracked, stained pavement. The strap of her dress is broken, her knees are bloody and bruised, and black lines of mascara are running down her pale cheeks. Her frantic eyes scan the area as her entire body shakes. I remove my blood-stained shirt, snubbing the trembling that has encroached my hands.

"Don't touch me. I don't want you to touch me," she stammers out.

"It's okay. I won't touch you."

I crouch down in front of her to carefully drape my shirt over her shaking body. She peers up at me, wide-eyed and in shock. Her lips quiver as a mass of moisture swamps her eyes. I return her stare, allowing my eyes to issue the words my mouth is failing to produce. My apologies for what she went through, while also relaying that I won't hurt her. When the sounds of sirens approach, Gemma leaps forward and digs her nails into *my arm, clutching onto me for dear life, like I'm her safety shield......*

I've never forgotten the terrified sobs that tore from her throat that night.

I lunge for Brandon, grabbing the scruff of his shirt before he can react. Hauling him to within an inch of my face, my furious eyes scorch his. The mad beat of his heart pounds the edge of my clenched fist that is pinning him against the car. He eyeballs me, wide-eyed and slack-jawed, but not a sound seeps from his lips.

"Who are you?" I query, my voice failing to conceal the shivers havocking my body as a flurry of memories delve into me.

Brandon's eyes dance between mine, but not a word parts his mouth.

"Who are you?" I scream again, tightening my grip on his shirt.

He stares into my eyes. "My name is Brandon James--"

My teeth grit, furious he's trying to play me for a fool.

"McGee," he adds on.

The air is vehemently removed from my lungs. I roam my eyes over Brandon's face, studying him in precise detail. Same hazel eyes, defined nose, wonky smile; it was just the blond hair that lead me astray. I take a step backward, overwhelmed by a surge of emotions pummeling into me at once.

"You're Grabby McGee's brother?"

Fury unlike anything I've ever felt makes it hard for me to secure a full breath when Brandon nods. I yank him forward before slamming his body back with vicious force. Metal crunching echoes in the quietness of the night. Even with his back slamming into his car with brutal strength, Brandon's face remains staunch, not giving any indication of the pain rocketing through his body.

"Do you know who I am?" I ask, my words a vicious snarl.

Brandon's nostrils flare as he inhales quick, sharp breaths of air.

"Yes," he mutters, his chin quivering.

My stomach tenses, copping an emotional blow as every secret I've fought to keep hidden becomes exposed. My panic doesn't last long, replaced with anger. Angry that I was ever forced to keep such a secret. Fury scorches through me, burning my chest with its ferocious heat.

"Do you know what they did?" I ask, my eyes blazing.

My lungs burn as my body battles to cool the furious heat of the blood scorching my veins. I'm spiraling out of control as a range of reactions crash into me. Anger, remorse, devastation. It all hammers into me in a flurry, nearly sprawling me onto my ass.

When Brandon remains quiet, I scream, "Do you know what they did to me?!"

"Yes," Brandon replies, his head jerking in a nod.

My whole body is trembling, my nostrils are flaring, anger is burning me alive. Brandon stares into my eyes, exposing his guilt and remorse. *His shame.*

"I'm nothing like them," he pleads, his eyes rocketing between mine. "I didn't change my name because I didn't want people to know who my father is. I changed it because I'm ashamed of it. I'm ashamed of them."

His wholesome eyes stare into mine, begging for me to believe him. I know what he's saying is true. Even with his eyes hazed by sorrow, I can see the truth relayed by them. I can feel his shame, his remorse, but it doesn't lessen my anger. I want to lay my fists into him. I want to make him suffer the way Gemma suffered. *The way I suffered, but* then, I'd be just as much a coward as they were.

So instead, I release my grip on his collar and stalk to my car.

SIXTEEN

HUGO

I stumble out of my room with my head pounding as fitfully as my heart. My confrontation with Brandon last night turned my mood woeful. Instead of remembering the lessons Avery has taught me the past five years, I once again sought the aid of a liquor bottle to guide me through the storm. I was desperate, doing anything I could to wash away the memories asphyxiating the joyful mood I'd been in the past four days. I wanted the grim memories that haunt my dreams to vanish. Normally, I could only achieve that with a bottle. Last night, alcohol did nothing. The only people who have the chance to stop my nightmares are seven hundred miles away. Just looking in Ava's eyes can appease any storm brewing on the horizon.

Noticing my stagger, Hawke opens a bottle of whiskey and pours two glasses, sliding one across the marble counter to me. The inexpensive brown liquor sloshes over the rim, landing on the glistening countertop.

"Hair of the dog?" I mutter, securing the glass.

Hawke arches his brow. Every man knows there's only one cure for a hangover – keep drinking. The bitter-tasting bile sitting in the back of my throat washes into my stomach when I lift the whiskey glass to my mouth and down the generous nip in quick succession. My face grimaces when the familiar burn scorches my throat before settling in my churning stomach. Hawke props his elbows onto the kitchen counter. His movements allow me to see the time on the microwave. It is nearly five PM. My brows hit my hairline. I slept for over twelve hours.

Hawke peers at me with uncertain eyes. "I wasn't expecting you back so early. Didn't go as you hoped?"

By the time Hawke walked in the front door of my apartment last night, I was well past tipsy. Assuming I was drowning my sorrows about my trip to Rochdale, Hawke gathered a second bottle of whiskey from the bar and joined my silent commiserations. We didn't talk; we just sat, side by side, staring into space, drinking in silence.

"Rochdale was good," I say, rubbing my temples, praying for the pounding drilling my skull into the next century to settle so I can get back on the road. *Back to my family.* "Actually, Rochdale was more than good. It was fucking great."

Hawke's eyes missile to mine. His brow is arched, and the expression on his face is even more uncertain than the glint in his eyes.

"I have a son," I enlighten him. Even having a hangover that rivals all hangovers, I can't stop an ecstatic smile stretching across my face. Joel has captured my soul even more quickly than Ava stole my heart.

Hawke's eyes bulge as his looks at me in utter shock. "Who's the mom?"

My brain screams blue murder when I throw my head back and boisterously chuckle. My hearty laugh booms off the laminated cabinets and ricochets into my ears. Hawke doesn't see the hilarity of the situation. His brows are stitched, and his lips are screwed. He looks utterly confused.

"Who do you think?" I ask once my laughter dies down.

"I don't know, that's why I'm asking," he replies, his tone deadly serious.

When I waggle my brows and smile, clarity forms in his baffled eyes.

"Ava?" His voice is super-alto.

I bite on my lip and nod. If I'd slapped Hawke in the face with a cold fish, it wouldn't have shocked him more. I slant my head to the side and eye him curiously when his eyes get a spark in them I haven't seen since the day he married Jorgie.

"She was right," he says, pushing off the counter and crossing his arms in front of his chest. "Jorgie always said you and Ava were destined to be together. Your son proves it. You can't--"

"Fight fate," I fill in, smiling.

Hawke nods and smiles. His eyes get a gloss of sheen in them.

A tingling sensation scratches my throat when Hawke lifts his gaze from the bench to lock his glistening eyes with mine. "I'm really happy for you, man."

I'm not going to lie, my eyes are welling with tears. Hawke may have only said six little words, but his eyes are expressing much more than his mouth ever could. His normally unreadable eyes expose fragments of a Hawke I haven't seen in years. The pre-heartbroken Hawke.

"Thanks."

After coughing to clear his voice of any hindrance, Hawke says, "I'm going to squeeze in a workout at the gym before heading to Nick and Jenni's. I'm on night watch."

He smacks me on the back before ambling to the door. Just before he exits, he cranks his head back and peers at me. His mouth is carved in a lopsided grin, and his eyes are sparked with mischief.

"You should consider heading to the gym yourself," he suggests, waggling his brows. "Get some testosterone pumping through your veins. I don't want you to run the risk of waking up in the morning with a vagina, since you're getting all sentimental and shit."

Catching sight of his shit-eating grin, I pick up an apple from the fruit bowl in the middle of the counter and peg it at his head. He chuckles raucously before darting out the front door. I snarl when my throw narrowly misses hitting his head and slams into the mirror hanging in the entranceway, shattering it into tiny shards.

Darn it. The last thing I need is seven years of bad luck.

AFTER HAVING a shower to wash off the funk of a heavy night of drinking, I clean up the shards of glass in the foyer. Half of me was tempted to leave it for Catherine's arrival tomorrow afternoon, but my laziness only lasted as long as it took for me to remember a quote my mom has always said: *A real man knows how to respect a woman. Because he knows the feeling if someone would disrespect his mother.*

While picking up the last shard of glass, my eyes catch sight of a white envelope sitting on the entranceway table. My heart smashes against my ribs. It isn't the fact I don't get any mail delivered to my home address that piques my interest. It is the fact it has my full name scribbled on the envelope. My full *deceased* name: Hugo Joel Marshall.

Snatching the lightweight envelope off the table, I rip it open and upend the contents onto the table. My eyes scan the official-looking document before I've even gathered it in my hands. The more my eyes speed-read the paper, the more my blood boils. Shoving the document under my arm, I snatch my keys and cell phone out of the crystal bowl on the entranceway table and race to the elevator at the end of my hallway. When the elevator dashboard announces the elevator car is still in the lobby, I push open the fire door and sprint down the stairs.

By the time I make it to the my car, I'm sweating profusely and shaking. Neither is from the effects of running down thirty flights of stairs. I jump into my car, crank the ignition and reverse out of my parking space. The smell of burning rubber and gasoline infiltrate my nostrils as I throw *baby* into gear and fly out of the underground garage, narrowly missing a blue BMW entering. I don't miss Brandon's curious glance as my car whizzes by, but I've got more important matters to deal with right now than him and his guilty conscience.

Drifting my eyes between the road and my phone, I dial Ava's cell phone. Ignoring the shake encroaching my hands, I press the phone against my ear.

"Hey, you've reached Ava; leave a message."

"Ava, please don't do this. Please don't take my son away from me," I beg, lowering my eyes to the paperwork sitting on the passenger seat. "I know I hurt you and broke your heart. I know you may never forgive me, but please don't do this. I need him. *I need you.* I'll do anything you want, anything at all, but I can't sign those forms, Ava. I can't give him up. I can't give *you* up."

I continue pleading into her voicemail until a message comes over the line saying her voicemail is full. I snap my untraceable cell phone shut and throw it onto the forms requesting my signature to sign away my parental rights to Joel, relinquishing full custody to Ava and Marvin. No request for child support has been included and no visitation rights have been stipulated.

As if that weren't already a low blow, the very last page gutted me. It is requesting a paternity test, wanting to prove Joel is my biological son. I know he's my son. I've never doubted it from the moment I laid my eyes on him, but now Ava is trying to deny it, pretending he isn't mine. It doesn't make any sense. I can't comprehend why her perspective has altered so greatly the past two days. She said Joel would be there waiting for me when I came back, that he wasn't going anywhere, but this paperwork says different.

APPROXIMATELY TWO HUNDRED miles outside of Ravenshoe, my untraceable cell phone rings. Not bothering to look at the screen, I flick it open and push it against my ear.

"Ava, please--"

"Who's Ava?" Hunter's voice is laced with mockery.

"Hunter, I don't have time. I'm—"

My words stop when Hunter says, "Izzy needs you."

"What's going on?" I ask, apprehension heard in my voice.

"Travis called to say she arrived at the Dungeon an hour ago. She's fairly intoxicated."

I smirk. *Sounds like something Izzy would do.* "Where's Isaac?"

After Izzy was cleared of murder charges, Isaac gave me the month off, clearly stipulating Izzy wasn't going to leave his sight until he "had his fill." Reading his coded statement, I was more than happy to take a leave of absence from my position. It is my first official vacation in nearly five years.

"Isaac is in Tiburon," Hunter replies. I hear him run his hand along his scruff beard. "I don't know when he's coming back. I've been trying his cell phones all day, they keep going straight to his voicemail."

My brow arches. Isaac is never unreachable. His cells are an extension of his body.

"Can you send Roger to keep an eye on her? He's as boring as bat shit, but he's good at his job. He'll make sure Izzy stays out of mischief."

"Can't," Hunter retorts. "He's at Vegas helping Parker secure Isaac's asset."

My eyes squint when a semi-trailer comes over the horizon, blinding me with its high beams.

After flashing my lights at the truck driver and flipping him the bird, I say, "What about you?"

Hunter sheepishly chuckles. It is a laugh I only hear when he is in trouble or causing it. "I'm a little *indisposed* right now."

He's not the only one.

"I'm two hundred miles out," I explain.

Normally, I wouldn't hesitate, but it going to take me at least three hours to get to Izzy, someone else in Isaac's team might be closer.

"That's means you're fifteen hundred miles closer to Izzy than me. I've tried everyone, but being New Year's Eve, I'm running out of options. Besides, you're the only man Isaac trusts with Izzy."

Muffled voices sound down the line before Hunter says, "I got to go; can you do this or not, Hugo?"

My eyes flick to the clock on my dashboard, displaying it is a little after nine PM. Even if I continue on my trip, I won't reach Rochdale until 3 AM. I don't think Ava would appreciate me rocking up to her door that early in the morning, and I don't need to add any more nails to my coffin by pissing her off.

"I'll do it," I say, pulling my car over to the side of the road. "But you're going to fucking owe me, Hunter."

Hunter chuckles. "I'll add it to the long list of favors."

Not giving me a chance to reply, he disconnects the call.

BY THE TIME I'm turning onto the street the Dungeon night-club is located on, I'm exhausted and beyond pissed. I promised Isaac I'd always protect Izzy, and I will, but her timing couldn't be anymore fucked.

I pull my Chevelle to the curb at the front of the club and peel out of my car. Travis, the bouncer, greets me with a dip of his head as I storm toward him.

"Cormack sent a town car to collect Cate," Travis advises. "That only leaves you Izzy to deal with."

I roll my eyes before entering the double doors he's holding open for me. The intoxicating scent of alcohol infused with sweat smacks me in the face when I enter the main section of the Dungeon. It is crammed to the rafters with patrons out enjoying the end of another year. *A year that packed more punch than I was prepared for.* I extend to my full height, seeking Izzy amongst the crowd. The quicker I get her out of here, the quicker I can get back onto the road. My brows furrow when I spot Izzy dancing with a man who has sandy blond hair. He either has a death wish or isn't a local, because no man in this town is brave enough to talk to Izzy, let alone dance with her.

"He has a death wish," I mutter, pacing closer to Izzy.

Not only is Izzy wearing a dress that leaves *nothing* to the imagination, he's grinding up on her like Robin Thicke grinded up on Miley Cyrus at the MTV Video Music Awards. *Isaac will kill him.* As the final minute of the year counts down on the clock shackled to the ceiling, I barge my way through the mass of sweating bodies cavorting on the dance floor. Just as the cheer of "Forty-eight" seeps from Izzy's mouth, I seize her elbow and drag to the edge of the dance space.

"What the hell are you doing, Izzy?" I ask, staring into massively dilated eyes that clearly expose the extent of her intoxication. She's *well* past tipsy.

"What does it look like I'm doing? I'm dancing," she replies, her slur not impeding her sassy attitude.

When she attempts to stumble away, I grab her wrist. Her head rockets back to me.

"Dancing? You're not dancing. You're provoking Isaac, trying to force his hand."

Izzy snarls, baring teeth before she shakes her head. Beads of sweat fling off her drenched nape and land on the floor.

"You don't know what you're talking about. He left, Hugo. He walked straight out of the house without a backward glance. He left me. So I'm free to do *whatever* I please."

Whatever or whomever?

With the determination of the little ninja she is, Izzy squirms out of my grip and stumbles back to her blond dance partner. I count backward to ten, trying to keep a grip on the anger bristling my spine.

Once I have a small sense of rationality, I step in front of Izzy, halting her wobbly steps. "Bullshit, Izzy. You, yourself, had to see if the claims were true, but you don't expect Isaac to react the same? You're using that guy all because you want to antagonize Isaac. All because you want to force him to react."

Her face scrunches as she shakes her head, denying my statement.

"If it isn't that, then why are you going to all this effort? What is the purpose? A free drink? A grope on the dance floor? A stupid midnight kiss?!"

"Yes!" she screams, her loud voice projecting over the blare of music booming out of the speakers. "Because that is probably what he's doing to her right now. He's probably kissing her right now!"

"That's what you want? A kiss? All of this heartache for a pathetic kiss on New Year's Eve?!"

Anger blackens my blood. I could lose *everything* because she wants a stupid midnight kiss. My son, the woman who owns my heart, I could lose them both because she's acting like a selfish little brat who didn't get every item on her Christmas wish list.

If she wants a stupid midnight kiss, I'll give her a fucking kiss.

I snag Izzy's wrist and pull her back to me. Her nipples pebble when her chest crashes into mine. A surprised gasp escapes her lips and flutters my mouth with a fruity cocktail scent when I press my lips against hers. I feel the quickening of her pulse through her wrist I'm still clasping. I run my tongue along the seam of her lips before plunging it inside her warm and inviting mouth. Weaving my fingers through her hair, I secure her mouth to mine and increase the intensity of our kiss. I kiss the living hell out of her. Not holding anything back. Giving it my all.

When she pulls away from my embrace, her lust-filled eyes wildly dart between mine. She runs the back of her hand over her red, swollen lips, vainly trying to remove the evidence of our kiss.

"Isaac will kill you," she mutters as tears well in her eyes.

I smirk and nod. "Yeah, well, at least I know what I'm getting myself into. That dumb fuck had no clue you were in the process of signing his death certificate."

I know Isaac. I know him better than he thinks I do. He won't let anyone come between him and Izzy. Just like I'm no longer willing to let anyone come between me and my family.

SEVENTEEN

HUGO

I feel Isaac's presence before I see him. His anger is so paramount, I feel it all the way in the guest bedroom I'm emerging from. I pull a shirt over my head before rounding the corner of the hallway and entering the main living area. After dumping my duffle bag near the entranceway, I lift my eyes. Isaac is standing in the middle of the sunken living room. He has his back facing me, his fists clenched and hanging at his side. I don't need to see his face to know he's aware of the kiss Izzy and I shared. I can feel his anger vibrating out of him. I also wouldn't have expected anything less. Isaac knows everything, especially when it comes to Izzy.

Sensing my presence, he spins on his heels to face me. I take a step backward when I see the despondent look on his stern face. His eyes are darker than I remember and his jaw more set. The veins in his neck thrum as he roams his thinly slit eyes over my face. He looks like he wants to kill me. Rightfully so, he should.

Exhaling a deep breath, I pace into the living room. My steps are hesitant, weighed down by the guilt my shoulders are carrying. I place the keys to my apartment and Chevelle onto the wrought iron and glass coffee table in the middle of the room. Although my *baby* was initially Jorgie's car, it was nothing but worthless scrap metal before Isaac had it rebuilt, so it belongs to him. My hand slips into the back pocket of my jeans, removing my wallet. Isaac watches my every movement, but doesn't speak a word. He doesn't need to. His eyes are relaying his disappointment and anger. *My firing.*

Isaac's eyes drop to my hands when I remove the first check he gave me in the limousine over five years ago. After everything he did for my family and me, I couldn't bring myself to cash it, no matter how tempting the figure written down was. After placing the check next to the keys, I dip my chin in farewell and amble to the door, cowardly walking away without saying goodbye since my mouth is refusing to relinquish any words.

Isaac's hand shoots out, seizing my arm and stopping my brisk strides. He grips my arm tight enough to display his strength, but not enough to warrant me to react. I wouldn't react, anyway. I deserve any punishment he wants to dish. His nostrils flare as his eyes burn into mine, searing my soul with their furious heat. Nothing but pain reflects in his uniquely colored eyes. They issue more punishment than any fists or words ever could. My betrayal cut him deep. His eyes are his battle wounds. My brows furrow when he releases me from his grip and strides toward the master suite of my apartment, his steps fast and efficient. *I expected a much harsher punishment.*

Once he enters the main bedroom, I slip out the front door

of my apartment and walk down the hall, not once looking back on my old life.

Hugo Jones is now dead.

My brows meet my hairline when I step onto the sidewalk of my apartment building and discover Hunter's Dodge Challenger SRT Hellcat parked at the curb. The passenger window glides down before his scruff-covered face pops into frame.

"Get in," he says, his tone rough.

When I slip into the passenger seat, Hunter slams his foot down on the accelerator, showcasing his car's 707 horsepower motor. After cracking sixty miles in under three seconds, Hunter flicks his eyes between the road and me. Even with a thick beard covering his jaw, I can't miss the twinge inflicting his jawline.

When we reach the T intersection at Tivot, his eyes glide to me. "Airport or train station?"

I smirk and shake my head. "How do you know I'm leaving?" *Running.*

"Come on, Hugo. Don't treat me like I'm stupid." Hunter responds, running his hand along his beard. "You knew he'd be watching."

He's always watching.

When Hunter takes a left, failing to signal, a motorist beeps his horn and curses.

"You couldn't have just quit? You had to force Isaac to fire you. It was a stupid move, Hugo. You know what he's like with Izzy. You're lucky you're still breathing."

"I have a son," I blurt out, no longer able to stand the disappointment in Hunter's eyes.

Hunter may be my supervisor, but he's also my friend. That

is a hard title for any man to achieve since I've spent the last five years being a ghost.

Hunter remains quiet for the next five miles. His brows are knitted tightly and his eyelids are twitching, but his lips remain rigid.

After a beat, he says. "Why didn't you just tell Isaac that?"

"You don't think he has enough on his plate? He's been dragged through the trenches the past month," I answer, my tone rough from the guilt strangling my vocal cords.

"So you thought you'd add to it?" Hunter interjects.

My eyes rocket to Hunter's. His dark eyes stare into mine, revealing what I already know. I just added more drama to Isaac's already drama-filled life.

Fuck!

"I don't work well under pressure," I mumble, running my hand over my head. "I tend to charge first, ask questions later."

Hunter pulls his car into the curb at the front of the domestic terminal at Ravenshoe Airport. He clicks the locks into place, trapping me in the car with him. "Take a week. Sort your shit out with your family, then come back here and wade through the shit you just dumped."

I shake my head. "I can't"

"Why not?" Hunter interrupts, his tone clipped.

"I can't do both. My family is over seven hundred miles away. I already missed four years of my son's life, I'm not willing to miss anymore."

"So you want to be a dad?"

I nod.

"A good dad?"

I nod again.

"Then lead by example, Hugo. Show your son how to do the right thing. You owe Isaac—"

"You don't think I know what I owe him?" My question booms around Hunter's car. "I know what I owe him. I owe him *everything, but* I *owe* my family more."

His hard-hearted eyes stare into mine. "There's no reason you can't have both. Be a man. Talk to Isaac. Don't thank him for everything he has done for you by messing around with the only good thing he has in his life."

A barrel of emotions pummel into me. I owe Isaac the world. Without him, I'd be dead, but I won't have a life worth living without my family. *Without Ava.* I barely survived the past five years without her, but now, knowing what I'm missing, I can't live without her and Joel. I can't give them up.

"Besides, how are you supposed to care for your son if you don't have a job? You're a ghost. A phantom. No one will hire a dead man."

Shit, I didn't even consider that. How can I entice Ava away from a man who has more money than sense with a dwindling bank account and no employment prospective? I know Ava doesn't love Marvin. She doesn't look at him the way she used to look at me. Not the slightest, but she's stuck between a rock and a hard place, struggling between putting her heart before the welfare of her son. *Our son.*

I understand her dilemma. It's why I stupidly kissed Izzy. When I first kissed her it was out of anger, furious her childish antics were risking my chances of seeing my son, but the instant I pressed my lips against hers, it dawned on me that Isaac would be watching. *He's always watching.* Instead of manning up and talking to Isaac, I took the coward's way out, doing what he hates. I forced his arm. Kissing Izzy was my way out. She was my golden ticket home.

I'll admit it, I was shocked as hell when Izzy kissed me back. It was only after a sleepless night did I realize why she did it. She was hurting, believing Isaac had left her for Ophelia. She wanted him to experience the pain she was feeling. It worked. I've never seen Isaac look so dejected. I never want to see that look again. Not on Isaac's face and not on Ava's. I'll make this right, for both of them. *I have to.*

Noticing my defiant stance weakening, Hunter continues with his campaign. "Take a week, then come back and we'll talk it out like real men. There's no reason you can't have both your family and your Ravenshoe family."

My lips twist. "That sounds like an ideal situation, but Isaac's not going--"

"Don't worry about Isaac, I've got him covered," Hunter interrupts, his tone cocky.

I arch my brow. "Who the fuck are you and where's the real Hunter Kane? No one has Isaac *covered.*"

It is only when I stare into Hunter's shimmering eyes does the *real* reality hit.

"Who has your dick wrapped around their little finger?" I ask, my tone not matching the heaviness of our conversation.

I can't help it, though. Hunter's longest relationship is the length of time it takes him to fuck her and walk her to the door. He's never had a girlfriend. Not once, but I can't miss the glimmer in his eyes. It is the same glimmer my eyes get every time I see Ava.

I chuckle when Hunter leans over, unlocks the passenger door and barges me in the shoulder, shoving me out of his car. A winded grunt escapes my lips when my backside crashes onto the sidewalk. Even with a jolt of pain rocketing through my shoulder, a broad grin etches on my face.

"Are you in *love?*" I jest, drawing out the last word in a long, husky drawl.

Hunter grabs my duffle bag from the backseat of his car and throws it into my chest, winding me with his brutal force.

"Get your ass back here in a week," he directs sternly, glaring into my eyes.

I smile, loving that I've finally discovered Hunter's weak spot. *It's taken me over four years to find it.*

"Is it true what they say about beards? Can you smell her hours later?"

Hunter's teeth grit before he throws open the driver's side door and peels out of his car. I scramble off the floor and hotfoot it to the entrance of the airport. I have a leering grin stretched across my face and am feeling the most carefree I've felt since tackling Ava to the floor three days ago.

Realizing he has no chance of catching my long strides, Hunter returns to his car and leans on the front quarter panel.

"I'll see you in a week," he says, his tone displaying it is a demand, not a request.

I nod. "I'll be back."

Just as I enter the double automatic doors of the airport, Hunter calls my name. Tilting my torso out, I stare at his chortling face.

"You have a week, Hugo; can you woo her in a week?"

A cocky grin etches on my mouth. "I've done it in less."

EIGHTEEN

AVA

"The wheels on the bus go round and round, round and rou--"

Joel's cheerful song stops halfway down the sidewalk, closely followed by his rushed footsteps. I adjust the heavy bag of groceries on my hip and lower my eyes to him. His eyes are opened wide; he has a broad grin stretched across his face, and the flutter of his pulse is pulsating through our joined hands.

"Daddy!" he yells at the top of his lungs before releasing his grip on my hand and charging toward our house.

My breath snags halfway to my lungs when my eyes follow Joel sprinting across the snow-covered ground, and I spot Hugo standing on the patio. *He came back.* He's wearing a pair of low-riding jeans and a long-sleeve shirt. He would have to be freezing as we had a fresh sprinkling of snow overnight, covering the ground with a thick layer of sleet. When Hugo notices Joel rushing down the path, he pushes off the patio and strides toward him, his steps long and urgent. Tears pool in my eyes when Hugo scoops Joel up in his arms and spins him around and around on the concrete path. Joel has missed Hugo so much the past three days, obviously just as much as Hugo has been missing him. Warmth blooms across my chest when I hear Joel's beautiful giggle bellowing out of him. Nothing in the world sounds as beautiful as Joel's infectious giggles.

I take that back. There's nothing more beautiful than Hugo and Joel laughing together. Their laugh is very similar, except Hugo's is deeper and rumbling. *Core-shattering.* Hugo puts Joel on his feet, gathers his knocked-off beanie from the ground and pops it back on Joel's head.

"Hey, buddy, I've missed you so much," Hugo says, adjusting the collar on Joel's coat to protect his neck from the chilly winter winds.

Hugo's eyes lift to mine when I walk down to the sidewalk.

"Hey," he greets me, his voice softer, somewhat reserved.

"Hey, you're back sooner than I expected."

He smiles a tight grin before nodding.

"Here, let me take that," he offers, gathering the grocery bag sitting on my hip.

"Thanks," I say, grateful to lighten the load.

When I walk to the front door, Hugo and Joel follow behind me, hand in hand. After pushing the key into the lock, I sweep the door open and gesture for them to enter. When Joel goes to walk inside, Hugo tugs his arm gently, pulling him back to stand beside him. Joel's brows stitch as he cranks his neck to peer at his dad.

"Remember?" Hugo says, gesturing his eyes sneakily to me.

Joel's face lights up before he eagerly nods. My heart melts when he says, "Ladies first," his little voice stuttering in excitement.

"Why thank you, kind gentlemen."

When I sashay into the foyer like I'm a crowned princess, Joel laughs hysterically. "You're silly, Mommy."

His laughter switches to an excited squeal when he notices a wrapped present sitting on a duffle bag on the porch. From the shape alone, I can easily perceive it is a football. Joel's eyes shoot to Hugo. When Hugo nods, shredded pieces of wrapping paper fly in all directions. Joel holds the football close to his chest like it is the Heisman trophy itself and not a regular leather stitched football.

"Can we play?"

Hugo shifts his eyes to me, seeking permission.

I smile and nod. "Go get changed into some yard clothes first."

"Okay," Joel replies before running into his room.

When he disappears down the corridor, Hugo chuckles. "Does he ever walk?"

I laugh. "No, he doesn't."

Hugo shadows me into the kitchen. When he sets down the bag of groceries on the counter, I pack away the perishable items in the fridge. Hugo props his hip on the counter and silently watches me. I eye him with curiosity, surprised by his quietness. Although his happiness at seeing Joel again is beaming out of him, there's something clouding his eyes, dampening their usual spark.

"Are you okay?" I query, no longer able to harbor my curiosity.

Hugo has always been a communicator. He's never had trouble expressing himself, but I know something is bothering him, and his reserved composure is setting me on edge. Hugo tilts his torso out of the kitchen, twists his neck and peers down the hall. When he returns his anxious eyes to me, my heart beats wildly. I set the carton of eggs on the table in the middle of the kitchen and pace closer to him.

"I've already missed so much time with him, Ava. Please don't make me miss anymore," he pleads, his words low and full of dread.

My brows furrow as quickly as my heart slithers into my gut. I'm utterly confused by his statement.

"I'll do anything you want to prove to you I'm not going to break his heart. That I won't break your heart... *again*. I just need you to give me a chance," he vows, his begging eyes adding strength to his request.

"I don't understand what you're saying."

Hugo rubs a kink in the back of his neck before attempting to settle my confusion. "The paperwork you sent me."

My brows shoot into my hair. "I didn't send you any paperwork," I shake my head. "I don't even know your address."

His Adams apple bobs up and down as his eyes bounce between mine. Remaining quiet, he walks to his duffle bag dumped at the entranceway and yanks down the zipper before pulling out a white envelope and walking back to me. He's gripping the envelope so tightly, it gets a crinkle down the middle. I can't miss the shake of his hand as he passes the envelope to me. My heart beats wildly as I lift the flap and pull out a four page document. The more my eyes scan the official looking letter, the more my pupils widen. I snatch the envelope off the counter and roam my eyes over the address it was sent from. Blood roars into my ears. *That son of a bitch!*

"Can you watch Joel?" I query, rushing into the hallway to gather my purse and keys.

My eyes shift to my cell phone on the entranceway table. Normally, I'd take it with me everywhere I go, but ever since the "ghost" dropped it into the toilet bowl, it hasn't been working. It fritzed at the exact same moment my answering machine went missing.

Hugo shadows me as I move from the hallway to the garage. I'm so angry, my thighs shake with every step I take. When I reach the side of my car, Hugo stops my frantic pace by grabbing the tops of my arms. His confused eyes dance between mine, his concern growing by the minute.

"I didn't send you those forms," I vow, returning his docile stare. "I'd *never* take your son away from you."

Hugo intakes a quick breath, seemingly astonished by my admission.

"But I can't fix this unless you let me go. Can you please watch Joel?" I ask again, peering into his anxious eyes.

His eyes bounce between mine before he nods. I place a kiss his mouth and jump into my car. Hugo's eyes expand when my heavy compression on the accelerator causes my tires to skid out of control in the ice-covered driveway. I raise my foot off the accelerator and inhale a deep, nerve-clearing breath. *I'm not going to do anyone any good getting in an accident.* Once I have a more rational head, I carefully push my foot down onto the accelerator, taking the necessary precautions required to drive safely in the snow. The panic marring Hugo's face eases when I reverse out of the driveway without incident.

When I enter the bustling main street of Rochdale, my eyes dart in all directions, seeking the first parking lot. I pull into an empty space across from my office building, not caring it is a handicapped space. I throw off my seatbelt and make a beeline for my office building across the street. The freezing cold air blowing in from the west does nothing to damper the fiery rage burning inside me. I throw open the glass door and rush into the building. Belinda's head lifts from her computer monitor when I enter the office. Smiling a tight grin, I rush down the hall before taking the third door on the left. Not bothering to knock, I storm into Marvin's office.

My brisk strides stop and my breathing shallows, shell-shocked at the scene I've stumbled into. Oddly, my first response is relief. You'd think walking in on my fiancé in the midst of a sexual act would have my claws hackled and ready to pounce, but all I feel is relief. *Sweet, heavenly relief.*

When Marvin's head lifts to the door, he balks and takes a step backwards. The half-dressed blonde sprawled on his desk whimpers from his loss of contact.

I roll my eyes. *Nothing on Marvin's body deserves that type of response.*

"Where are you going, sweetie?" she meows, her sickly sweet voice making her sound like a porn star in the middle of a film production.

Marvin's eyes dart between the blonde and me, his panic growing with every second that ticks by.

"This isn't what it looks like," he stammers, fixating his eyes on me.

I raise my hand into the air, stopping any more of his pathetic excuses. Following Marvin's fretful gaze, the blonde shifts her head to the side. Her eyes widen and her throat works hard to swallow when she notices me standing in the doorway, displaying she's aware of who I am and what my significance in Marvin's life is. In my book, that makes her just as guilty as Marvin. She scampers off the desk, yanking her skin-tight pencil skirt down on the way. Her stiletto heels shuffle on the tiled floor as she darts to the door, stuttering an apology to me on the way by.

When the unnamed blonde exits Marvin's office, I pace to his desk. I only came here for one reason, and the shock of discovering him cavorting with an unnamed blonde on his desk isn't enough to dampen the violent anger pumping through my veins.

"You had no right to intervene in my son's life. No right at all. Joel is *not* your son!" I yell, slamming the paternal forms he sent to Hugo onto his cherry oak desk.

Marvin paces around his desk, tucking his disheveled shirt into his undone trousers on the way. "I want him to be my son, Ava. I want to legally adopt him. For him to have my last name."

"Why?" I fire back, skepticism in my voice. "Why would you want that? Joel knows the local dog walker better than you, and we don't even own a dog!"

When Marvin lifts his hand to clutch my arms, I violently yank away from him.

"Don't touch me," I sneer. "I have no clue where your filthy hands have been."

I take a step backward, widening the distance between us. "Why did you do it, Marvin? Why are you trying to create a rift between them? Joel wants Hugo in his life. He needs him in his life. He *loves* his father."

"I can give him more, way more than Hugo ever could," Marvin argues, his jaw quivering as his anger is unleashed.

"It isn't about money or possessions. It is about love and understanding. Taking the time to give Joel the attention he needs—he deserves."

"I give him time and attention. You're acting like I don't give him anything. Everything he has is because of me!" Marvin roars, his angry snarl bouncing around his office.

I laugh a witch-like cackle. "Everything my son has is because of *me*, not *you*. He doesn't even know you."

"Your reaction has nothing to do with me filing adoption papers, and everything to do with Hugo being back in town."

I grit my teeth and shake my head. "This has nothing to do with Hugo. I might have gone along with your little game to keep you in your daddy's good graces and myself employed, but Joel was *never* part of our agreement."

"The instant you slipped that ring on your finger," Marvin says, nudging his head to my engagement ring sparkling in the office lighting. "You not only became *my* property, so did Joel."

Fury unlike anything I have ever felt before scorches my veins. I step closer to Marvin, so close my furiously heaving chest smacks into his. I stare him straight in the eyes, internally cursing the day I ever agreed to his stupid ploy. "Joel was *never* up for negotiation. He will *never* be your son. He has a dad. He doesn't need another."

I rip the diamond engagement ring off my finger and place it on top of the paperwork. "Our agreement is over."

I dash out his office and race down the hall. My steps are urgent, not wanting to give Marvin the satisfaction of seeing my tears. *Today will be the last time he will be the cause of my tears.* Belinda's eyes dart between Marvin leaning in the doorjamb of his office with lipstick smeared on his face and my quickly retreating frame. Her eyes bulge when she notices my finger is void of the engagement ring I was wearing when I entered. Her eyes question me. *Did you really do it? Did you leave him?* When I nod, she jumps from her desk, snags her coat off the coatrack, then briskly marches out of the office behind me.

When we reach the sidewalk outside, I glide my eyes to her. "What are you doing?" I ask, my eyes bouncing between hers. "I thought you said you couldn't come with me?"

I begged Belinda for months to leave Gardner and Sons and come be my receptionist at the practice I'm endeavoring to get off the ground. She always said she would if she could, but she never agreed. I understood her hesitation. Who in their right mind would leave an established company for one that has more chance of collapsing than getting off the ground?

Belinda slings her arms around my shoulders. "Who needs a dental plan when you'll be working for the best dentist in the country?"

Our panicked breaths is visible in the frigid air. "Are you sure this is what you want? You've worked at Gardner and Sons for years. There's no guarantee my practice will get off the ground, let alone be viable."

She rolls her eyes and a lewd smirk curls on her lips. "Please, Ava, anything you set your mind to is viable."

I stare into her glistening green eyes. Nothing but admiration reflects back at me.

"Can you start Monday at 9 AM?"

A SQUEAL RIPPLES from my lips when a loud tap sounds on the window of my car, startling me half to death. Clutching my chest, I peer outside. My brows stitch together tightly when I spot Mrs. Marshall standing next to the passenger side door, rattling the door latch. Her hair is covered with silver foils and she has a hairdressing towel wrapped around her shoulders. Grimacing, I lean over and unlock the door. A freezing breeze blasts into the car when she opens the door and slips inside. She doesn't say anything, she just sits quietly in the seat next to me, staring straight ahead. It is only when I see the shadow of Mrs. Mable moving away from her front window does it dawn on me what has caused Mrs. Marshall's sudden arrival.

I've been sitting in my car in the driveway of my home for the past twenty minutes, futilely trying to unjumble the mess of confusion in my head. I can't comprehend what is happening to me. When I stumbled into Marvin's office, all I felt was relief. I should have been angry at catching my fiancé in a midst of an affair. I should have stormed into the room and gouged the blonde's eyes out before running my nails down her abhorrent face. I should have felt something, but I felt nothing. Not anger, not jealously. *Nothing.*

"I'm a terrible person," I mutter to myself. "I broke off my engagement and I don't even care."

Mrs. Marshall adjusts her position to face me. She clutches my hand in hers and secures my attention with her dazzling green eyes. "Don't feel guilty for what happened, Ava. Your heart has only ever belonged to one man. Marvin knew it wasn't him. He used that knowledge to his advantage."

I shake my head. "I can't just blame Marvin for our pathetic attempt at a relationship. I'm just as bad as him. I knew I was never going to love him the way I loved Hugo, but instead of telling him that, I continued to lie. I dragged him down as much as he did me."

I've wanted to leave Marvin for months, but I never did it. I was too scared about losing my security blanket. Although I've never allowed Marvin to financially support me, I liked the security that came with having a partner. As callous as this makes me sound, I wanted an emergency backup. For years, Marvin has been my safety net.

Mrs. Marshall screws up her nose and waves her hand in front of her face. "Please. You supported him for years – not the other way around. You stroked his gigantic ego and stood by his side while he accepted all the praise from the wonderful things you *both* achieved."

When I shake my head, Mrs. Marshall squeezes my hand tighter. "Tell me one thing that man did solely for *you*, Ava, without expecting some type of reward for it?"

I peer into her empathy-filled eyes while racking my brain, trying to think of something. I'm truly stumped. The only time Marvin and I were ever seen together as a couple was at fundraising events or work functions. We never went on dinner dates alone; he never attended a Marshall family brunch until Hugo arrived back in the picture, and I had to beg him to accompany me to the Christmas Day celebration at the Marshall's residence this year. The only reason he agreed to go is because I agreed to continue with the ploy of us being engaged.

Noticing I'm unable to answer her question, Mrs. Marshall cocks her brow. "Exactly. Now what has he given you?" She waves her head to Hugo zooming past the front window of my house with Joel in his arms.

Joel has his arms outstretched, like he's soaring through the air. I never thought I would have the opportunity to witness this, father and son standing side by side, playing airplanes. I dreamed it would happen, but I never thought my dreams would turn into reality.

"Joel," I answer without a hesitation. "Hugo gave me Joel. The best thing that has ever happened to me."

Mrs. Marshall smiles as she squeezes my hand.

"And this." I press my palm against my madly beating heart. "He gave me his heart. It is the reason Marvin's betrayal didn't hurt, because it wasn't my heart Marvin was deceiving, it was Hugo's, but even being Hugo's heart, Hugo's betrayal still *hurts.* It hurts so much. I don't know if I can get past this."

Mrs. Marshall's tear-glistening eyes lock with mine. "I'm not saying this because Hugo is my son. I'm saying this because you're my daughter, Ava, and I know you. I've watched you grow from a girl into the beautiful woman you are today."

A tear escapes my right eye and rolls down my cheek, overwhelmed by the pride radiating in her words.

"If you don't give Hugo the chance to fix the mistakes he made, you'll never forgive yourself. You've wanted this for years. Every wish you've ever made the past five years was for Hugo to come home. Your wish came true. Cherish it, Ava. We learned from Jorgie's passing that we have to make the most of every day we have. No one is saying you have to forgive and forget, not at all, but harboring anger will only diminish your quality of life, not improve it. Live the best life you can, as you only get one."

My face scrunches, battling to keep my tears at bay. Everything Mrs. Marshall said is true. Every time I blew out the candles on my birthday cake or saw a shooting star, I wished for Hugo to come home. I swore I wouldn't care where he'd been or why he left, all I wanted was for him to come home and meet his son. *To come back to me.* My wish came true, but instead of relishing in having my greatest wish granted, I'm letting anger ruin a true miracle.

"Do you remember the promise you made to Joel the day you walked through those doors with him cradled in your arms for the first time?"

I wipe my hand under my nose before nodding.

"You kept your promise to Joel. Now it's time to keep the promise you made to yourself."

NINETEEN

HUGO

"Mayday, mayday, we are experiencing catastrophic engine failure." A big boom sounds from my mouth, startling Joel flying in my arms. "Mayday, mayday, our engines are on fire. We're going down."

I jolt Joel in my arms, replicating the shuddering of an engine. A grin carves on my mouth from the hearty chuckle bellowing from his lips.

"Prepare for crash landing, select emergency fuel." My voice mimicks the helicopter pilot in the movie *The Day After Tomorrow.*

Joel squeals in excitement as we race through the living room, zooming around the couches and past the antique clock. He holds his arms out like a plane, making engine noises with his lips. When I round the rock-hard couch I slept on a week ago, our makeshift plane crashes to the ground. I roll and land on my back, ensuring Joel lands safely on my chest. Blood surges to my heart when he giggles loudly into my chest before wrapping his arms around my torso to snuggle in close.

"That was the best game ever!" he screams at the top of his lungs, his voice coming out in a flurry, overcome with excitement. "Can we do it again?"

I chuckle. "Yep, just give Dad a minute to recover, and we'll get this bad boy back into the air."

Joel nods against my chest before cuddling in deeper. Joel is as light as a feather, but my shoulder has been giving me grief the past week. I could ease the stabbing pain rocketing through my body by taking the pain relief tablets Dr. Jae prescribed, but with the box clearly warning that side effects may include dizziness, tiredness, and delayed response time, I refuse to take them. I don't want to impede my response time, especially because Ava has entrusted me to take care of Joel alone.

I run my fingers through Joel's hair as we catch our breath, preparing for round two in our game of airplanes. The tips of Joel's curls are damp from our exhaustive playdate. We haven't stopped mucking around since Ava left nearly an hour ago. I want to squeeze in every moment I can get. I can't make up for the time I missed, but I can make the most of the time I have left.

Joel's head pops off my chest when the creak of the front door opening sounds through the room. He inhales a quick breath before he pushes off my chest and dashes to the foyer. Ava's beautiful laugh sounds through my ears when Joel wraps his arms around her thighs and squeezes her tightly, nearly knocking her over. Anyone would swear she has been gone for days, not an hour, from Joel's reaction.

I scramble off the floor and pace toward them. My long

strides slow when I notice a shimmering of wetness on Ava's reddened cheeks. My eyes dart up to her face, assessing her in careful detail. She has red rims around her eyes and her lips are cracked, clearly displaying she has been crying. After running her fingers through Joel's hair, fixing his messy curls, she lifts her glimmering eyes to mine.

"*Are you okay?*" I mouth, not wanting to alert Joel to her distress.

She smiles and nods. "I'm good."

The crippling pain in my chest dampens when she playfully winks before crouching down to Joel's level. After adjusting the collar on his shirt, she asks, "What do you think we should have for dinner?"

Joel's lips pucker and a serious mask slips over his face. He takes his food selections very seriously. Just like his father.

"Because I was thinking we could have.... *Pancakes,*" Ava says, her tone falsely portraying apprehension, like she is concerned Joel may not like her suggestion.

Joel's eyes bug out of his head as he jumps into the air. My insides are also bouncing around like a ho on crack, but thankfully, my outward appearance gives no indication of my excitement. I can still recall the horror of the last time Ava made pancakes in this house, so I can't let my excitement get away from me.

"Pancakes! Yay!" Joel squeals in an ear-piercing scream.

Ava laughs. "Do you want to help me make them?"

Joel eagerly nods.

"Alright, go and wash your hands then."

I laugh when Joel pivots on his heels and charges down the hall. I swear I've never seen the kid walk. My eyes shift from the hall to Ava when she stands from her crouched position.

"Do you have any plans tonight?"

I smile and shake my head, ignoring the mad beat of my heart.

"Did you want to stay and have some pancakes with us?"

My brow arches. Even if I missed the hidden innuendo laced in her simple question, I can't overlook the glimmer in her eyes. Ava's never been good at hiding her true intentions. She wears her heart on her sleeve, clear as day for all to see. I can also read her like an open book. To strangers it may seem as if she's asking me to stay for dinner, but her eyes are relaying much more than that.

She inhales a quick breath when I take a step closer to her, closing the space between us. Her eyes linger on my thrusting chest for several heart-clenching seconds before she tilts her neck back. When her eyes lock in on mine, the shift of air between us is so great, a current of electricity surges through my body, sparking my heart with a renewed hope. Her eyes are exposing that I haven't lost them yet. That I still have a chance. Not just with Joel, but her as well.

"I'd love to stay." My voice is strangled by the flood of emotions hammering me. "But I should warn you. I have a slight obsession with *sweet* things. Once I taste them, I can't stop."

Her breath fans my lips when she expels a large gasp, proving she didn't miss the innuendo in my reply. I stare into her eyes, wanting to ensure she understands I'm not just here for Joel. I want her too. We stand across from each other, staring, but not speaking. The connection between us is as strong as it's ever been, if not stronger. *Joel makes us stronger.* I look at the woman I've loved from before she even became a woman, my eyes expressing the words my mouth is refusing to relinquish. *I'm sorry. Please forgive me. I love you.*

When I run the back of my fingers down her feverish cheek, removing a tear tracking down it, she nuzzles into my hand. I want to kiss away every tear falling down her beautiful face. I want to fall to my knees and promise I'll never be the cause of her tears again, but before I get the chance, Joel tugs on the hem of my shirt. I was so mesmerized staring into Ava's beautiful eyes, I didn't hear him approaching. He stands between Ava and me with his head rocketing side to side. A smile curves on my mouth when he screws up his nose and gags.

"Girls are gross," he mumbles, glaring at me with reprimanding eyes.

Who is this kid? I had no clue about girls until I was well into middle school. He's only four and can already read the undeniable connection between Ava and me.

"I'll show you gross," Ava threatens, shifting her squinted eyes to Joel.

When she puckers her lips, making gaga kissy faces, Joel screams a window-shattering squeal before racing to the other side of the room. Ava's on his tail before he even makes it halfway across the living room. She tackles him onto the ground and holds him down similar to how I normally pin her down. She smothers his face in kisses, smooching noises and all. Joel screams in protest, but the smile etched on his adorable face is giving away his deceit. He's loving every single moment of his mom's attention. And rightfully so, he should.

"Daddy, help me," Joel squeals between giggles. "Save me from the girl germs!"

I throw back my head and laugh. I don't want to be saved by Ava's girl germs. I want to be smothered in them.

"IS HE ASLEEP?"

I nod. "Yeah, he was asleep before his head hit the pillow."

Ava laughs. I wasn't joking. The poor little guy was exhausted. After Joel and I ganged up on Ava, tickling her into submission, we went into the kitchen to prepare pancakes for dinner. Joel's excitement was beaming out of him the entire time. As was mine. After a good dose of sugar, Joel was literally bouncing off the walls. We played a few more rounds of the airplane, then Ava gave him a bath. He didn't stop yawning the entire time Ava was dressing him in his air fighter pajamas. Only after promising to take him to the park tomorrow did he agree to go to bed. I'm not going to lie, I was as smitten as the President on Inauguration Day when Joel asked me to read him a bedtime story and tuck him into bed. We never got to read a story... *maybe next time?*

"Did you want a wine?" Ava offers, pacing to the kitchen.

My face screws up.

Ava chuckles softly. "Beer?" She arches a brow, noticing my expression.

I nod before plopping onto the rock-hard coach. My shoulder is screaming in pain. Not a faint scream, an Alex Koehler from Chelsea Grin scream at the start of the song "Sonnet of the Wretched" scream.

I'm still rubbing the knot out of my shoulder when Ava paces into the living room with a refilled wine glass and a bottle of beer. I lower my hand when I notice the direction of her gaze.

"What's the deal with your shoulder?" She hands me the beer before filling the spare seat next to me. "I've noticed you rubbing it a few times tonight."

I take a swig of my beer before angling my torso to face her. If I want any chance of regaining the trust I lost when I vanished, I need to be honest with her. *About everything.*

"I got shot."

Her wine traps in her throat. She wheezes and coughs, spraying the coffee table and my shirt with red wine splatters as she fights to keep her lungs full of oxygen and not wine.

"You alright?"

I set my beer on the coffee table so I can pat her back. It takes her a few moments to recover from her coughing fit before she lifts her tear-glistening eyes to mine. I can't tell if her eyes are welled with tears from her coughing attack or because I was shot.

"Shot? Like shot with a gun shot?"

I nod.

"By whom? Why?" Her words come out in a hurry as a panicked mask slips over her face.

"The girl I was protecting was kidnapped. Her kidnapper didn't appreciate my presence," I report, shrugging my shoulders, acting like it's no big deal. I'll do or say anything to remove the cloud of concern plaguing her beautiful eyes.

Ava stares at me, her eyes widening more with every second that goes by.

After a beat, she mumbles, "And here I was thinking root canals and extractions were exciting."

I laugh. Only Ava would find the lightheartedness in a somber conversation. I shouldn't be surprised, though. Ava doesn't have a judgmental bone in her body. She has never judged me. Not once. Not even if she was bursting at the seams to know something, she wouldn't ask, preferring only to be divulged information when the informant felt comfortable sharing it. She doesn't understand the meaning of the word "strong-armed."

Setting her wineglass on the counter, Ava props her legs under her bottom and swivels to face me. "Can I see where you were shot?"

When I nod, she licks her lips, leans forward, and gently pulls down the neckline of my shirt. I grab the back of my shirt and yank it over my head. Ava's eyes enlarge as her throat works hard to swallow, somewhat surprised by my impromptu strip.

"I was shot in the chest, but the bullet exited my shoulder," I explain, peering into her eyes. "You won't see the wound properly with my shirt on."

I manage to catch my eye roll halfway. I sound like a slack-jawed idiot. It is nearly as good as the fake yawn maneuver I regularly used on her when we were watching re-runs of *Friends*.

Ava gasps when her eyes drift over my chest, assessing the wound from a safe distance. The thrum of her pulse thuds through my hand when I clasp her hand in mine and run two of her fingers over the wound site. She inhales a sharp breath when her fingers glide over the roughness of the wound and the sharpness of the stitches that still haven't dissolved. Although it has healed well the past two weeks, the grittiness of the wound will never fully diminish.

"Did it hurt?"

I smirk. "Like a bitch."

Only one knock has hit me harder: leaving her. My stomach muscles bunch when Ava gently runs her finger over the edge of the wound site before she leans forward and presses her lips on the border of the scar tissue.

My dick turns to stone when she mutters, "I better kiss it better then," before placing another kiss on the other side of the wound.

My heart thrashes against my chest when she lifts her eyes and locks them with mine. Ava's eyes have always been expressive, and today is no exception. Her eyes are crammed to the brim with desire, and it isn't a hunger for food. I gather her hand off my chest, kiss the tips of her fingers before jerking my shirt back over my head.

Ava sinks deeper into the chair as her eyes shift nervously around the room. The look of rejection is darkening her beautiful eyes. I scoot across the loveseat, leaving not an ounce of air between us. Gripping her chin with my hand, I tilt it back, lifting her pessimistic face to me.

"I want you. I want you more than anything. More than my next breath, but I can't have you yet."

"Why?" she whispers, her shaking words relaying her rejection.

"Because I need you to know the truth, to ensure you aren't walking into this relationship blind."

She shakes her head, sending tears flinging into the air. "I'm not. My eyes are open. I know you, Hugo."

When she fists my long-sleeve shirt, I notice her ring finger is void of the large diamond engagement ring she was wearing earlier.

Spotting the direction of my gaze, she mutters, "It was a lapse in judgment. A mistake."

Any further words about to spill from her mouth stop when I place my index finger against her lips. "We all make mistakes. We can't change them. We can only learn from them."

She drags her bottom lip through her teeth before nodding. Her tear-welled eyes bounce between mine. She does know me. Better than anyone. So I can be assured she will never judge me. *She never has.*

I capture both of her hands in mine and peer into her shimmering eyes.

"I have made plenty of mistakes I'm not proud of. My very first was in Afghanistan."

TWENTY

HUGO

Ava tries to put on a brave front, but I can see her remorse for Gemma dimming the spark in her eyes the longer my story goes, let alone the way her hand rattles as she runs it under her eyes, capturing her tears before they roll down her face.

"She endured so much, and it still wasn't enough. It took months for Gemma's case to make it to court. We thought the main fight was over. Little did we know, the battle had only just begun."

My knee bounces up and down, a nervous twitch exposing my agitation. Leticia, the assigned DA leans over and places her hand on top of my knee, moving the twitch from my knee to my jaw.

"There has to be something you can do?" I say, tilting into her side. "Interject, argue bias, something?"

Leticia shakes her head. "The accused has the right to be represented by a lawyer of his choice."

"Even when it is his father?" I interrupt, disbelief heard in my voice.

Leticia's green eyes float from the terrified Gemma getting slammed by the defense attorney in the witness stand to me. "Yes." Her answer is swift and precise.

"That's fucking bullshit. He's treating her as if she's a criminal." My angry sneer reverberates off the whitewashed walls.

Leticia doesn't respond to my outburst. She can't. Everything I said was true. Gemma is getting grilled by the defense attorney. The same defense attorney who is the father of her accused. He's absurdly declaring that Gemma is using the courts as a way to clear her guilty conscience. He's proclaiming Gemma initially agreed to the "liaison" with his clients, and only sought medical treatment after her "boyfriend" caught wind of her indiscretion. He's implying if I failed to aid Gemma that night, no charges would have been filed against his clients because I would have been none the wiser about her activities.

My eyes drift from the tear-stained face of Gemma to Madden McGee and three of his fellow accused sitting next to him. Madden has his fingers laced together and a callous smirk etched on his face. When a painful sob rumbles from Gemma's quivering lips as she denies the defense attorney's blatant lies, he sinks deeper into his chair, seemingly pleased Gemma is rattled. I fist my hands into tight balls, battling the urge to wipe the smug smirk right off his face. The desire turns potent when Madden's older brother leans over the wooden barrier separating them and pats him on the shoulder, like he's commending him on a job well done, oblivious that his brother is in the middle of a court hearing facing charges of aggravated battery and sexual assault.

By the time Gemma has finished giving her testimony, she's

just as rattled as she was the night in the alley. I stand from my chair and move toward her when she rushes out the swinging doors that separate the well of the court from the seating area. My fast steps stop when she briskly shakes her head, sending tears flying off her ashen cheeks.

"Just give her a few minutes to calm down, Hugo," Leticia suggests, enclosing her hand over my shaking one.

I slump into the hard wooden bench, feeling the most help-less I've ever been. I run my trembling hand through my shaggy mane, struggling to maintain enough strength for both Gemma and me. The past few months have been the most draining weeks of my life. Just getting Gemma to agree to press charges was a hard-fought battle. She wanted to pretend it never happened. To sweep it under the rug. It was only when I asked her how she would feel if another woman had to endure what she went through did she finally agree to meet with Leticia, on one condi-tion: no one in our squadron was to be aware of what was happening. I instantly agreed. It wasn't my news to share anyway.

"Have you had any luck finding the witness from the alley?" I ask Leticia.

She shakes her head. "No, but the Air Force isn't exactly forthcoming when I request personnel records for every enlistee called Brody. Are you sure he was in the Air Force?"

I nod. "I'm certain he's in the Air Force. I have a knack for remembering faces. He isn't in my section, but I've seen him around base."

Leticia smiles a tight smirk. "Hopefully he will grow a conscience and come forward."

He never did......

"The defense attorney was a real snake, conniving and low-handed. The moment I met him, I was on guard." I peer at Ava, who is watching me with compassion in her eyes. "I had a reason to be wary. He was a deadly snake hidden in the long grass. Not only did the jury believe him and his clients' side of the story, he twisted everything Gemma said on the stand."

I swallow a brick in my throat. "Eight weeks after Madden McGee was cleared of all charges, I was arrested."

Ava's brows scrunch as her eyes dart between mine.

"For the sexual assault of Gemma."

She sucks in a quick, sharp breath. "What? How? You saved her. Protected her. That doesn't make any sense." She scoots across the couch and encloses her hand over my shaking one. "What happened?"

Her eyes are void of the judgment I expected to see when I shared my story.

"I was on my way to...."

"KEEP WALKING, Hugo, he isn't worth the effort."

Tyrell wraps his arm around my shoulders and guides me down the hallway, past the snickering face of Madden McGee. We only arrived back on base earlier this week, preparing to re-deploy to Afghanistan. I just finished a grueling workout in the gym and could hear the showers beckoning me all the way from the fitness center. The instant I spotted Madden, any thoughts on enjoying the remainder of my rec time disappeared. It is the first time I've seen Madden in person since a jury of our peers found him and his three co-accused not guilty of sexually assaulting Gemma. I assumed even with the jury handing over the verdict of not guilty that some type of reprimand would still be given to Madden by our superiors in the Air Force. Nothing happened.

Gemma's entire life was upended in an instant. She was left unemployed and on the verge of a nervous breakdown. Madden didn't suffer the slightest. He took an extended period of absence for "personal" reasons before returning to his original rank of Captain. Pictures of him riding a jet ski in the Caribbean have been circulating the dining facility most of the day, spurring on my agitation. He was vacationing in paradise while Gemma was living in a hell.

My long strides down the corridor falter when Madden snickers, "If he'd been giving it to her right, she wouldn't have been looking elsewhere."

I hardly hear the roaring laughter of the group surrounding Madden over my pulse shrilling in my ears when I pivot on my heels and charge for him. When he notices me approaching, the veins in his neck thrum, and his eyes widen. My fist lands on his right cheek before lowering to his stomach. I don't know how many punches I inflict before Tyrell pulls me away, but my punishment was severe enough for Madden to be sporting a black eye and split lip as he gave his statement to the Air Force Police, requesting for them to press battery charges against me.

I sit in a holding cell at Security Forces compound of our base for nearly sixteen hours before being ushered into a cold, sterile interrogation room. I'm surprised when I shuffle into the room, dragging a pair of metal shackles behind me, to discover Madden's father standing in the corner of the room talking to a

JAG officer. Since when did a civilian have any input in a case involving an Airman?

After removing the shackles from my hands and ankles, the JAG officer, whose name badge states "Christopher," gestures for me to sit in a wooden chair pulled up close to a steel table.

Christopher pulls out the chair across from me and takes a seat, his eyes arrested on a document in his hand. "These types of cases are generally hard to prove. With the whole She Said-He Said notion coming into play, it falls to the jury's mood for how the verdict will swing."

My heart rate kicks up, but I continue with my fifth amendment right, remaining quiet. I've already decided to plead guilty to the charges of battery against Madden, but I'm not going to disclose that to the DA, deciding it is in my best interests to wait it out for a plea.

When I take a seat, Christopher's eyes lift from a manila folder to me. "But in your case, it's a slam dunk. I can't lose," *he states, his voice smeared with cockiness.*

I give him an arrogant wink. Madden's blood on my knuckles is pretty incriminatory.

"So, instead of wasting our time dragging this through court, we're going to be kind and offer you a plea deal."

My lips twitch, fighting to suppress the smile trying to cross my face. I knew they wouldn't have brought me in here without a having a pre-drawn plea agreement.

"If you sign this statement, admitting to all charges, you'll avoid doing jail time and tainting your honorable family name with mud."

My brows furrow. My mother would be proud I defended Gemma, not dishonored. *The confusion on my face amplifies when Christopher slides a pre-typed statement across the table for me to sign. His abrupt movement causes the ballpoint pen to roll off the name on top of the Alford doctrine.*

"Why do you have Gemma's name written in the victim field?" I query, my words as uneasy as the swirling of my stomach.

Christopher smirks. "The victim's name is generally placed in the victim section." The pompousness in his tone fuels my annoyance.

"Gemma is not my victim. I didn't hurt her; I protected her," I retort.

Christopher's eyes turn to Madden's father in the corner of the room. The shrewd look that crosses Mr. McGee's face is only there for the tiniest second, but I didn't miss it. It was cunning and judicious.

The churning of my stomach ramps up when my eyes return to the document and I speed-read the charges against me.

"I want a lawyer," I request, my eyes floating from the document accusing me of the sexual assault and battery of Gemma back to Christopher. "I'm not speaking another word until I have a lawyer present."

Madden's father pushes off the wall, reaching the edge of the table in three lengthy strides. "Even the best lawyer in the state won't help you." His tone is a deep rumble that bounces off the stark white walls and bellows into my ears. "They have your DNA and skin fibers in Gemma's rape kit. Your blood was even discovered under her fingernails."

"Because I protected her!" I standing from my chair, toppling it over. "You're not pinning your son's crime on me because I taught him a lesson. Maybe if you'd spent more time with him as

a child instead of hobnobbing with golf buddies, he would have learned the difference between right and wrong, but I guess lining your expensive threads with money was more important than raising your son with morals."

Before I have the chance to react, Mr. McGee grabs my shirt to pull me to within an inch of his face. I stare into the eyes of a snake with my nostrils flaring. My body shudders with fury, but I don't back down. He raised a monster, and I'm not scared to tell him of that.

"Your son is a rapist," *I sneer, staring into his bleak, desolate eyes. "And a fucking coward."*

I TURN my eyes to Ava, who is watching me sympathetically. "I pleaded guilty to the sexual assault of Gemma three weeks later."

Her eyes widen before darting between mine. "What! Why, Hugo? Gemma would have never testified against you. You saved her; she would have done the same for you."

I shake my head. "She tried, but Madden's father offered to chair with the DA. Everything Gemma said during her testimony was twisted by him. He even made out to the jury that the time I walked in on Gemma showering in the male latrine was what started my 'obsession' with her."

I run my hand down my tired face, scrubbing away my tiredness while wishing I could erase the memories that haunt my dreams just as easily.

Exhaling a deep breath, I turn my eyes to Ava. "I've always had a knack for reading people." An edgy smile stretches across her face before she nods. "I could tell the jury was believing the lies the DA was telling them. Even with Gemma testifying on my behalf, they were going to find me guilty. To save my family name being tarnished, I requested a plea."

Ava's smile becomes a tight grin when she wraps her hand around mine. She doesn't speak. She doesn't need to. The compassion in her eyes is all the comfort I need.

"On the agreement that the nature of my charges were to remain undisclosed, I pleaded guilty to the sexual assault on Gemma and for battery in the second degree on Madden. I was issued with a criminal record, stripped of my ranking, and dishonorably discharged from my position within twenty-four hours of signing the plea bargain."

After wiping a tear off her cheek, she crawls across the minimal space left between us. A whizz of air parts my lips when she straddles my hips, wraps her arms around my torso, and presses her ear over my heart. I'm not going to lie, even with a morose mood suffocating my usual persona, I'm smiling, relishing having her in my arms again.

A length of quiet crosses between us. It isn't awkward, but rather comforting.

"What happened to Gemma?" Ava queries a short time later, her voice low and filled with concern.

I run my hand down the waves hanging halfway down her back. "She never returned to her position after the incident in the alleyway. We stayed in contact sporadically six months after I was dishonorably discharged, then I met you, and everything went a little crazy."

Her head pops off my chest, so her eyes can bounce

between mine. A grin tugs on my lips when the corners of her mouth droop downward.

"A good type of crazy." I pinch her chin, angling her head up. "Those weeks we had together are the only thing that kept me going the past five years. Without them, I don't know how I would have survived. *If* I would have survived."

She chews on her bottom lip, battling to keep her tears from flowing. "Me too," she whispers. "Our memories, then finding out I was expecting Joel were the only things forcing me to get out of bed every morning."

I run a finger across her cheek, capturing a tear rolling down her pale face. "Please don't cry." I've seen enough tears seep from her eyes to last me a lifetime. "I'm so sorry, Ava. For everything I did, for everything I put you—"

My words stop when a salivating pair of lips press up against mine, stealing my words and my ability to think. When she drags her tongue along the crest of my lips, I open my mouth. She slips her tongue inside, entangling it with mine and controlling the pace of our kiss. *She tastes even better than I remember.*

I wrap my arms around her waist, drawing her in close, not wanting even an ounce of air between us. The husky moan spilling from her lips hardens my cock even more. I slide my tongue around her mouth, tasting and savoring every inch of her. I kiss her like a man starved of her taste, because I am. It's been years since I've tasted anything as sweet as Ava's mouth.

She kisses me back with a sense of urgency, like she's afraid she may open her eyes and discover she's dreaming. I rub my hardened cock against the seam of her sweatpants, making sure she's aware she isn't dreaming. Her hands glide under my shirt to run over the ridges of my stomach before they lower to tackle the belt of my jeans.

Just as Ava slips her hand inside my jeans to grasp my erect cock, a little voice pops up to the side of us.

"What are you doing?"

TWENTY-ONE

AVA

My hand shoots out of Hugo's jeans like I've been scorched by an open flame instead of his thick cock. My bug-eyed gaze dances between Hugo's smiling eyes for several terrifying seconds before I slowly filter them to the side. Joel is standing at the end of the couch. He has his sock monkey in one hand and an empty glass in another. I'm at a loss for how to respond to what he has just stumbled upon. Although I was in a "relationship" with Marvin the past nine months, Joel has never walked into a situation like this. Unless you include kissing Chase and Mr. Marshall on the cheek goodbye, Joel has never witnessed me kiss another man, let alone participate in anything as graphic as the sexual activity I was about to undertake. *God, imagine if he was five minutes later?*

Joel rubs sleep out of his eyes while yawning. "I'm thirsty. Daddy forgot to fill my glass of water."

Hugo shifts his eyes to Joel. "I'm sorry, buddy. I didn't realize you still woke up during the night."

From the leering grin on Hugo's face, I can't tell if he's apologizing for forgetting to fill Joel's glass of water, or reprimanding him for interrupting us. There's one thing I do know, though, I need to get off Hugo's lap. Just the vibration of his deep voice rocketing through my aching-with-need core is surging my libido to a never-before-reached level.

"Let's get you a drink, then it's back to bed, mister."

A grin tugs on my lips when Hugo inconspicuously conceals his erection with a pillow after I slide off his lap. Joel shadows me into the kitchen, his steps sluggish and slow. I fill his glass of water to the very brim, eager to ensure he won't require any more refills tonight.

Nothing against my son—I love him more than anything in the world—but it has been years since I've had this level of rampant horniness surging through my blood. Just the stimulation I got from Hugo's enthralling kiss was enough to have my orgasm sitting precariously on the edge of a very steep cliff. Keen is an understatement for how eager I am to get back to my make-out session on the couch.

After giving Hugo a hug goodnight, Joel climbs back into his bed and snuggles into the pillow, his glass of water remaining untouched. I switch on his nightlight, carefully close his door and amble into the living room. My fervent steps falter when I reach the end of the corridor and notice Hugo standing in the entranceway, putting on his shoes. His eyes lift to mine when he hears my shuffling, dejected footsteps.

"I better get going." He puts on his last shoe. "It's late, and you've got work tomorrow, and Joel has pre-school."

Putting the feeling of rejection to the side, I move into the kitchen to gather the Tupperware container full of pancakes I set aside for him earlier.

A grin furls on his kiss-swollen lips when he spots me walking back into the foyer with the container in my hand. "There's only one thing sweeter than your blueberry pancakes." His baby blues lift to my face. "You."

I have no chance in hell of concealing the grin stretching across my face. Hugo accepts the container from my hand before running the back of his fingers down my inflamed cheeks. I try not to nuzzle into his embrace, but the urge is too great for me to inhibit. I'm drawn to Hugo like a moth to a flame.

"I really enjoyed tonight." He peers at me with smoldering eyes. "Can we do it again?"

He chuckles when I nod. I swear, nothing has changed. I'm once again rolling over begging for my stomach to be scratched, but I can't help it. It wouldn't matter how much time passes, when Hugo is in my presence, I become the braces-wearing teen flabbergasted by her high school crush. Everything Mrs. Marshall said this afternoon was true. Hugo has owned my heart longer than I have. And even having my heart torn from my chest and stomped on when he left, nothing will ever change the fact he is my one true love.

"How long are you back for?" I query, my words juddering as nerves dangle on my vocal cords.

When I open my front door, goosebumps prickle my spine when a freezing cold air blasts through the crack of the door.

A new type of coldness freezes my heart when Hugo mutters, "A week. I have some stuff I have to go back and sort out."

Noticing my despondent appearance, he cradles my cheek

with his warm hand, covering my entire face. "I promise you, I'm doing everything I can to ensure I'm not away from Joel too long." He lifts his gaze from my lips that are still tingling from our kiss to my tear-welling eyes. "I never want to be away from *either of you* ever again." His chest thrusts up and down as he stares at me with beseeching eyes. "If I could take it back, Ava, I would. If I could take away your pain, make it disappear--"

"The past cannot be changed, forgotten, edited, or erased. It can only be accepted," I interrupt, quoting what he said to me over five years ago. The same mantra I repeated every time he dropped Joel off last week, fearing he may not arrive the next morning as promised. Just from peering into Hugo's contrite eyes, I'm certain my fears will never transpire.

Hugo places the Tupperware container onto the entranceway table before running his thumbs over my cheeks, removing my tear stains.

"Accept the past, embrace the present, and believe in the future," he recites, staring into my moisture-filled eyes.

The coldness of the crisp winter night is a forgotten memory as we undertake a mesmerizing stare-down. As always, the dynamic between us is electrifying, sparking the air with enough heat to make it feel like we are in the middle of summer. Hugo's eyes, which had darkened during his confession about Gemma, get a familiar sparkle as fragments of the old Hugo, the teenage boy who stole my heart at the tender of sixteen, emerges from the dark shadows crippling his usual carefree composure.

"I'm going to make this work," he vows, glancing into my eyes. "*Us* work."

The saltiness of my tears flavors his kiss when he presses his plump lips to my mouth. "I'll see you tomorrow?"

I smile and nod. "I wouldn't miss it for the world."

I watch Hugo slip into a rental car and drive away through the peep hole of my front door. He was adamant he wasn't leaving the front porch until he heard the deadbolt click into place.

Once his tail lights disappear, I lean my back against the door and inhale a deep breath of air. I've known Hugo more than half of my life, and I've never seen him be as open as he was tonight. He was raw and unguarded. *Honest.* Hugo has always been a communicator, but as he matures, his actions are out-speaking his words. The love he displays to Joel... *to me,* is greater than I could have ever imagined. I've always said there's no love greater than a love a mother has for her child. I'm starting to think that saying also applies to fathers.

"Can I have a brother?"

I slant my head to the side and peer down the corridor where the little voice is coming from. Joel is leaning on the wall outside of his bedroom. His eyes are narrowed tightly, and he's yawning. If he didn't occasionally blink, I would have assumed he was sleepwalking.

"I don't want a sister. Angie and Katie are so *annoying.* Please, Mommy, can I please have a brother?"

A grin curls on my lips from the tired slur of his words, making him sound like the little four-year-old he is. I'm not biased when I say Joel is a genius. He speaks well above his age, reads better than any six-year-old I know, and slaughters me anytime we play a game of monopoly. It is only moments like these do I realize his true age. He's a sweet little boy who has confused his nursery rhythms, believing it is the girls made out of snips, snails, and puppy dog tails.

"How about we discuss the possibility of siblings after a few hours of sleep?" *And a few glasses of wine.*

"Siblings?" Joel mutters, trying on the new word for size.

"Siblings is a term for brothers and sisters," I explain, gathering him in my arms.

My heart warms when he slings his arms around my neck and nuzzles into my chest. I love Joel more than anything, but it was only when Joel was born did I realize the love you have for your partner is entirely different than the love you have for your child. Although both are as consuming as the other, they're unique and beautiful in their own way.

When I lay Joel in his bed, his twinkling eyes lift to mine. His brows are stitched together, and his lips are pursed. "Does that mean I can have more than one?"

"More than one what?" I query, tucking him in nice and firm, ensuring he can't escape for a third time this evening.

"Siblings." He rubs his eyes with his balled fist. "You said 'siblings' not 'sibling.'"

I laugh. There's no greater innocence in the world than the innocence of a child. Not even a twenty-four-year old virgin.

I grimace when Joel says, "I want five brothers."

Pressing a kiss onto his forehead, I switch on the lamp on his bedside table before ambling to the door. I'm knackered. Not just physically but emotionally as well. The past week has been a hazy blur of confusion. Hell, the past five years has been one devastating blow after another, but it feels like everything has changed in a matter of hours. My mind tonight is the clearest it has ever been. It is remarkable how much can change in a couple of hours, and how one man can alter my perspective of life so greatly.

"Mommy," Joel whimpers when I reach his door.

I crank my neck and look at him.

"I love daddy," he whispers through a yawn before cuddling into his pillow.

A vast grin etches on my face. "So do I, sweetheart, so do I," I mutter to no one.

TWENTY-TWO

HUGO

Dumping my duffle bag onto the ground, I turn my eyes to Ava and Joel. Joel has his arms wrapped around his mother's thigh and his big blue eyes are peering up at me, pleading for me to stay. I don't want to leave my family. Leaving them is one of the hardest things I've ever done, but I need to settle the tension between Isaac and me. I want the chance to explain my fool-hardy action to him before leaving his empire in an honorable way. I've already left one position dishonorably in my life. I'm not going to do it again, especially not with a man of upmost importance to me. Once I've settled the dust between Isaac and me, the heavy burden weighing down my shoulders will lift, and I'll be free to begin a new chapter in my life. A phase surrounded by my family.

I've spent every waking moment with Ava and Joel the past week, not willing to miss a single minute. The majority of the second half of my week has been spent in a blur of playdates and fatherly duties with Joel while Ava settles into her new practice, but the past two days have been a little more subdued as the countdown to my return to Ravenshoe creeped upon us. Although neither Joel or Ava has verbalized their concerns about me returning to Ravenshoe, I've seen a shift in their personas the last two days. I'll often discover Ava watching my interactions with Joel with a misting of tears in her eyes, and for the past forty eight hours, Joel hasn't let me leave his side, even going so far as requesting for me to sleep on his bedroom floor.

A grin tugs on my lips when Ava rolls her eyes as I noogie Joel's head, messing his curls she just finished wrangling into order.

"I'll see you soon, buddy," I assure him, crouching down to Joel's level.

The heaviness weighing down my chest increases when I spot the little tears pricking in the corners of his eyes.

"Yes, Daddy," he replies, his words coming out in a whimper.

I wrap my arms around his trembling shoulders and pull him into my chest. The pain in my heart turns lethal when his little sobs sound through my ears.

"I'll be back soon. I promise, Joel," I swear, drawing him in tighter.

"We've got all that practice we need to do before try-outs," I murmur into his ear, saying anything to stop his concern that I'm not going to return.

His quivering lips tremor against my neck when he nods his little head. It breaks my heart knowing I'm the cause of his tears. Every small tear directly impacts me.

"Don't tell Mommy, but I snuck a few packets of candy into your sock drawer," I whisper into his ear.

His head shoots off my neck and his eyes dart between mine. Seeing the truth projecting from my eyes, a grin stretches across his face, rapidly drying his tears. I return his smile while wiping away the tear-stains from his pale cheeks. After giving him a final noogie on the head, I rise from my crouched position and shift on my feet to face Ava.

For Joel's sake, she's putting on a brave front, pretending she isn't upset about my departure. When Ava initially suggested she could drive me to the airport, I declined her offer. Not because I didn't want to spend every moment with her and Joel, but because I can't stand the thought of leaving her at the airport crying. The memories of her walking away from me in this exact airport still agitate me. I thought those six years would be our longest separation. *How wrong was I?* Only after Ava assured me she wouldn't cry did I agree for her to drop me off. I wrap my arms around her shoulders and pull her into my thrusting chest.

"This time is different, Ava. We were young back then, just kids. Nothing could keep me away from you now. Not a single thing," I say, intuiting that the memories of that day are also steamrolling into her.

She runs the edge of her sleeve under her eyes before nodding.

"Don't tell Joel, but you might want to check his sock drawer when you get home. I may have gotten a little excited with the amount of candy I left in there."

A winded grunts sounds out of my mouth when Ava elbows me in the ribs. The weight on my chest eases when she pulls away from our embrace and I see the grin tugging her lips high.

"Leave him a couple of packets?" I plead, my words barely a whisper to ensure Joel doesn't overhear our conversation.

A smile etches on my face when Ava gently nods. After snagging my duffle bag off the ground, I place a kiss on Joel's head before pressing one on the edge of Ava's lips. The battle not to slip my tongue inside her sweet, inviting mouth is tortuous. The ball-clenching kiss Ava and I shared a week ago has been the only kiss we've shared. Don't construe my confession the wrong way. I'm more than interested in devouring every single inch of Ava, but it was only after Joel interrupted us with an expression of shock on his face did I recall Ava was only engaged to another man mere hours before our kiss. Not that Marvin will be a hard act to follow, but I don't want to be the rebound guy. Once Ava becomes mine, there will be no going back - ever. So I need to ensure she has enough time to properly evaluate what she wants, because I know as well as the next man, rushed decisions can cause dire consequences.

When the final boarding call for my flight sounds over the speakers, I shift my eyes between Ava and Joel. "I'll see you soon?"

A smile curls on my lips when they nod their heads in sync. Even with the feeling of a knife being stabbed into my chest, I spin on my heels and walk to my departure gate. I need to do this. I need to make things right with Isaac. Then I'll have a clear conscience to move onto the next stage of my life.

THE FLIGHT back to Ravenshoe is thankfully uneventful and void of the nail-biting I experienced when I flew to Tiburon with Izzy last week. I can't believe it has only been a little over a week since that day. So much has changed since then.

Exiting the domestic terminal, I spot Hunter's hellcat parked illegally in a loading zone at the side. He's sitting behind the wheel of his car, either oblivious to the police officer filling in a citation for his illegal parking or he doesn't care.

"I'll be there in thirty. You better get that little red number out," I hear Hunter murmur as I crank open the passenger door of his car and slide into the dark gray leather seat.

"I'll call you back in a few," he states into his cell phone, his tone more stern than earlier.

Snapping his untraceable cell shut, he throws it into the middle console of his car and turns his eyes to me.

"Who was that?" I ask, not bothering to hide the innuendo in my voice.

Hunter tries to hide his smile behind his scruffy beard, but I can't miss it. Even if I could, the vibrant blaze flicking in his eyes is all the indication I need to know his heart is flipping in his chest.

"You'll meet her in a few." He snatches the parking ticket out of the officer's hand then tears out of the loading zone.

When we reach the highway, he scrunches up the parking fine and throws it onto the pavement whizzing by. Once his window glides back into place, his eyes drift to me. He eyes me with curiosity but remains silent. My brow curves when he leans over and vigorously sniffs the edge of my jaw.

His lips quirk. "Hmm sweet," he mutters, curtly nodding.

I adjust my position, moving away from him and his out-of-character awkwardness as I can in the confines of his car.

Hunter grins and winks before jutting his chin out.

"Your turn." He peers at me from the corner of his eye.

I eye him with even more curiosity than earlier.

"You want to know if a beard captures a woman's scent. Check." He thrusts his beard-covered chin out further.

His chuckle booms around the interior of his car when I punch him in the bicep. He rubs the area, feigning injury before slanting his chin back in and returning his eyes to the road.

Inhaling deeply through his nose, he mutters, "Never smelled anything so delicious."

I'm about to argue that there's no sweeter scent in the world than Ava, until I remember, what is one man's meat is another man's poison. A man may see one woman as a precious diamond, whereas another may only see her as a dirty stone stuck in a rock. Although I'm certain Ava is the sexiest woman alive and the sweetest smelling, it isn't my place to convince Hunter. Actually, I'd prefer it if more men were unaware of the fact. Then I may have a chance of keeping my inane jealousy that only Ava incites intact.

"Does Isaac know I'm back?" I ask, endeavoring to return my focus to the task at hand. The quicker I fix things between us, the quicker I'll return to my family.

Hunter nods. "Yeah, he requested your assistance with a task this morning."

My brow arches. "What task?" I query, my words juddering. "Digging my own grave?"

Hunter chuckles. "Come on, you know as well as the rest of us, Isaac doesn't mind getting his hands a little dirty if he needs to. If he wanted your grave dug, it would have already been done."

I smirk and nod. "True," I drawl out.

Hunter shifts his eyes between the road and me. "His asset is arriving this morning. You were an integral part of securing her. He wants you there to see Izzy's reaction."

I shake my head. "I don't deserve any credit for what Isaac did. He put up the money, and pushed his empire into dangerous territory to secure her. All I did was recognize a pair of distinctive eyes."

"Yeah, but a lesser man wouldn't have cared what happened to her. You knew Isaac. You knew he would have responded to your discovery. If you didn't care about him or Izzy, you would have just hidden that little girl's existence to save your own ass. You didn't. That deserves credit."

I grunt. It is the only plausible reaction I can give. Although some would see my decision as loyalty to Isaac, I've been anything but loyal. Neither Hunter nor I have been totally forthright with Isaac the past three months. After Isaac ran into Izzy at the airport, he requested for Hunter to gather any information he could on her. Hunter did as requested. He just failed to disclose *everything* he found on Izzy. Although, I'll admit, it took Hunter a lot of effort to unearth the real Isabelle Brahn from the deep pile of rubble Brandon hid her under, but since Hunter is the best hacker in the world, he eventually found a channel.

Both Hunter and I saw a change in Isaac the day he met Izzy. We knew without a doubt she was his Achilles heel. So that night, we made a plan. Izzy had a month. If she didn't disclose her true identity to Isaac within a month of them being a couple, we were going to out her. Isaac was arrested before we got the chance.

My palms begin to sweat when Hunter pulls his hellcat into

the front entrance of Isaac's property and enters the security code into the black security panel. The beat of my heart climbs astronomically as he guides his car up the driveway and parks at the front of the double French doors. My eyes lift to the half-circle window on the top floor of Isaac's residence as I climb out of Hunter's car.

"You coming?" I ask when Hunter's seatbelt remains latched.

Hunter smirks and shakes his head. My pupils widen as I swallow the brick in my throat. Spotting my panicked expression, Hunter chuckles.

"This is the first time I've ever seen you scared," he cackles.

Rolling my eyes, I slam the passenger door shut. With a laugh, Hunter tears out of the driveway, leaving nothing but the smell of dust and burning gasoline in his wake. I'm going to be honest, I'm shitting bricks. Before, I never had a reason to fear Isaac. I had nothing to lose, so I never worried about retribution when I'd taunt him. Now, I have *everything* to lose.

Running my sweaty palms down the front of my jeans, I walk up the small flight of stairs to the front door. Before I can grab the gold engraved door handle, the French doors swing open. Isaac's dark eyes stare into mine for numerous stomach-churning seconds before they lower to absorb my long-sleeve shirt and ripped jeans.

"There's a spare suit in the guest bedroom." He gestures his head to one of the numerous rooms in his private residence.

Unsurprisingly, his tone is clipped and stern. Surprisingly, this is the first time he has spoken to me as if I'm a member of his staff and not his friend. I'm not going lie, his coldness stings my ego and bruises my heart.

"Isaac, I--"

Any further words preparing to seep from my lips are cut off from the stern glare he directs at me. His furious wrath causes the guilt I'm carrying on my shoulders to become more weighted.

"Not now," Isaac demands, glaring into my eyes. "This day is not about me or you. It is about Isabelle. I know you care for her." His jaw gains a twitch from his last sentence. "And she cares for you. So for her, I'm willing to push aside the overwhelming urge to *destroy* you like your *betrayal* gutted me."

After seeing Isaac fight in the charity UFC match last week, I thought his fists were his greatest weapons. They aren't. His words and the desolate look in his eyes are inflicting more damage to my already guilt-ridden heart than his fists ever could.

"We leave in five minutes."

When I nod, he paces into the living room at the side of the foyer. I move into the spare room and change into my work attire: a black suit and a crisp white dress shirt. My movements are sluggish, weighed down by the guilt strangling my heart. After I'm dressed, I return to the foyer to await further instructions.

My eyes lift from the ground when I hear a tiny pair of feet padding down the stairwell. Izzy stops halfway down the stairs. Her hand shoots up to clamp over her mouth and her eyes well with tears. After brushing away a few stray tears, she gallops down the stairs and throws herself into my arms.

"Hey, Isabelle," I greet her, returning her embrace.

Deep down in my heart, I knew Isaac would take care of

Izzy, but it still feels good to see her back to her carefree, happy nature.

When I place Izzy onto her feet, her eyes drift over my face. From the corner of my eye, I catch sight of Isaac exiting the living room, carefully watching the exchange between Izzy and me. Even though his gaze remains stagnant, I know he sees it. Izzy is like family to me. Nothing more. Nothing less. There are no fireworks or sparks. There's nothing but friendship and mutual respect.

When Izzy spots Isaac standing to the side, she gnaws on her bottom lip before she scurries across the room to greet Isaac with the same enthusiasm she bestowed on me. Well, minus the kissing part. Watching them interact should settle any concerns Isaac has. The fireworks he's searching for are exploding before his very eyes – between him and Izzy.

"I'll bring the car around," I advise, slipping out the front entrance.

The heaviness of my steps soften when my cell phone buzzes in my trouser pocket. Lugging it out, my chuckle sounds over the gravel crunching under my feet when I peer down at the screen. Ava snapped a picture of her and Joel playing Monopoly last night. Instead of using fake money, they used the multiple bags of Skittles I left in Joel's sock draw as leverage.

I quickly type a message as I move to the garage at the side of the main house.

Me: *Lucky his mom is a dentist?*

There's no doubt who the real estate mogul is in the photo Ava snapped. Joel has a pile of candy nearly bigger than his head. Ava has a small scattering of Skittles that wouldn't even fill half of her small hand.

Ava: *Lucky he agreed to save his candy gorging until his daddy returns.*

As I type a message, eclipses trickle across the screen. A grin stretches across my face when my message is sent at the same time Ava's is received.

Me: *I miss you guys.*

Ava: *We miss you.*

I've only been away from them for a few hours, and I'm already missing them more than I could possibly express. That proves, without a doubt, my life will not be complete until they're in it. Both of them.

When I hear Isaac and Isabelle walking toward the garage, I quickly type a message and hit send before housing my cell phone into my trouser pocket. I rush to the driver's side door of one of Isaac's many town cars and crank the ignition.

Halfway to the private airstrip Isaac instructed me to drive to, my cell phone buzzes in my pocket. Dying to know what Ava's reply is, I shift my eyes between the road and my trousers while retrieving my phone. My hearty chuckle traps in the front partition of the car since Isaac has the privacy divider lifted between us.

Ava: *That was even more pathetic than that time in your office.*

It takes me several tedious minutes to type a reply since I'm gripping the steering wheel with one hand and typing with another.

Me: *Come on, cut a guy some slack. I've never done this before.*

I can't wipe the grin off my face as I pull into the private airstrip on the outskirts of Ravenshoe.

Ava: Well, for one, you missed a box.

Me: No, I didn't.

Ava: Yeah, you did.

I scroll up the screen to check the original message I sent her: *Will you go out with me? Yes or Maybe. To dinner. I meant to say, will you go out to dinner with me?*

Me: I don't see what the problem is.

Ava: Imagine a rolled eyes emoji here if I could work out how to do them on my new phone.

Me: Lol. Ask Joel. He would know.

Ava: I can't believe you type Lol. How old are you? Anyway, you forgot the "no" box.

Me: And? What's wrong with that?

Ava: You can't ask a girl out without a no box.

Me: Hell yes, I can. Saying I can't do something is pretty much daring me to do it. And we both know, I never back down from a dare.

I place my phone into my lap and pull Isaac's town car beside Cormack's private jet Isaac regularly uses.

Me: There isn't a no box as I'm not going to take no for an answer. Come on, Ava. It's dinner. A guy's got to eat.

Ava: What if the restaurant stops serving breakfast at 11 AM?

I chuckle.

Me: We'll go to another restaurant.

Although I'm loving Ava's playful banter, on the inside, I'm dying. I haven't inhaled a full breath since her first reply was received.

I stare at the screen of my phone, willing for it to hurry up and deliver Ava's reply.

Ava: Alright. Let me know the day and I'll ask Mrs. Mable to watch Joel.

Fuck yes!

Me: Let me take care of everything.

My eyes lift from my phone when the door of the private jet swings open. My brows hit my hairline when the guy who was dancing with Izzy steps out of the jet with a little girl wrapped around his legs. My eyes snap to Isaac, wanting to gauge his reaction to being confronted by the guy who had every intention of adding Izzy's name to the notches on his bedpost. My brows furrow when Isaac seems oblivious to the man's significance in Izzy's life. Isaac's reaction can't be true. He's always watching Izzy. *Always.*

I turn my eyes back to my phone and quickly type out a message.

Me: I gotta go, babe, I'll call you later.

Ava: Okay. Talk to you later.

I sit in the car for several minutes, quietly watching the exchange between Isaac, Izzy and Izzy's half-sister, Callie. You'd think witnessing Isaac spend millions of dollars to secure Izzy's sister would be the most admirable thing I've witnessed him do the past five years. It isn't. It's not even close.

AFTER SETTLING Callie into her new room, Isaac strides into his office. His brisk pace slows when he notices me standing at the side of his desk, glancing at a photo of Izzy he has there. He seems to have an odd obsession with watching Izzy sleep, as this is only one of many photos he has of her dozing.

I place the photo on his desk and turn around to face him. "You knew what Izzy was going to do. You knew why she went to the Dungeon," I say.

Although you could construe my statement as a question, it isn't. I know Isaac. I know him *very well*. So I'm well aware my statement is factual, not fiction.

Isaac unbuttons his suit jacket, removes it, and slings it over the coatrack in the corner of the room. Remaining quiet, he ambles to a crystal bar set up at the edge of his desk and pours a generous serving of whiskey into a crystal glass.

"You intuited Izzy's next move before she even knew what she was going to do." *Just like I knew Ava would accept my invitation to dinner before I even sent the message.*

The corners of Isaac's mouth lift in a wry smirk. "A game of chess is not a hard game to win if you study your opponent in great depth."

My eyes widen. "You sent Ayden in knowing he was going to kiss her?" I ask in disbelief.

The smirk on Isaac's face vanishes and a set of hard-lined lips ruefully take its place. "No," he growls. "I sent Ayden in to *stop* Isabelle from kissing someone."

He pivots on his heels to face me. "Isabelle knows me better than anyone. She knew I'd kissed Ophelia without me even needing to confess. In her heart, she knew I betrayed her. So she went to the Dungeon to exact her revenge. Ayden was the closest man I had on the ground. I sent him there to *stop* her kissing another man."

He slams his whiskey glass onto the bar so roughly, the crystal chips from his brutal force. His nostrils flare as he inhales deeply, filling his thrusting chest with air.

"Ayden had one task: use any tactic he could to keep Isabelle safe until you arrived. What I didn't expect was to be blindsided by the man I trusted. I never suspected the man I would have bled for would be the one to cut me open and *tear* my heart straight from my chest."

The heaviness in my chest turns lethal. "Isaac, I did--"

"You did it because you knew I'd be watching," he interjects, his tone lowering to a vicious snarl. "Because you wanted me to see it."

Isaac's face lines with anger when I nod, agreeing with his statement.

"What I can't comprehend is why you did it. I've seen you with Isabelle. I know you care for her, but I never suspected it to be anything more than friendship. I've only seen the spark of admiration in your eyes once before. It wasn't directed at Isabelle."

"Izzy is my family, Isaac. Just like you," I state, staring into his pained eyes.

Isaac's face reddens, and his jaw muscle spasms.

"I wanted you to fire me," I confess, taking a step closer to him, putting myself in the danger zone by moving within reaching distance. "After everything you did for me, I didn't feel like I could leave your empire of my own freewill. So I took the coward's way out. I forced you to do it for me."

Isaac's stern eyes bounce between mine, but he remains quiet, allowing his eyes to demand an explanation.

"I have a son," I enlighten him.

Even in the seriousness of our conversation, I can't stop the smile tugging on my lips. Isaac's strengthen posture weakens, and he eyes me as if he misheard what I said.

"Ava was pregnant before I snatched Roberto from the compound," I explain, still smirking.

Isaac inhales a quick breath before shaking his head. "No, she couldn't have been. I had a member of my family keep an on Ava the weeks following your disappearance. I wanted to ensure Col wasn't aware of her significance to you."

I curtly nod. "I know that." Isaac would have ensured Ava was safe. "Ava didn't discover she was pregnant until she was nearly six months along. Joel is my son, Isaac. Even without a DNA test, there's no doubt in my mind."

Isaac swallows harshly before scrubbing his hand along his jaw. After a small stretch of silence, he paces around his desk and takes a seat in his leather chair. This is the first time I've seen him look wholly stumped. He's not used to being divulged information second hand. He's normally the informant of vital information, not the receiver.

His leather chair creaks as he leans back and lifts his eyes to me. "If I'd known, I would have never--"

"I know," I interrupt, taking the chair across from him. "I didn't kiss Izzy because I thought you hid my son from me. I kissed her because I didn't take the time to properly judge the repercussions of my actions."

The deep V groove in between Isaac's eyes smooths. "I've warned you before. Haste decisions--"

"Cause unforgiving mistakes." I fill in, nodding.

I rest my ankle on my trouser-covered thigh. "I don't expect you to ever forgive me. What I did to you was wrong, but I need you to understand why I did it. I was hurting as I thought Ava was going to take my son away from me. I let my anger get the better of me... as did Izzy."

Isaac shifts his eyes to the side of his office, like he can see Izzy through the walls separating them.

"I made a foolish mistake, and stupidly threw Izzy under the bus with me. You don't need me to tell you this because I can see in your eyes you are already aware, but I'm going to say it anyway. Izzy is your Achilles heel, just like Ava is mine."

Isaac returns his eyes to me. The catastrophic storm brewing in his eyes earlier has been downgraded to a tropical shower.

"I wasn't man enough to talk to you last week, but I'm man enough to admit I made a mistake. I'm sorry for what I did to you, Isaac. For breaking your trust, and for messing around with the best thing that has ever happened to you. I don't expect you to accept my apology, but I hope one day, you'll understand if I had the chance, I'd go back in an instant and fix all the wrongs I've done. Not just this week, years ago as well."

Isaac inhales a ragged breath as he stands from his chair. He paces around the desk and props his hip on the side. His arms are crossed in front of his body, and his jaw is ticking, exposing his agitation, but the pain in his eyes has eased from my confession.

"I'm only going to say this once, so you better listen." His voice is rough, like his throat is raw and bleeding. "I was once told family isn't the people related to you by blood. It is the people you chose to be a part of your life that makes them family."

I smile and nod. I've quoted that saying to him numerous times the past five years.

"No matter what happens, Hugo, you'll always be my family." He coughs, clearing his throat of any encumbrance. "But in saying that, I'll *fucking* kill you if you *ever* touch Isabelle again," he warns, glaring into my eyes to ensure I'm aware his warning is not an idle threat. If I so much as touch a strand on Izzy's head, he will slit my throat.

I swallow the brick lodged in my throat before nodding. Smirking at my agreeing gesture, Isaac pushes off the desk and takes his original position behind it. After running his eyes over a barrage of paperwork in front of him, he lifts them to me.

"Are you planning to sit there all day?" When I shake my head, he says, "Then get the fuck out of my office. Some of us actually have to work for a living."

Even exulted by Isaac using part of a quote he said to me many years ago, my brows furrow. I'm happy I've repaired some of the damage I instigated between Isaac and me, but I can't just step back into my old role. My family needs me, but even more important than that, I need them.

Sensing my hesitation to leave, a smirk etches on Isaac's mouth. It is only small, but it is enough to appease some of the guilt maiming my heart.

"Go back to your family, Hugo" Isaac responds to my silent thoughts. "Mark might have pulled in the female clientele back in the day, but he's shit at operations. My clubs in the New York region are taking a hit with him behind the wheel. Maybe with someone steering him in the right direction, I might not have to fire his ass."

A broad grin stretches across my face. I'm not bragging, but when I was at the helm of operations in New York five years ago, Isaac's clubs saw substantial growth. *Alright, maybe I'm bragging.*

When I stand from my chair, Isaac gestures his head to the door. "Make sure you say goodbye to Isabelle before you leave."

He tried to suffocate it, but I didn't miss the slight smear in his tone, but I appreciate his effort in lessening the vehement jealously he has when it comes to Izzy and me being friends.

Never being the talkative type, Isaac returns his eyes to the paperwork spread on his desk as I amble to his office door.

"Hugo," he calls out just before I exit.

I crank my neck. "Yeah?"

His gray eyes stare into mine. "You should consider upgrading your suit. It just looks tacky walking around in a thousand dollar suit when you have over two million dollars in your bank account."

I stare at him, more confused than ever.

Isaac stands from his chair and walks around his desk. "Those checks belonged to you. What I did for you and your family wasn't under the stipulation that you had to repay me. I did it because I wanted to."

A smile curls on my lips before I curtly nod. Isaac has always been generous, but I never felt right accepting his money. For the past five years, he has fed me, sheltered me, and kept me safe. What more did I need than that? So instead of cashing his checks he printed every month, I shredded every one of them, with the exception of the original one he gave me over five years ago. I kept it as a memento of how far I'd come, and what I'd given up to get here.

My eyes lift from my shoes when Isaac finalizes the distance between us, stopping directly in front of me. "Ravenshoe has grown substantially the past few years."

I nod. Under Isaac's guidance, it's grown phenomenally in the five years I've lived here.

"A rapidly developing city could use a world class dentist," he suggests, his tone rapidly changing from my boss to my friend.

A vast grin stretches across my face. "I'll talk it over with Ava. See what she thinks."

I don't have a chance in hell of hiding the excitement in my voice. Although Rochdale was where I was born and raised, Ravenshoe became my home the past five years. It wasn't the location that earned it that title. It was the people who live here. People like Isaac.

Spotting my slack-jawed expression, Isaac smirks. "I'll have my team look into suitable locations. Just in case Ava is interested."

Not giving him the time to react, I throw my arms around his broad shoulders and give him a quick bro hug. Although he stiffens, he doesn't pull away from my embrace. That is good enough for me to accept.

My brows meet my hairline when Isaac strengthens his grip around my shoulders. "If Ava is your Achilles, pull your head out of your ass before you lose the best thing that's ever happened to you."

I crank my neck back and peer into his eyes. "You were close, but I said 'pull your *fucking* head out of your ass before you lose the best thing that's ever *fucking* happened to you,'" I say, quoting what I said to Isaac the night he was arrested by Izzy.

Isaac shrugs his shoulders. "Extending your vocabulary with offensive language doesn't make you any more of a man." His lips curve into a smirk. "Besides, my memories of the night are a little fuzzy, hazed by a liquor bottle or two."

I chuckle. "True," I drawl out. I'd never seen him so intoxicated.

When he lowers his arms from my shoulders and locks his eyes with mine, his amorous gaze spears me in place. It is the same spark he had in his eyes when I collected him from the airport the day he met Izzy. The glimmer that told me he had just met his match.

"Don't waste a day, Hugo. Because when you breathe your last breath, it won't matter how many breaths you took, but how many moments took your breath away."

TWENTY-THREE

AVA

My office chair gives out a squeak when I slump into it and swivel around to face the window in the corner of the room. I've officially been operating my practice for the past week. Thankfully, for the most part, the experience has been positive. With keeping my prices reasonable for the average Rochdale community member, I've managed to secure a handful of new patients. I even snagged a few loyal clients from Gardner and Sons who prefer the appeal of quality dental work over a lavish office space. Although it has been a good trading week, I have a long way to go before I'll be turning a profit.

"Even Bill Gates had to start somewhere," I mumble to myself.

A soft sigh spills from my lips when I peer down at the screen of my phone and discover it is void of any missed calls or text messages. Ever since our exchange of text messages earlier this morning, Hugo has maintained radio silence. The craziness of my day has ensured I only sneaked peeks at my phone every thirty minutes, instead of every minute of the day like I did the months following his disappearance. I'll be the first to admit it will take me some time to adjust to Hugo's conflicting work schedule, but it's a compromise I'm willing to make if it maintains his relationship with Joel and me.

Hugo has only been gone a little over twenty-four hours, and I'm missing him like crazy. Even though we are not an "official" couple, my moods have already become dependent on Hugo's presence, which sounds like a terrifying notion. After being controlled by my father, I grew up striving for independence, often vowing no man would ever have that type of hold over me again. Although some may see my dependency on Hugo in such a short period of time as a negative, I see it as anything but. The fact Hugo and I have years of friendship as the foundation of our unique bond undoubtedly proves our relationship isn't based on propaganda. It is based on mutual respect and admiration.

The past week has been surreal. Hugo stepped into the role of devoted spouse and father without a single qualm seeping from his lips. He's mastered the school drop-off without getting any citations from the parking mothers who govern with an iron fist, and he even attended a PTA meeting with me Tuesday night. Although I'll admit, from the blank, desolated look he wore during the entire meeting, I'll have more chances of getting him to sit in my dental chair than through another PTA meeting.

Although Hugo has only been back in my life for two weeks, it feels like years have passed. Our relationship has always been like that. Small moments make a lifetime of memories.

Don't read my admission with foggy glasses, though. I know Hugo is anything but perfect, but for years, he has been my drug of choice. And just like every addictive drug, he's been the cause of life-altering highs and devastating lows in my life, but like all things in life, I greedily accept the good and wade my way through the bad. It is the sacrifice every woman makes for the man she loves.

I rub my throbbing temples before stretching my arms above my head. After an exhausting day, I'm dying for a long, hot shower and a nice glass of wine. I place my phone on my Ikea desk and crank my head to the side when a knock sounds on my office door.

"Come in," I say, my high tone, exposing my interest. It is a little after six PM on Friday night, so my office doors are officially closed for the weekend.

My excitement dampens when Belinda glides through the door with a imploring look on her face. "I know we are closed, but we've just had an emergency case come in. Do you think you could squeeze them in?" Her nose screws up as she stares at me with pleading eyes.

Even though I'm beyond exhausted, and I've reached my quota of peering into smelly mouths for one day, it would be injudicious of me to turn down a prospective new client. Strength and growth only come through continued effort and struggle.

I raise my eyes to Belinda. "Sure, just give me five minutes so I can advise Mrs. Mable I'll be late collecting Joel, then send them into the exam room," I instruct.

A big grin carves on Belinda's mouth before she nods and exits my office, closing the door behind her. I leave a quick message on Mrs. Mable's home phone when my call is sent to voicemail. I'm not shocked by her failure to answer. She can barely hear Joel's earth shattering screams, let alone a telephone ringing.

I'm scrubbing my hands in the sink of the washroom when the exam room door attached to my office creaks open.

"Hi, I'm just washing up. Please take a seat in the dental chair, and I'll be right with you," I call out, snagging a paper towel from the dispenser mounted on my right.

After thoroughly drying my hands, I crumble up the paper towel and throw it into the bin before walking out of the washroom. The ghastly dentist smell I've always hated hits my senses when I pace into the sterilized treatment area at the side of my office. The space is deadly quiet; only gloves being removed from a cardboard box is heard.

After tying a face-mask around my head and putting on my gloves, I amble further into the room. My breath hitches halfway between my lungs and my throat when I discover who is sprawled on the dental chair. I cough and wheeze, struggling to breathe through the saliva now sitting in my lungs instead of my throat.

The panty-melting smile on Hugo's face sags when he hears my breathless coughing fit.

"Are you okay?"

Through watering eyes, I nod. I try to speak, but the shock of seeing him sitting in *my* dental chair is too great for me to harness. My mouth can barely move, let alone relinquish words. Hugo *hates* dentists. Not a small dislike, he openly admits that he hates, *HATES*, them. Even putting aside the shock of his sudden arrival in my office, I only dropped him at the airport yesterday afternoon. And although I wished for him to return soon, I never fathomed it would be the very next day.

Rolling my shoulders, I level out my erratic breathing and try to portray that I am a responsible, career-oriented twenty-nine-year-old woman, not the teenage, braces-mouthed girl Hugo's presence always incites. Although my posture is alluding to professionalism, my shaking steps and quickening pulse thrumming in my neck is giving away my deceit.

"What has brought you to my practice today?" I ask, finalizing the last three paces between us.

I manage to catch my eye-roll halfway over the dimness displaced in my words. Anyone would swear I'm performing dental work on Beyoncé for how much my voice is juddering.

"I have a toothache on my lower left molar," Hugo mumbles, his words low and croaky.

And just like that, professional obligation to my patient overtakes my nerves.

The butterflies impinging my stomach settle when I notice a beading of sweat glistening Hugo's forehead. He appears even more rattled than me. After switching on the dental operatory light above my head, I take a seat on my swivel chair and roll in close to Hugo's side. He remains as quiet as a church mouse as I adjust the height of the dental chair. His lips tug into a seductive grin when I clamp a drool cloth around his neck and hand him a pair of protective glasses. His cheeky smile is wiped straight off his face when I gather a dental mirror and probe from the sterilized stainless tray at my side.

"Open up," I instruct when I spot his clamped-shut mouth.

Through quivering lips, he does as instructed. Leaning over, I glance into his wide-opened mouth. My lips purse. For someone who *loves* sweets and *hates* dentists, Hugo's teeth are beautiful. *He must be a regular flosser.*

After a deep exploration of his mouth, I fail to locate anything that would cause him any concern. There are no cavities or shadows that allude to an internal problem; his mouth is clear of any signs of an abscess, and his gums appear healthy. *Perhaps it's a sinus issue?* More times than not, some dental pain is associated with severe sinus infections.

"I can't see anything pointing to a reason why you're experiencing pain. Can you explain what the pain feels like?" I ask, mumbling through my face-mask.

Placing my probing tools back onto the tray, I yank down my mask. "Sometimes sinus infections can cause--"

My words stop, halted by a delicious pair of cinnamon-flavored lips. After licking the seam of my O-formed lips, Hugo's tongue dips into my mouth to explore every inch with more vigor than my cavity search of his mouth undertook. His tongue dances with mine in a toe-curling kiss that renders me breathless. He kisses the living bloody hell out of me, bestowing me with a kiss that makes every other kiss I've experienced pale in comparison. He holds nothing back, and neither do I. I've wanted this, and so much more the past week, but no matter how many corny one liners, seductive poses, or inappropriate teases I did, nothing could deter Hugo from his resolve to give me time to process my failed relationship with Marvin.

In all honesty, at the start, I was confused about my ease on leaving a relationship without feeling a morsel of remorse, but after spending thirty minutes having a deep and meaningful in my car with Mrs. Marshall, any doubts festering my mind vanished. The facts were as clear as the sun shining in the sky. I never loved Marvin. I've always loved Hugo – even after years of absence and more tears than I can count. A minute, an hour, or a week of deliberation will never change that fact. Hugo is my one and only true love.

When Hugo pulls his sinful lips away from mine, my head is dizzy, stuck in a crazy blur of lust and devotion. His eyes dart between mine before his kiss-swollen lips curve high in the corners. He runs his index finger over my tingling mouth before he stands from the dental chair and paces to the middle of the room. I watch him, more stunned than ever, shocked he can function so normally after a mind-hazing kiss. I can barely breathe, let alone walk.

"You coming?" he asks, grasping the handle of the door separating my office from the treatment area.

Nodding, I slip off the stool and pace toward him. The shake of my knees increases with every stride I take, as does the grin on Hugo's face. Once I'm standing in front of him, he runs the back of his fingers down my cheeks before swinging open the door. My heart leaps out of my chest and tears prick my eyes when the splendor of the scene unfolds before me. Joel is standing in the doorway, swamped by a giant bunch of red long-stemmed roses in his hands. His usually unmanageable hair has been wrangled into glossy curls, and he's wearing a pair of dark blue trousers and a buttoned-up shirt. He looks adorably cute and grownup all at the same time. The rest of my office has vase upon vase of long-stemmed roses in every color you could imagine. Pink, blue, yellow, white. It is like a rainbow of color, and it smells divine, overpowering the ghastly dentist smell I hate.

The tears welling in my eyes escape when Hugo kneels down on one knee in front of me and gently grasps my left

hand. The glistening of moisture in his eyes gathers my attention, but the admiration beaming out of them secures my utter
devotion.

"The biggest mistake I ever made was letting you walk away
the first time, but the past cannot be changed, forgotten, edited
or erased, it can only be accepted. I've learned from my
mistakes, and I'm not going to let them happen again. I never
want to be away from you again. Not a second, not a minute, not
a single day. This ring is a symbol of my promise to you. A vow
that I'll always be there, standing by your side, supporting you,
loving you, and cherishing every single inch of you until the end
of time. I can't change the past, but I can shape my future. I
want to shape it with you, Ava. My very existence begins and
ends with you. Will you do me the honor of becoming my
wife?" He cracks open a red heart-shaped box to showcase the
beautiful dusty pink diamond ring nestled inside.

I run my hands over my tear-drenched cheeks before
nodding. I don't need time to formulate a response or an objection, or to evaluate his proposal. All I need is him. Hugo places
the ring on my finger and stands from his crouched position as
Belinda captures the entire precious moment with her phone.
Joel squeals excitedly before dumping the roses onto the ground
and encircling his arms around mine and Hugo's thighs. His
elated cheers dull into a hum when Hugo seals his plump lips
over mine, finalizing the most romantic proposal of all time with
an even more heartfelt kiss.

TWENTY-FOUR

AVA

"Thank you so much for watching Joel," I say, wrapping my arms around Belinda's shoulders.

After Hugo proposed, he took Belinda, Joel, and me to a fancy restaurant in the middle of New York City. I'm not going to lie, when I saw the price they were charging for a regular glass of wine, I choked on my glass of water. Then panic set in. If a standard glass of wine cost hundreds of dollars, how much was a sparkling glass of water going to set me back? It was only when Hugo assured me we would be paying wholesale prices as he knew the owner did my flipping stomach settle down and excitement took over. As we exited the elegant restaurant, I spotted two limousines at the curb. Hugo explained that one was to take Belinda and Joel home and the other was for us.

"Our night of celebrating is only just beginning," Hugo said after bidding farewell to Belinda and Joel.

Memories of our first night we went out dancing at the club flooded my mind when Hugo gathered me under the nook of his arm and dashed to the black stretch limousine. Those memories turned into real-life flashbacks when the limousine pulled onto the curb at the exact club he originally took me to. Even though it was over five years ago, the vibe at the club was just as exciting as it was the first time we visited it. It was a wild mix of sex and seduction, but even more intoxicating than the thumping club was the boyish grin on Hugo's face. It never once waned, not even with us being bumped and elbowed as we danced for hours. Tonight was the most carefree I've been in the past five years. My clipped wings grew back and I was once again free to fly. It was perfect.

"You're welcome, Sweetie," Belinda replies, returning my embrace. "I'm just sorry I didn't get Joel settled for you so you could enjoy the rest of your night in peace." Her lips purse as a heavy set of lines indent her forehead. "I think I'll adhere to your advice about lowering his sugar intake after dinner. That boys goes a little bit crazy when the clock strikes eight."

I laugh while pacing to my front door to open it for Belinda. Crazy is an understatement for Joel's antics when he stays up too late. Instead of his tiredness wearing him down, it seems to heighten his excitement.

"I'll see you Monday?"

Belinda nods before slipping out the door. "Have fun."

After ensuring Belinda has entered her car and exited my driveway safely, I amble down the hall. My brisk strides slow when I hear Hugo's deep voice quietly whispering. When I reach Joel's room, I lean against the wall and prick my ears.

"So, if you hear Mommy calling out, don't worry, I've got her covered," Hugo whispers, his tone self-assured with a dash of cheekiness.

Interested in what their conversation is about, I sneakily peer into Joel's room. His brows are furrowed together tightly as he looks at Hugo with confusion in his eyes. After a beat, he cautiously nods.

"Do we have a deal?" Hugo peers into Joel's anxious eyes.

"Yep," Joel replies, his words muffled by a big yawn.

"Alright, let's go over it one more time, just to make sure you have the details right."

Joel nods. "If I stay in my bed *all* night, I get five dollars."

My brows arch high at the same time a dash of euphoria pumps into my veins.

"Uh huh," Hugo mutters softly.

I lean deeper into the hallway when Hugo slants his head to the side and glances out Joel's door, no doubt checking that the coast is clear. Once Hugo's focus returns to Joel, I peer back around the door.

"And?"

Joel rubs his droopy eyes. "And if I ask Mommy to make pancakes in the morning, I get ten dollars," he confirms, resting his head on his pillow.

"That's right," Hugo praises before standing from Joel's bed to tuck him in. "That's called a bonus. An incentive for a job well done."

"I like a boganus," Joel replies, his lips quirking.

I laugh quietly over his mispronunciation of the word.

Once Joel is tucked in tight, Hugo places a kiss on his forehead, switches on his nightlight, and ambles toward the door. I spin on my heels and sprint down the hallway, vainly pretending I wasn't eavesdropping on their private conversation.

When Hugo spots my contemptuous face, his long strides down the hall slow. His head angles to the side and his brow curves high. "You heard that, didn't you?"

"No." I overdramatize the short word while nodding. I've never been good at deceit.

Hugo cockily winks, not the slightest bit concerned I heard him bribing our son to stay in his room. I'm not shocked that he devised a tactic for us to have uninterrupted adult time, I'm just astonished I didn't think of it first. It would have been helpful when I was attempting to seduce Hugo last week. At times, my vigorous ploys seemed to be working, until we were interrupted by the patter of little feet.

With a crass grin on his face, Hugo continues on his original journey.

I quirk my lips. "Sounded like someone was planning on sleeping over?" I try to keep the excitement out of my voice. My attempts are fruitless.

"No," he replies, shaking his head.

My bottom lip drops into a shameful pout at the same time a pathetic whimper ripples through my lips.

My heart beats double time when Hugo says, "Neither of us are going to get any sleep, so I can't really call it a sleepover."

My eyes drift between the beast of a man prowling toward me and my dowdy work attire-covered body. Hugo is dressed in a well-fitted black suit with a light gray pinstriped dress shirt. His jacket has been removed and slung over the rock-hard couch he slept on weeks ago, and the sleeves of his shirt have been rolled up to the elbows. Even with every inch of his alluring torso covered, I can't miss the mouth-watering ridges of his chiseled abs and pecs as he prowls toward me, like a lion on the hunt. My brows furrow as I take in my clothing selection. I'm wearing a black pleated pencil skirt with sheer black stockings, and a white blouse with decorative cuffs. My waist-length jacket has been hung on the coatrack in the entranceway, along with my heavy wool coat.

I'll be the first to admit, I'm panicked. I didn't thoroughly evaluate all avenues when I attempted to seduce Hugo last week. My brain was too overwhelmed with unbridled horniness to think rationally. Now, while watching the muscles in Hugo's thigh flex as he struts toward me, I realize I should have given it a little more thought. In both good and bad ways, I'm not the Ava Westcott Hugo remembers from five years ago. I've changed. Some things have improved, like the strength of my backbone and my sense of self-worth. Others, mainly my body... not so much.

"I've changed," I warn, slowing Hugo's fast pace. "My body is no longer that tight twenty-four-year old body you're used to seeing."

I straighten my slumped posture when Hugo's eyes run the entire length of my figure, from the tips of my toes to the top of my head, studying every inch in great depth. When his eyes return to my face, my breath hitches. His gaze is uninhibited and brimming with lust, causing my pulse to quicken.

"My boobs hang a little lower, and my stomach isn't as flat as it used to be," I notify him, wanting to ensure he fully comprehends my warning. I've given birth; no woman's body bounces back to its original perkiness after that.

Arching his brow, Hugo glares into my eyes. "Insult yourself one more time, Ava, and your ass will be as colorful as my tattoos by the time I'm done with you."

My breathing pattern quickens as my lady garden throbs. I stand still, openmouthed and frozen in excitement.

A beguiling grin etches on Hugo's sinful lips. "I need to devise a new punishment for you. You like spanking a little too much for it to be classed as a reprimand."

Blood surges to my pussy when he bands his arm around my waist and pulls me in close to his body, allowing me to feel what his avid inspection of my figure has done to him. He's thick, hard, and rip-roaring ready to go.

"Your body incited that fully clothed." He rocks his hips so the crown of his cock rubs my throbbing pussy. "Imagine what seeing you naked will instigate."

Leaning in, he presses a kiss to the side of my mouth before moving his dedication to my neck. His teeth sink into the sensitive skin above my collarbone before the lash of his tongue soothes the sting. I slant my head to the side, giving him full access to my neck. Soft, provocative moans spill from my lips with every gentle nib and suck he does.

He grips the back of my thighs, encouraging my legs to wrap around his waist. A breathless pant erupts my lips when the thickness of his cock brushes against my sensitive clit. After sealing his lips over mine, he paces toward my bedroom at the end of the hall. By the time we make it down the corridor, fumbling with each other's clothes on the way, any doubts festering my mind have vanished. If the look of desire in his eyes isn't enough to assure me he's attracted to me, the thickness of his cock is a sure-fire indication.

When he places me down onto my feet, a grunt of air leaves his parted lips. On the short walk, he managed to nimbly undo all the buttons on my blouse, exposing my Carmina black and red push-up bra. Growling, he lowers his head, tugs down my bra and sucks the peaked bud of my nipple into his mouth. A surge of desire floods my nether regions when his teeth graze over the sensitive bud. My hands shoot up to grasp his hair so I can run my hand through his thick mane while also securing his wicked mouth to my breast that has been aching for his attention for nearly five years.

Keeping my nipple in his mouth, he wraps one arm around my waist and steps me backwards until the fluffiness of the duvet quilt on my bed brushes against my stocking-covered legs. His stealthy movements cause my blouse to slip off my shoulders and plunge to the floor around our feet. Releasing my nipple from his mouth with a pop, he stares at me with a heavy-lidded gaze. With a cheeky smirk, he pushes my shoulder, sending me toppling onto the bed. My hair fluffs out wildly as a breathy huff escapes my lips. Any laughter preparing to spill from my mouth entombs in my throat when Hugo removes his dress shirt before fisting the scruff of his undershirt and yanking it over his head. I don't know what it is, but there's nothing sexier than the way men remove their shirts.

I take that back. There's nothing sexier than Hugo biting on the corner of his lip as his eyes rake over my half-dressed body. His gaze is predatory and sets my pulse racing. My eyes assess him with just as much vigor as he is instilling me as he undoes the belt of his trousers and lowers the zipper. Even covered by an immense amount of colorful tattoos, I can't miss his chiseled abs, rock-hard pecs, and drool worthy V muscle. Every inch of him is hard. And by every inch, I mean every goddamn rock-hard inch.

Raising my eyes from his thick, glorious cock he's just freed from his trousers, I lick my lips and lock my eyes with his. My knees curve inward, battling to settle the mad throb between my legs from the panty-wetting visual in front of me. Hugo's seductive grin enlarges as he places his knee between my thighs, denying me the ability to ease the tingle that may have me falling into ecstasy before he's even touched me.

He stares into my wild eyes while undoing the fastener at the side of my skirt. His eyes absorb my thrusting chest as he pulls the zipper on my skirt down. He drinks in every inch of my body as he slowly slips my skirt down my waist and hips. His lusty gaze compels a peppering of goosebumps to form on my skin and wetness to saturate the area between my legs.

"Beautiful Ava, every inch of you is perfect," he praises, his words deep and tempting.

A rush of heat forms on my cheeks nearly as quickly as an inane smile stretches across my face. A hiss of air escapes Hugo's mouth when my skirt glides down past the matching garter and lace-topped stockings I'm wearing.

"Fuckin' hell," he mutters under his breath.

When his eyes rocket to mine, I bite my lower lip. His gaze is full of desire, sending my libido to an all-time high.

"I wanted to be prepared for your return," I inform him, my tone a low purr, shamefully exposing my pleasure at the approving look beaming from his eyes. "Since I didn't know when that was going to be, I brought a weeks' worth of supplies. This is day one of my seven day lingerie selection I prepared for you."

The surge of desire pumping into my veins thickens my blood when a seductive growls emits from his lips. "If I'd known you were wearing these the entire time we were dancing, we wouldn't have made it past the club's storeroom."

I throw my head back and gasp when he flicks the suspender, slapping my skin with a pleasurable jolt of pain. The pounding of my clit nearly matches the hammering of my excited heart rate from his playful tease.

"Nothing's changed," Hugo murmurs in a low, deep tone. "Not a single fucking thing."

Lowering his head, he slips my panties to the side and runs his tongue along my pussy in one slow, tantalizing motion. Although shocked he hasn't removed my panties, I'm also happy. He did the exact thing the first time we slept together – the night we conceived Joel.

I fist the duvet on my bed and arch my back when his tongue delves inside my quivering labia. He tongue fucks me with just as much eagerness as his cock usually instills. The battle to keep my excited squeals to a bare minimum ramps up when he devours my pussy like a man who's never been fed. It's a mind-hazing blur of licks, sucks, and bites that have my orgasm building at a rapid pace. When he slides his index finger into my throbbing womb, adding another mind-blurring element to the already overstimulating mix, my teeth gnaw on the side of my palm, battling to hold in my cries of pleasure.

Before I have the chance to warn Hugo of its arrival, a climax shreds through my body, hard and fast. An ear-piercing scream erupts from my lips as my whole body quakes. My pussy tightens, trembling around his finger before my cries switch to a low, long moan as I ride the intense wave that feels like it is never going to end.

"Please. Oh god. Please. I."

Constructing a full sentence is above my caliber at the moment. I can barely breathe, let alone formulate a response to the flood of excitement coursing through my veins, overheating my body with feverish heat. Hugo continues to devour me in a torrent of greedy lashes and gentle nips, not the slightest bit impeded by the sudden arrival of my orgasm. His holds down my hips bucking against him as the intensity of my climax becomes too much for me to bear. Too overwhelming.

"I want every drop, Ava," he mutters against my trembling lips, sparking even more ardor to surge through my body. "Every sweet drop of your cum belongs to me."

Like it could get any stronger, my climax gains momentum. I snag the pillow at my side and throw it over my head, attempting to suffocate the erotic screams shredding from my mouth as a second climax claims my body. I've never experienced an orgasm with this much intensity, let alone two so close together. Not once. Not ever.

I've only just returned from the clouds when Hugo places one last lash on my clit before rising from his kneeling position at the end of the bed. When the room falls into silence, I flutter open my eyes and remove the pillow from my flushed face. My excited breathing lowers to a pant when I catch sight of Hugo's hard, thick cock fisted in his hand. Keeping his eyes arrested on my shimmering bare mound, he runs his hand down his engorged length to the very tip before gliding it back to the base. His cock is thick, hard, and undoubtedly beautiful, and I can't wait to be claimed by it.

A new type of anticipation courses through my veins when I see the glistening of pre-cum beading on his knob. Scampering off the bed and onto my knees, I wrap my hand around the base of his cock and lick off the drop of excitement from his crown. A groan tears from Hugo's throat as his knees buckle. Weaving his fingers through my hair, he secures a tight grip and guides my pace. The sting of pain from his ardent tugs on my hair spurs on my pursuit to unravel him as he just unraveled me. I lap him up, drinking in every inch of him. His seductive scent, the warm silkiness of his glorious cock, and his delicious taste. *God, I've missed his taste.*

I draw him in deep, working hard to untangle him, wanting to force him to lose all rational thoughts. The corners of my mouth burn as they stretch to accommodate his girth, but nothing can snuff my enthusiasm. I glide my moist lips over the smooth crest of his cock, then down his shaft with palpable eagerness. My tongue flicks and teases his knob while gathering up every drop of his enjoyment. My cheeks hollow, revealing my keenness to suck him dry.

"Slow down, babe, I don't want to come yet," Hugo demands, his words throaty. "We've got all night."

I increase my pace, loving that I can push him to the brink just as quickly as he can me. I stare up at him, peering past the bumps of muscles carved in his impeccable six pack. My hankering eyes advise him that I have no intention of slowing down until I've swallowed every drop of his spawn. A cocky grin carves on Hugo's mouth when he spots the determination in my eyes.

"Be careful what you wish for, Babe," he mutters.

Before I have time to prepare my throat, hot, thick cum spurts out of his silky smooth crown, drenching my mouth and throat with his magnificent goodness. I moan before swallowing vigorously, battling to ensure every bit of his cum is consumed. I don't want to waste a single drop. The throb in my pussy intensifies when the hardness of his cock doesn't lessen any, even with every drop of his cum expelled. If anything, it gets thicker, more veined.

I guide his still rigid cock out of my mouth before staring up at him wide-eyed and highly aroused. Smiling, he bands his arms around my waist and repositions me back onto the bed. His eyes absorb my naked, feverish skin as he glides my panties down my legs. When my panties are dumped to the side, my thigh muscles sweep open to accommodate Hugo kneeling between them. My body tenses when the crown of his cock hovers over my drenched pussy.

Hugo stares into my eyes as he sheaths me one glorious inch at a time. I'm so wet, he can slide in without too much hindrance. My breathing stills and a nib of pain rockets through my body when he finalizes the last three inches. I'm so full, so taken, so overwhelmed, tears prick my eyes and dribble down my face.

Spotting my tears, Hugo intakes a quick, sharp breath. "Babe--"

"I'm fine," I interrupt, my voice husky, strangled by an upwelling of emotions. "I'm more than fine. Please don't take my tears the wrong way. They're sentimental tears, not tears of pain. I'm just overwhelmed with having you here, with me, doing this," I blubber.

Hugo's concerned eyes bounce between mine, seeking any untruth in them. The strain hampering his gorgeous face relaxes when he sees the candor spoken by my eyes. Every word I spoke was the truth. I can't believe he's here, in my bed, in my home, and I'm not dreaming. *I may have pinched myself earlier just to make sure.*

"I'm not going anywhere, Ava. Never again," he assures me, intuiting what has caused my sobbing.

Fresh tears well in my eyes when he leans over and kisses away the ones falling down my heated cheeks. Once every teardrop has been lapped up, he seals his mouth over mine and kisses me senseless, expressing his promise with actions instead of words.

By the time he pulls away, my heart has just as much fluid surging through it as my lady garden does. He watches me, patiently waiting for my body to adjust to the sheer girth of him while also ensuring no more tears spill from my eyes.

Only once I nod, giving him permission to move, does he slowly withdraw his cock. My pussy ripples around him, greedily trying to hold him inside. It doesn't care about the bite of pain shooting through it, all it cares about is being consumed by him.

"Fuck, you feel good, Ava. Tight, wet," he mutters, his eyes burning into mine. "You feel even better than I remember."

His words have me on the verge of another mind-hazing orgasm. I just need a little more to push me over the edge. Hugo rocks into me harder, reading my body's desires without a single word needing to seep from my lips. He places his hand on the small of my back and tilts my hips high before wrapping my legs around his sweat-slicked waist. A husky moan rumbles through my lips when the hardness of his V muscle rubs against my pulsating clit with every perfect stroke he inflicts. Our bodies mold together and move in sync, like two pieces of a puzzle, perfectly matched for one another.

Over time, my skin dampens with sweat and my whole body is overheated, but nothing can weaken the excitement coursing through me. I've dreamed of days like this. Hell, I prayed for days like this, and now, it is coming true.

I run my nails down Hugo's sweat-slicked back before grasping the globes of his perfect ass. Just like every other part of his body, it's gotten better with age. His body moves with such ease, showcasing how in tune he is with himself. He's a sexual creature who holds nothing back as he possesses and claims every inch of me, inside and out.

The tightening of my coil strengthens with each precise stroke he inflicts. He's like a machine, designed to unravel me.

The room is thick with humidity and the smell of sweat and sex filters through my nose as his body guides me to a core-shattering climax. His name is torn from my throat and goosebumps prickle my skin as my orgasm hits fruition. My nails claw into his back as I fight my way through a blinding scattering of stars forming before my eyes. A carnal groan sounds from Hugo's parted lips when my pussy squeezes his cock, greedily begging for his hot cum.

My earth-shattering orgasm sets Hugo off. He sheaths me to the very root of his cock before he stills. Hot, violent cum spurts from his cock, like lava exploding from an active volcano. Unlike me, he manages to keep his cries of ecstasy to a bare minimum. Although from the strained look on his face and the way his veins are bulging, it was a hard-fought battle.

A snuggle into my pillow, beyond exhausted and eagerly anticipating a few solid hours of sleep. Hugo arches his brow and peers into my sleepy eyes.

"No sleep, Babe. I'm not even half done with you yet."

A squeal emits from my lips when he flips me over and yanks my ass into the air. Dynamite explodes in my womb when he rubs his cum into the cleft of my pussy with his hand, coating me with his slickness to lessen any friction before his slides his *still* rock-hard cock inside me. I crank my neck and peer at him, both shocked and incredibly aroused by his determination.

Any thoughts on catching a few hours of sleep turn into a forgotten memory when the sting of his hand spreads a fiery heat across my butt cheek from a perfectly placed spanking. The final act to confirm our fire-sparking reunion.

TWENTY-FIVE

HUGO

TWO WEEKS LATER...

My heart pounds hard as my lungs fight for air. I feel like I'm dying, suffocated by the heaviness weighing down my chest. The face of a monster is before me, snickering as he seeks his revenge, evening the score between us. I took his son; now he's taking mine. Joel's big blue eyes stare at me, pleading for me to save him from the devil holding a knife to his throat. Even with tears flooding his eyes, and his entire body uncontrollably shaking, he maintains a brave front, appeasing the fear of his mother standing beside me.

"It's okay, sweetheart, Daddy will save you," Ava stutters through the tears streaming down her pale face.

When Joel is jerked backwards, I lurch for him, pulling through the heaviness asphyxiating me with fear. I outstretch my arms, frantically trying to reach him, but no matter how hard I fight, no matter how far I stretch, I can't reach him. Col is too quick.

"No!" My back arches as a tormented scream tears from my

throat. "Please, don't hurt my son." I plead as Col drags Joel through a sea of black, soulless shadows. "I'll do anything you want, just don't hurt my son."

I thrash against a heaviness entangled around my legs, fighting to be released from their stranglehold. I *need* to save my son. I *have* to save my son. I suck in quick blasts of air, filling my lungs with oxygen as I race toward Joel. The ice cold fear clutching my chest impedes my usually lengthy strides. My thighs burn as I chase the white Range Rover that has an unconscious Joel in the backseat. My lungs are heaving, and my entire body is covered in a dense layer of sweat, but I don't give up. *I'll never give up.*

Confusion envelopes me when I race past distinguishable landmarks in Ravenshoe: Harlow's bakery, the office building where Izzy worked, and the Dungeon nightclub flash by as I sprint down the narrowing street.

The heaviness on my chest increases when the Range Rover vanishes before my eyes, not leaving a trace of its existence.

"Joel!" I yell out.

I run my hand through my hair as I spin around in a circle on Tivot street. My brows furrow as an overwhelming volley of confusion steamrolls into me. Only now do I realize, Joel was snatched from his bed in Rochdale, not Ravenshoe. My bewilderment intensifies when an image of a blond-haired man resuscitating another surfaces before me. My wild eyes dart up and down the street, seeking assistance. Surprisingly, the usually packed sidewalks of Ravenshoe are empty. Not a soul is in sight.

My focus returns to the two men in the middle of the street when the blond man releases a heavy grunt as he pumps furiously on the chest of the unconscious man sprawled on the ground.

"Come on, Hugo," he commands, thumping the unconscious man's chest with his enclosed fist.

I shift my feet and slant my head to the side, unsure exactly how I can aid them. The air is forcefully removed from my lungs when I discover who the blond man is resuscitating. *It's me.*

"Don't give up! Do you hear me? You're *not* allowed to die!" screams the resuscitator.

I step around the scene, wanting to see the face of the man saving me. I don't recall the events after I was shot. All I remember is landing on my backside with a sickening thud and waking up to the devastated face of Izzy. Everything in the preceding seven hours was a complete blur.

When I peer down at my rescuer, my pupils dilate to the size of dinner plates. "Blondie?"

I crouch down on the ground, unable to comprehend what I'm seeing. *The son of the man who ruined my life is saving my life?*

As the sounds of sirens approach, the buildings surrounding me distort before I'm suddenly swamped by eerie blackness. It is so dark, not even a star in the sky can be seen.

My head cranks to the side when a familiar voice screams through the darkness. "Hugo, wake up!"

I stand from my position and walk toward the voice. "Ava?"

Lifting my hand, I shelter my eyes when a blinding light streams through the darkness.

"Wake up!" Ava screams again.

I jerk awake, gasping for air. My massively dilated eyes shift around the unfamiliar room as I suck in deep pants of air. It takes me several moments to realize where I have awoken. I'm not in my apartment, my childhood home, or Regan's penthouse. I'm in the guest room of Jorgie's home. Ava's bedroom. Gratitude envelopes me when I discover the bed is empty. Catching sight of the alarm clock on the bedside table, I see it is a little after seven AM. Ava and Joel will most likely be in the kitchen getting ready to start their day.

Kicking my legs, I break free of the sheets wrapped around me and run my trembling hand over my head. My body is cool from the combination of sweat and the remnants of my nightmare still clinging to me. A new type of fear clutches my heart when my surveillance of the room stumbles upon Ava crouched on the ground halfway across the floor space. She has her hand covering her mouth and fresh tears staining her cheeks.

"*Ava.*"

I scramble off the bed and kneel in front of her. Grief and despair smack into me when I see the terrified haze clouding her beautiful eyes.

"Did I hurt you?" I ask, panicked as my eyes rake every inch of her, seeking any injuries from the brutality I can display in my dreams.

Ava shakes her head. "No," she whispers, her voice hoarse. "I remembered what Dr. Avery told me about ensuring I'm at a safe distance before waking you."

I peer into her eyes, seeking any untruth in them. I inwardly sigh when nothing but honesty reflects back at me. Wrapping my arms around her quivering shoulders, I slump onto my bottom and lean my back against the bed. The pain twinging my heart weakens when Ava presses her cheek onto the sweat-drenched skin on my chest and nuzzles in close, not the slightest bit concerned about the dampness. She sobs quietly. She's so discreet, if her tears weren't adding to the wetness of my chest, I wouldn't be aware she's crying.

I gather her hair off her cheeks and lift her tear-stained face to me. Her lips twitch, itching to speak, but no words spill from her mouth. I already know what she's going to ask without her needing to speak. Ava's eyes have always been expressive, revealing way more than her mouth ever could. Today is no different, but even if I couldn't read her eyes, she knows me well, better than anyone. She would have determined what my nightmare were about the instant she heard my tormented screams begging for Col not to hurt Joel.

My voice shakes as I begin to speak. "I tried, Ava. I swear to you, I tried every legal avenue available. When that failed, I took matters into my own hands. I couldn't let him get away with it. He killed Jorgie and Malcolm, but was free to live his life how he saw fit. He didn't suffer at all. I'd already seen Gemma endure the injustice of the courts. I wasn't going to let the same thing happen to Jorgie."

Ava's moisture-swamped eyes stare into mine, but she doesn't speak; she doesn't need to. The understanding in her eyes is all I need to see to ease my concern about revealing a secret only a handful of people know.

"I wanted him dead. I wanted him to suffer the way Jorgie suffered. The way *we* suffered." I peer into Ava's forgiving eyes as my chest rises and falls with every inhalation I take. "I wanted to make him pay."

Ava takes a quick breath as her pupils dilate, but remains as quiet as a church mouse......

I load .38 caliber bullets into the magazine of my gun before clicking it back into the chamber. After sliding across the safety mechanism, I house my gun into the back of my jeans, swing open my truck door, and walk toward the compound I've been surveying the past two weeks. I have one plan on my mind: exact revenge on the man responsible for killing my sister and unborn nephew.

I tried to follow the necessary legal channels. I spoke to the DA, the detectives assigned to Jorgie's case, and I even pleaded with the media. No one listened. Jorgie's killer was a free man, exonerated of all charges. That is about to change.

A sense of calm settles over me as I pace toward the warehouse surrounded by a six-foot steel wire fence. A Rottweiler charges out of a kennel at the back of the compound, barking and growling. His fang-baring snarl only lasts as long as it takes for me to throw a juicy bone over the fence. He gnaws on the half frozen turkey leg as I cut a hole in the mesh wire with a pair of bolt cutters. After returning the bolt cutters to my duffle bag, I conceal it in a bush at my side and climb through the hole.

When I enter the unsecured grounds at the edge of the warehouse, I take a sharp left. I've witnessed the same routine every day the past two weeks at this compound. Three men enter the complex at nine AM, two guards, and one asset – my target. One armed man stands at the front entrance of the warehouse while the other follows the asset inside. Within ten minutes of entering, the second armed guard cranks open a door on the left hand side of building, his nicotine habit too strong from him to overcome the desire for a quick hit. Within twenty minutes of arriving, my target leaves the warehouse flanked by the two guards and carrying a black briefcase in each hand. Their routine hasn't altered the past two weeks I've been watching them. Their complacency is about to cost them dearly.

When I reach the edge of the warehouse, I slow my pace, ensuring my heavy stomps don't cause the gravel under my feet to crunch. I lean my back against the sun-heated outer wall of the warehouse, vying for a prime opportunity to react. When the door next to me cracks open not even five minutes later, I pounce.

Grabbing the handle, I yank the metal door forward before slamming it back with brutal force. A grunted noise echoes in the quiet, closely followed by a hard thud. Gliding my hand into the back of my jeans, I retrieve my revolver before peering around the door. A man easily six feet tall lays sprawled on the dirty concrete floor. A nasty bump is forming on his forehead, his eyes are closed, and his half-lit cigarette is dangling from his mouth. My eyes scan the inside of the warehouse as I crouch down to remove the two semi-automatic weapons strapped to his hip and a knife wrapped around his thigh.

Housing his Glock and Bulpap into the back of my jeans, I brace my gun in front of my body and move through the warehouse. The smell of freshly printed Benjamin Franklins filters through my nose the closer I amble to an office on my right. Years of sniper training ensure my fast pace goes undetected. I push open a heavily weighted wooden door and sweep my eyes over the room. Roberto's suit-covered back faces me as he piles bundles of money from a black safe bolted to the floor into an open suitcase sitting on a polished wooden desk.

"Give me another five minutes, and I'll be ready to go," Roberto instructs when he senses my presence.

"How about we leave now." I aim the barrel of my gun at the back of his head.

Roberto freezes. "Do you have any idea who you're robbing? Leave now and this matter will remain between us."

"I'm not here for your money. The only asset I want to secure is you." I lift my eyes to the flashing red light in the corner of the room.

Roberto spins on his heels, his movements steady and alert. A V grooves between his brow as his rich brown eyes roam over my face. His expression remains stagnant until he registers the similarities between Jorgie and me: same nose, same eyes, same smile. No one could deny we were siblings. Roberto's throat works hard to swallow before his lips spasm, preparing to speak.

"Move," I say, gesturing my head to the door, not giving him the chance to protest.

He had his chance to speak up when he was arrested at the scene of Jorgie's accident for driving under the influence. If he'd pled guilty, I wouldn't be standing before him.

I follow Roberto out of the warehouse with the butt of my gun aimed at a patch of gray hairs in his dark, clipped hair. When we exit the frosted glass door at the front of the compound, the armed guard spins around, clearly shocked by Roberto's early arrival. When he notices me standing behind Roberto, with a gun pointed at his head, his hand slips into his suit jacket, no doubt to reach the gun he has holstered on his waist.

"Roberto will be dead before you even remove your gun," I warn, my words rough, like they were dragged through a whole heap of gravel before spilling from my lips.

The guard's dark eyes shift between Roberto and me. His gaze is vehement, fueling my agitation.

"Unless you want splatters of Roberto's brain on your fancy suit, unclip the Seven Eagle strapped to your hip, remove the bullets, and throw it into the bush," I instruct, motioning my head to the thick bush at the side of us.

Other than his eyelids twitching, the guard remains motionless, refusing to follow my demand. He only does as solicited when I squeeze my finger on the trigger. A bead of sweat rolls down the nape of Roberto's neck as his entire body shakes in fear. Through gritted teeth, Roberto's protective detail removes the gun holstered on his hip and empties the magazine chamber.

"Now the Magnum strapped to your ankle," I demand, glaring into his thinly slitted eyes when he dumps his first gun into the prickly bush.

His lips set into a hard line before he bobs down to remove the magnum strapped to his left ankle. After removing the bullets from the barrel of the 44, he throws it into the bush and pivots around to face me.

"You're a dead man walking," he snarls, his tone vicious.

I snicker before pushing the barrel of my gun deeper into Roberto's skull, using it as a way of directing him to my truck parked at the side of the compound. The guard's stern threat causes me no concern. I'm already dead. An empty, soulless man who has no chance of emerging from the hell I'm living in. That is why I didn't bother covering my face. I want everyone to know I'm the man who is going to ensure Roberto pays his repentance.

"DO IT." Roberto peers at me over the barrel of the gun pointed at his head. "Do it already! I killed your sister! I ran her down!"

I slam the butt of my gun into his left temple with vicious

force. Roberto's head ricochets to the side and a trickle of blood streams down his face, pooling at his bound feet.

"Shut the fuck up." My angry words reverberate around the desolate basement in Jorgie's house.

In the haste of my decision, I didn't properly evaluate what I was planning to do once I secured Roberto from the Petretti compound. I acted on impulse, knowing it may have been the only viable time I could secure him. Rumors were running rife in our hometown that Col was moving his underground fighting circuit to a new location. I couldn't run the risk of losing my tail on Roberto. I also couldn't stand the thought of another day of injustice rolling by. Needing a place free of any encumbrance, I brought him to Jorgie's house. Roberto has been bound to the water boiler in her basement for the past two hours. I only left him twenty minutes ago to call Ava.

Roberto's head returns front and center. He smiles a blood-tainted grin, seemingly pleased to have sparked a reaction out of me. He has spent the majority of the last two hours goading me, not caring that his very existence is balancing precariously on the edge of a steep cliff. Just from his taunts, I can tell he has chosen death by suicide, but instead of using a gun as his weapon of choice, he is using me.

I push a gag into his mouth, not just to stop his callous words, but to also ease the pain shredding my heart, crippling me with grief. Snubbing the shake of my hands, I push the barrel of my gun against the skin between his eyes. Unable to speak through the gag, Roberto's eyes beg for me to issue the punishment the courts failed to decree: to free him from his miserable existence.

I push the barrel in closer, pinching the wrinkled skin on his forehead. When I lower my finger to the trigger, Roberto closes his eyes, accepting his fate with a sense of dignity. Gritting my teeth, I squeeze the trigger. Blood roars in my ears when a metal click bellows over the rampant beat of my heart.

Seconds felt like hours as I stare at Roberto, shocked I claimed another man's life. My shock doesn't last long. I take a step backwards, exasperated when Roberto's eyes flutter open. I pulled the trigger, he should be dead. It is only when I sense a presence at my side do I realize the clicking heard wasn't my gun firing, it was the old bolts clanking together in Jorgie's basement door.

My eyes swing to the side of the room, closely followed by my gun. Isaac stands at the entrance of the basement. He's wearing his standard suit, accentuated with a murderous glare. His stance is firm, not the slightest bit concerned about having a pistol pointed at his chest. One slip of my finger and he would be dead.

"You need to leave," I say, returning the barrel of my gun to Roberto. "This is between me and Roberto, not you."

"You're my family, Hugo. What happens to you affects me," Isaac responds, his deep timbre booming around the room.

My nostrils flare as I glare into the eyes of the man who killed my mom's spirit, leaving a shell of a woman I no longer recognize. The man who tore her heart out of her chest, threw it onto the stained floor and stomped on it. The man who shattered her soul.

"He killed my family. He tore them apart."

"No," Isaac argues, his composure stern and unwavering. "He didn't kill your family, but you will, if you don't leave now."

My neck cranks to the side faster than a missile being launched out of a jet. I stare into Isaac's eyes, unable to comprehend any of the words coming out of his mouth.

"*The instant you took Roberto, you signed your family's death certificates. Trust me, Col will not stop hunting you until you have suffered the same loss as him,*" Isaac explains to my confused face.

My stomach lurches when I see the truth relayed by his frank eyes, but nothing can lessen the fury blackening my veins.

"*He deserves to die. He killed my sister. My nephew!*" I roar, my veins bulging with every syllable I speak. "*I want him to suffer!*"

"*He will suffer,*" Isaac declares, stepping closer to me. "*I'll make sure of it. I'll take care of this.*"

He stares into my eyes. "*He won't get away with it. You have my word,*" he assures me. "*There are two types of people in the world, Hugo: healers and hurters.*"

Before I can react, Isaac snatches my wrist holding the gun. He stares at me with murky eyes. "*You're a healer. I am a hurter.*"

AVA REMAINS CRADLED in my lap with her eyes flicking between mine, staring but not speaking. Although the stretch of silence passing between us is thick and somber, the unspoken words relayed by her beautiful eyes are the greatest ally in repairing the damage my foolhardy mistake made. Even crammed with qualm, the glimmer her eyes get every time she looks at me doesn't dampen from my confession. Her eyes reveal she understands the reason I reacted the way I did. She empathizes with the pain I went through, as it wasn't just parts of my soul that vanished the day Jorgie died; it was parts of Ava's soul as well.

TWENTY-SIX

AVA

I'd like to say I'm surprised by Hugo's confession, but I'm not. When the news circulated about Roberto's disappearance, I suspected Hugo was involved in some way. Mr. Marshall had raised his sons to protect their mother and sisters. That notion didn't just stop because Jorgie passed away. Even after her death, I knew Hugo would continue to defend her. I just hoped the justice system would issue Roberto's punishment so Hugo didn't have to, but once again, the legal system failed him. Although I would have preferred that Hugo seek justice in a legal manner, I can understand what he was going through all those years ago. He was riddled with so much grief, he was unable to form a rational decision.

I still recall with crystal clear memory looking in Roberto's eyes when he was placed in the back of the police cruiser the day of Jorgie's accident. Even with his eyes jammed with remorse and a gold cross hanging around my neck, I cursed him to death. I wanted him to suffer the way Jorgie did when she held my hand and cried as she couldn't feel Malcolm moving in her stomach. I prayed for him to experience the pain that was shredding through my heart, crippling me with devastation. So I understand what Hugo was going through, because at the time, I also wanted Roberto dead.

My opinion on the matter only changed when Joel was born. When I was looking down at his little face and big, worldly eyes, I realized it wouldn't matter what he did, no matter how heinous, he would always be my son, and I'd always defend him. It was in that instant, I realized Roberto wasn't just the man who killed Jorgie, he was someone's son. His mother would have grieved his death just as deeply as Mrs. Marshall grieved Jorgie's. No mother should go through the pain of losing a child. Not even one who gave birth to a monster.

Hugo's eyes dance between mine as he lifts his hand and removes my tears from my cheeks. Once all my tears are cleared, his eyes stare into mine. "If I'd known my hasty decision would have the consequences it did, I would have evaluated it with more diligence. I would have taken the time to properly assess the repercussions of my decision."

Guilt darkens his eyes. "But I was hurting too much. Losing Jorgie and Malcolm, then you... the pain was too great. It killed any chances of my grief-riddled brain forming a rational decision. Losing Jorgie gutted me. Losing you utterly destroyed me." His words comes out gravelly and deep.

From the despondency in Hugo's eyes, I have no doubt if he could take back every wrong he did, he would. *All of it.* Not just hurting me and missing out on the first four years of Joel's life. *Everything.* Even what happened to Roberto.

Hugo's sorrowful eyes peer into mine. "I wanted to punish

Roberto, to issue the penalty the courts failed to administer." He exhales an uneven breath of air as his eyes flick between mine. "But when I peered into Roberto's eyes, all I could see were your eyes reflecting back at me."

I gulp in a jagged breath as my widened eyes dart between Hugo's, searching for the answer to the question my mouth is failing to ask.

"I got close. I held the gun to Roberto's head, and I pulled back the trigger, but no matter how strong the desire was to make him pay, I couldn't do it. I couldn't pull the trigger."

I release the breath I'm holding in as a mass of liquid swamps my eyes. "You didn't kill him?" My words come out in a shaky tremor as a torrent of emotions flood into me.

Tears roll down my cheeks when Hugo shakes his head.

"I couldn't. I didn't want you to *ever* look at me the way I was looking at him. I didn't want you to think of me as a monster."

"I would have *never* looked at you like that," I declare, cupping his jaw and staring into his eyes, wanting to ensure he can see the honesty in mine. "You not being able to pull the trigger proves how strong you are."

My gut twists when Hugo shakes his head. "I'm not strong. I might have failed to pull the trigger, but I didn't stop the man I knew could," he interrupts.

My breath snags halfway to my lungs when I see the dishonor clouding his eyes.

"I was a coward who left the integrity of defending my baby sister to a man who was a stranger only months earlier," Hugo mutters under his breath. "I didn't even ask Isaac what he was going to do to Roberto, because, at the time, I didn't care. Isaac said he would take care of him, and I trusted he would. That not only makes me a coward, it makes me just as much of a monster as Roberto."

I viciously shake my head, sending tears sprawling into the air. "No. That does not make you a coward or a monster. That makes you a man with morals. A man who was raised right. *Not* a coward. Even with your soul shattered, you still knew the difference between right and wrong. That makes you a man, Hugo. That makes you *brave.*"

Hugo stares at me in shocked silence, unable to relate to what I'm saying. I return his robust stare minus the calamity his eyes are sparked with. I stare at him with nothing but love and admiration, wanting to ensure he's aware his confession hasn't altered my opinion of him. I love him. I always have, and I always will. Nothing he could ever say or do would change that fact. Not one single thing.

As a stretch of silence crosses between us, the cloud dulling the usual impish glint in his eyes dissolves, but even with his mood shifting toward his regular persona, it isn't enough to ease the pain festering in my heart from the melancholy expression on his face. Deciding to test Hugo's theory of using actions instead of words, I press my mouth against his stern, snapped lips. The muscles in his thighs tense when my tongue brushes along the ridges of his lips, requesting access to his mouth. His unease only lasts for a fleeting second before he parts his lips and accepts my kiss.

I delve my tongue into his warm, inviting mouth in a slow, sweeping wave. His tongue follows the pattern of mine, tasting and devouring every inch of my mouth in lengthy, gentle strokes. Our kiss expresses all the emotions surging through our bodies: our sorrow and anguish, and my understanding of why he initially reacted the way he did. It is a controlled and emotion-packed kiss that relinquishes my heart from the stranglehold that's been asphyxiating it the past five years. Our kiss mends wounds I never thought could be healed. I should have known only Hugo's touch would have the chance of doing that. Only he has the ability to return the parts of my soul I lost when Jorgie passed away.

Inhaling deeply, I breathe in his scent. My senses savor being engulfed by his familiar woodsy smell. He smells heavenly. *He smells like home.* When I pull back from his delicious lips, his eyes slowly flutter open. Our kiss has removed the fog obscuring the eyes I fell in love with well over fifteen years ago. His eyes are the clearest they've been since he returned to Rochdale for the first time four weeks ago. He runs the back of his index finger over my cheek in a slow, tantalizing maneuver, prickling my nape with goosebumps. I lean into his hand, wanting every inch of my skin to be touching him in some way.

The muscles in his stomach contract when I run my hand along the bumps of his abs, over the Princess Peach and Luigi tattoo inked above his right hipbone, and by the replica of the tree I engraved our names into at Lake George over fifteen years ago covering the majority of his left ribcage. Every tattoo that adorns Hugo's god-crafted body is a reference to our life together. Whether it is the pair of black, thick-rimmed glasses floating on top of a pool of water, the *Friends* sitcom logo on his right shoulder blade, or the three letters of my name integrated in multiple locations on his body, every tattoo has some significance to our time together.

Snubbing the tears forming in my eyes, I lean forward and

place a kiss on the outer edge of the bullet wound scar in his chest. My lips land just to the side of Joel's freshly inked name above Hugo's heart. My breath hitches when I pull back and catch the cajoling look in Hugo's eyes. Gone is the cloud of remorse and despair, replaced with a new voracious look only my kisses incite.

My pulse quickens when Hugo rocks his hips, ensuring I'm aware of what my simple peck did to his body. I'm not going to lie, I love that I can spark such a carnal desire from him from the meekest brush of my lips against his bare skin, but even with the desire to throw caution to the wind and undertake crazy wild sex on the floor of our bedroom, I won't. Not because I don't want to, but because I refuse to relinquish my eyes from Hugo's demanding gaze. He's staring at me with zero restrictions or complications. Nothing but love and awe is beaming from his devoted eyes. This affects me more intensely than any earth-shattering orgasm ever could.

The unbreakable connection between us only bends slightly when little feet padding into the room sound over the furious beat of my heart. Warmth blooms across my chest when Joel sleepily rubs his eyes before plopping down onto the ground next to us and leaning his crazy curl-covered head onto Hugo's forearm.

A giggle bubbles up my chest when Joel's tired eyes peer up to Hugo as he asks, "Do I still get a pancake boganus since it's Monday?"

Hugo cranks his neck back and laughs. "Yeah, buddy, if you can convince Mommy to make pancakes, you'll still get a bonus."

Joel's little eyes widen before they dart to me. His lips

pucker as he gives me his best puppy dog eyes. Like a dog rolling over and begging for my tummy to be scratched, I nod. A squeal emits from Joel's lips before he jumps up from the ground and charges to the door.

"I'm going to wash my hands!"

He charges out of our room so quickly, nothing but a blur flashes before my eyes.

Laughing, I drift my eyes back to Hugo. "You know you're going to end up broke if you keep bribing him."

"It will be worth it. Besides, it's not bribery. It's an *incentive*," he retorts with a grin tugging on his lips.

I screw up my nose. "An incentive to stay in his room so you can screw his mom senseless before you gorge on pancakes?"

Hugo doesn't attempt to answer my question. Lying has never been his forte.

EPILOGUE

Hugo
Six months later...

"And just like that, Hugo Marshall is undead."

After a few more lightning keystrokes, Hunter snaps the screen of his laptop closed and puts it back into the hemp bag dumped at the side of the chair where he's sitting.

"Was it that quick to make me dead?" I ask, shocked it only took him five minutes to undo something that caused Ava years of pain.

Hunter arches his brow and stares into my eyes. "I didn't make you dead," he advises with a shake of his head. "If I did, you'd have no chance of being resurrected."

I watch him in shock. For the past six months, I'd assumed it was Hunter who made me dead to keep me hidden from Col Petretti. If it wasn't him, who was it?

Hunter throws his hemp bag onto a chair before running his

hand along his scruff-covered jaw. I eye him with even more curiosity when a sly smirk peeks out from behind his scraggly beard. Before I have the opportunity to ask what his odd look is about, his spine straightens and his dark eyes shift to me.

"Did you want me to file the paperwork for you today? Or do you want to do it the legal way?"

I smirk and slap him on the back. "Now that I'm undead, the legal way will be great."

Snubbing the confusion muddling my brain, I move to the corner of the room and check my tuxedo in the full length mirror. Today, Ava and I are getting married. Putting it bluntly: I shit bricks the day I asked her to marry me. It wasn't a fear of commitment that had me quivering like the earth was shaking beneath my feet, it was the fact I had to lure Ava away from her office long enough to give Belinda and Joel the chance to decorate it with the two hundred long-stemmed roses I'd purchased that caused my greatest concern.

It's no hidden fact I'm not a fan of dentists. I love Ava, but my fear of sitting in her dentist chair is the cause of my greatest panic. Thankfully, Ava's constant reminders to make sure I floss regularly were implanted into my brain from a young age, ensuring her dentist drill remain holstered on the side of her dentist chair and not buzzing in my mouth.

While I'm being forthright, I'll admit my proposal to Ava was brazen, particularly as we weren't even an official couple, but I'd already lost so much time with her that I didn't want to miss one more moment. Since my last two attempts at asking her out were pathetic, worse than any fifth grader could have conjured, I decided I either had to go big or go home. I went gung-ho. Thank god she said yes.

After loosening the constricting bowtie around my neck, I run my hand through my hair to fix it into place. I grimace at the small scattering of gray hairs forming on my temples. *Getting old sucks.* Even with the room air-conditioned at seventy degrees Fahrenheit, a beading of sweat glistens my forehead. My eyes shift to the side when a white handkerchief is placed on my tuxedo-covered shoulder. With a grin, I accept the handkerchief and run it over my sweat-drenched head before spinning on my heels to face the smirking face of Isaac.

"Why are your shoulders so tense?" he queries, his voice its normal deep, demanding tone. "You and Ava are already a family. Nothing screams of lifetime commitment more than raising a child together."

I cock my brow and stare into his jeering face. "Who are you trying to convince? Me or yourself?" I ask, my tone doused with cheekiness.

Isaac's nostrils flare as his face lines with anger. Although he's tried numerous times the past six months to drag Izzy down the aisle, her feet have remained firmly planted on the ground – outside of the church. I don't see Izzy's strong stance budging an inch until Isaac takes the pre-nuptial agreement he had Regan draft off the table. Since I don't see Isaac's position weakening anytime soon, I don't expect to hear the sounds of wedding bells for them in the near future.

Catching sight of Isaac's furious scowl, I cockily wink. Most men would be shaking in their boots from the wry look he's directing at me, but I know his threat doesn't hold any heat. No amount of scowling can hide the massive heart he has in the middle of his chest.

"Don't make me fire your ass," Isaac warns in a vicious snarl when he spots my grinning face.

"Again! What will that make it? The sixth time he's fired you the past year?" Hunter asks in a cheeky tone. "That's nearly a new record, even for someone as fire-able as you, Hugo."

Hunter's boisterous chuckle bounces off the wall and jingles in my ears when I punch him in the bicep.

"It's not my fault Izzy is always up to mischief," I mutter.

Neither Isaac or Hunter attempt to refute my accurate claim.

Hunter is still rubbing his arm, feigning injury when my mom enters the room. Her hair has been pulled back in a fancy up-do and she's wearing a pale light blue dress.

"We will meet you out there," Isaac advises, gesturing his head to the door my mom just entered.

Once Hunter and Isaac exit the room, my mom paces to stand in front of me. With tears in her eyes, she adjusts the collar of my light blue dress shirt before running her hands down the lapels of my jacket, smoothing everything into place. When her eyes lift to my face, a smile curls on my lips. Nothing but pride is projected from her eyes. *There's my mom I remember.*

"Ava is five minutes out. Are you ready?" Her voice shakes with both nerves and excitement.

I nod. "I've been ready for at least five years."

The hammering of my heart kicks up when we exit the vestibule at the side of the church and amble down the aisle Jorgie and Hawke walked down six years ago. This is the same church Chase, Helen, Jorgie and I were christened at. The same church Jorgie and Malcolm were laid to rest.

My heavily weighted strides down the white carpet come to a standstill when the suit-clad man standing next to Isaac turns around to face me. I shake my head, certain my brain isn't registering the prompts my eyes are relaying. Even after a brisk shake of my head, the unbelievable image remains. *Hawke has returned to Rochdale.* I'm not going lie, my nose is tingling and fresh tears are pricking my eyes.

After assisting my mom into the front pew to sit next to Mrs. Mable, I span the distance between the congregation of wedding attendees and the altar, only stopping when I'm standing directly in front of Hawke.

"You came," I mutter, bouncing my eyes between his.

Ava sent Hawke an invitation with a note attached stating we understood his reluctance to return to Rochdale and he was under no obligation to attend, but neither of us felt right not inviting him. When he failed to RSVP, I assumed he decided not to attend.

Hawke's lips twist before he nods. "Couldn't miss seeing my best mate getting married."

Although his voice cracks, exposing the surge of emotions pummeling into him, I can also see sparks of the old Hawke in his eyes. This is, no doubt, a tortuous step for him to take, but it is a step in the right direction. A giant, scary leap toward healing his heart and giving him the chance to move on from his grief.

My eyes drift from Hawke to the end of the aisle when "All of Me" by John Legend begins playing over the speakers. Hawke, Isaac, and Hunter take their spots next to me as the bridesmaids commence walking down the aisle. The pounding of my heart increases as Belinda, Izzy, and Helen make their way down the aisle to take their positions on my right. As they glide past the pews of attendees, my eyes spot a flurry of blonde. A smile curls on my lips when I see the smiling face of Gemma. Our reunion occurred not long after my return to Rochdale. When she walked into my office nearly six months ago, I automatically assumed Ava tracked her down. It was only when I saw the look of surprise on Ava's face when she arrived at my office not long after Gemma did I realize she didn't have the faintest clue who Gemma was. Ava's claws were sheathed when I promptly introduced her to Gemma. They've been close friends since that day.

My hearty chuckle rumbles over the beat of my heart when I spot sight of Joel charging down the aisle. Nothing has changed the past seven months. He still doesn't know how to walk. He dumps his frilly satin ring-bearer pillow halfway down the aisle, making me glad I succumbed to Ava's pleas for Isaac to look after our platinum wedding rings and not put them on Joel's pillow.

When Joel reaches the end of the altar, he wraps his arms around my thigh and turns his eyes to the end of the aisle. My lungs take stock of my oxygen levels when the song switches to "How Would You Feel" by Ed Sheeran. This song reflects Ava and my relationship to a T. I just wish I got to tell her I loved her years earlier.

My breathing halts the instant Ava steps out of the alcove of the church. Just like the first time my eyes landed on her at Jorgie's wedding, she takes my breath away and renders me speechless. She's beyond beautiful, a unique mix of innocence and seduction with big, rich eyes, gorgeous tanned skin, and a body created with the sole purpose of making me drop to my knees, but even with having off-the-Richter scale sexiness, Ava's heart is one of her most admirable assets. And thankfully, it belongs to me.

When Ava reaches the end of the altar, she kisses my dad on the cheek, and hands her bouquet of flowers to Belinda before pivoting around to face me. The smile of her face eases the nervous cramps hammering my stomach, and the happiness in her eyes smothers the agitation over the previous times I visited this church. Only Ava can calm any storm building on the horizon before the first cloud has even formed.

I gently run the back of my fingers over her pale cheeks before lowering them to brush by her beautiful rounded belly. "Is she being a good girl for Mommy?" I query, only loud enough for Ava to hear.

Ava's face scrunches as the color in her cheeks drains even more. Unfortunately, Ava has been suffering with dreadful morning sickness from the day she discovered she was pregnant with our little girl, exactly four weeks after we first slept together.

Although we caved and found out the sex of our baby, we haven't informed anyone that we are expecting a little girl. Joel is already struggling with the concept of sharing his parents' devotion in two months' time. We're moving to Ravenshoe at the end of the month, so we don't want to add even more uncertainty into the mix by declaring the baby brother he so desperately wants is actually a baby sister. I'm sure with some time and a good dose of candy, he will adjust to the idea of having a sister. If not, he has a 50/50 chance of getting a brother the next round. With how easy Ava gets pregnant, I have no doubt the odds of her being pregnant within a year of giving birth swings the pendulum in Joel's favor of having a large family. He's happily declared on numerous occasions to anyone willing to listen that he wants five brothers.

Ava screws up her nose. "Don't even think about it," she reprimands me, glaring into my eyes like she can hear my private thoughts.

I smile, loving that she can read me so easily. I shouldn't be surprised, though. She's always been the only woman who can see through my bullshit. Well, except for my mother, but she doesn't count.

The flutter of Ava's pulse spasms up my arm when I enclose my hand over hers and glance into her beautiful eyes. Every uncertainty, concern, or worry I've ever had vanishes the instant she peers up at me with her uniquely beautiful eyes. I have no doubt, Ava is my beginning and my end. *She's my everything.* And although we've lost years we can never get back, in a short period of time, we've created enough memories to last us two lifetimes.

People will often quote that there are no guarantees in life, but I'm *certain* Ava and I will never be parted again. Because although there are no guarantees, you can't fight fate.

THE END...

THE NEXT STORY IN THE ENIGMA SERIES IS:

Spy Thy Neighbor
The story of Hunter Kane.

Join my author page for updates on the next instalment in
the Enigma Series.
https://www.facebook.com/authorshandi

Join my READER's group:
https://www.facebook.com/groups/1740600836169853/

Hunter, Hugo, Cormack, Hawke, Ryan, Rico & Brax stories
have already been released, Brandon, Regan and all the other
great characters of Ravenshoe will be getting their own stories at
some point during 2019.

Join my newsletter to remain informed:

subscribepage.com/authorshandi

If you enjoyed this book - please leave a review.

ALSO BY SHANDI BOYES

Perception Series:

Saving Noah

Fighting Jacob

Taming Nick

Redeeming Slater

Saving Emily (*Novella*)

Wrapped up with Rise Up (*Novella - should be read after Bound*)

Enigma:

Enigma of Life

Unraveling an Enigma

Enigma: The Mystery Unmasked

Enigma: The Final Chapter

Beneath the Secrets

Beneath the Sheets

Spy Thy Neighbor

The Opposite Effect

I Married a Mob Boss

Second Shot

The Way We Are

The Way We Were

Sugar and Spice

Lady in Waiting

Man in Queue

Couple on Hold

Enigma: The Wedding

Silent Vigilante

Bound Series:

Chains

Links

Bound

Restrained

Psycho

Russian Mob Chronicles:

Nikolai: A Mafia Prince Romance

Nikolai: Taking Back What's Mine

Nikolai: What's Left of Me

Nikolai: Mine to Protect

Asher: My Russian Revenge

Nikolai: Through the Devil's Eyes

RomCom Standalones:

Just Playin'

The Drop Zone

Ain't Happenin'

Christmas Trio

Falling for a Stranger

Coming Soon:

Skitzo

Trey

Printed in Great Britain
by Amazon

71111756R00169